# Dog Binary

# Dog Binary

by

## Alex Macdonald

Beautiful
Books

Beautiful Books Limited
36-38 Glasshouse Street
London W1B 5DL

www.beautiful-books.co.uk

ISBN 9781907616280

9 8 7 6 5 4 3 2 1

Jacket design by Ian Pickard.
Photography by Mike McCartney.

Printed & bound in the UK by CPI Mackays, Chatham ME5 8TD.

*To Penny*
*With Love*
*Alex*

*but you open the door and you open it wide and the
little bad monkey, it stepped inside* - RL Burnside

# NO TEETH INDIAN BEARS

The radio's on. The window's open. The only difference tonight, the temperature outside. Everything else, it's just the same: the paint on my hands, the alcohol in my bloodstream and Jabba, down the hallway, lying there collapsed, making more money unconscious than I have on my knees in three days.

You don't have to see him to know what the situation is in that room.

His recently dialled gourmet history raising every horizontal surface to the skew. Him and his TV. The surround sound and big bass box punching out whatever's on his planner loud enough to permeate everything but the MDMA and the cocaine and the first-press pollen hash that's in his brain as a big buffer to the real world.

I'm holding a letter. My hands a mess of paint. Holding Beatrice's letter and watching the curtains billow.

Fragmented rectangles of light lift over everything.

There's an item on the radio about dancing bears in India. A man from an animal charity, he's telling you all about it, these gypsies and their dancing bears. He's telling you more and more dreadful things about the bears. As if you might need that much information to decide these bears aren't happy.

I'm picturing the bears along with the gypsies. Gypsies who've been keeping dancing bears for generations. The charity man's saying how he's very concerned for the gypsies, for their plight, as well as that of the bears. He proceeds to interview a young Indian gypsy—who, apparently, is standing right there with his bear. The charity-man's saying to the young Indian gypsy that maybe he'd be happier if he gave up his dancing bear. If he took up doing something else that didn't involve being cruel to bears. The young Indian gypsy is agreeing completely. He's saying he's really looking forward to giving up his dancing bear and doing something different. He's desperate to be doing something that doesn't involve being cruel to bears.

He can't wait.

I'm picturing the bear being right there. Close to the microphone. With a rope through its nose, no teeth and its claws all cut off.

I can't hear a sound from the bear.

The bear is completely silent.


I turn the radio off.

The madness of Beatrice's letter, it's salve enough to everything:

*Dear Mr. Lipman,*

*There's nothing nice to write about, it's been a terrible year—no holiday, no days off, just work, work and more work, and at seventy-seven it's all a bit much.*

*Elijah is at the moment in sheltered accommodation, having become too difficult for me to cope with alone. He's as slow as a snail, can be* quite rational, but does most peculiar things at times. I take him out for a meal twice a week, and he has embarrassed me by trying to drink from the teapot, but most recently by pouring tea onto his half-eaten lunch. When asked why, he said, 'There's nowhere else to put it and I've already put the sugar on.' At this point he glowered at me and defiantly emptied the remaining tea onto his plate.

He's also tried to sign a document at the bank with his finger and when wanting a visitor to read something or other, the visitor said:

'I can't, I haven't brought my glasses.'

'Here use mine,' said Elijah—and handed him the scissors!

It's been taking me two hours a day to clear leaves from the drive, when rained upon they are as slippery as black ice, and I've still got some of the lawns to clear. I've also had the cottage cellar to pump out twice daily and the streaming windows (all 21 of them) to wipe each morning.

What a life!

There are lots of apples on the trees and roses in bloom and our family of squirrels delight me daily with their antics.

Told you I had nothing to say.

Love Beatrice.


I picture Beatrice and Elijah.

The plight of Elijah, every letter it's just getting worse.

I think that no matter how bad things get for me, I've at least got them, Beatrice and Elijah. Courtesy of Mr. Lipman. Mr. Lipman being a previous tenant in this flat. Living here sometime before me and Jabba. Mr. Lipman, God knows what to Beatrice. Him, long gone, but the letters from Beatrice still coming.


I watch the curtains billow.

All hemmed in with the silent no teeth bear and Jabba. With

Elijah, Beatrice and her squirrels.

I open a drawer and take out a piece of paper. There's a telephone number on it.

The drawer's full of things I've been meaning to do.

I read the number.

Type it into the phone:

'Hello, how're you doing?'

'OK, darling. How can I help you?'

'Who's working tonight?'

'Miki, darling. She's very-pretty-size-eight. Very-toned body. She has long hair. She does all services including A. She's well worth a visit.'

I smoke a cigarette, drink two beers, take a bath and drive to a cash point machine.

I'm thinking all of this is more than likely another huge mistake but now we're talking prostitutes I might as well introduce my mother.

# A LITTLE LIQUORICE CIRCLE OF DOOM

Sitting there in this gloomy cottage in a hill-top-town with the dehumidifier always on. That's the way she is when I first see her. When I'm ten years old and 'Manny, this is your mum,' my father says, before leaving me and this woman to it.

All this being news to me.

I've got a feeling, as my dad's car creeps up that steep hill and into cloud, that something strange's happening. I'm thinking a profanity like it might actually be of practical help. Profanity already skirting the periphery of every waking moment.

One hand with some rings and a cigarette burning away in-between two fingers, it's resting on the TV remote, as if the TV remote smokes and she's being generous. The other hand feeling in a paper bag like a blind bird, nuzzling in there for something, as my dad's car's turning and going back down the hill and out of this cloud and away from me, this woman, and the dog on her lap.

The one that's staring at her like it's been hypnotised.

My eyes all snagged and caught amongst her wrinkles.

She looks really old.

'Does his face look a little bit twisted? Just a *bit,* Manny? Don't you think?' That's the first thing she says. I'm supposing she's asking me about the dog. Like that's the correct way to acknowledge a son who's never seen you before. Who's never heard a thing about you. She's not even looked at me yet.

I hear a machine noise then and focus in on it. Like that could change anything.

'What is it?' I ask.

'What's what?' she says, still looking at that dog.

Amongst more dog-talk she tells the dog it's a dehumidifier. She asks the dog for clarification.

The dog's like her crystal ball.

'What's a dehumidifier— ?' I ask. Not knowing what to call her, just leaving a gap where I might have said something more personal.

Like Mum.

She doesn't seem to mind.

'It pulls the moisture out of the air,' she says, 'The *wetness.*' She does something with her face as she looks at the dog. 'It's wet,' she says, nudging her head across to indicate the outside world. 'It *is.* Here it's *so* wet, isn't it *darling*? Sucks it in, doesn't it?' She makes a sucking noise as if the dog might like it.

The dog's wide eyed and staring.

I'm thinking she's like a person in a film. And in that film everything depends on her not breaking off from looking at that dog. Like the whole world would end if she did.

I wonder whereabouts on the road back my dad is and picture the back of his car. The red lights and the one head where there should be two.

All this five minutes away from me staring at her dog's hairy head and imagining a pulsating pink tube in there all ridged up and waiting to go. Like the fat concertinaed lump you get half way down particular worms. Because this woman is the new director in my life, the new conductor who's already making a strange music familiar to the tiny hapless orchestra that's me. Her being the kind of woman that tells a ten year old boy she's worried about the veins in her dog's head going bang. This woman, the mother I never knew I had, she moves her jaw as though she's trying to bite off her left ear. There's a thin black ring around the inside of her lips from whatever's in that bag.

A little black circle of doom.

The dehumidifier goes silent and shudders like it knows it's all bullshit. Only then she takes her eyes from that dog, slides them towards the dehumidifier, as though it's family that's just farted or something.

She hugs me and kisses the top of my head and my cheek but she never does let go of that dog.

The one that never has a stroke but dies from lung cancer like all the others.

Never *veins* in their *heads*.

Her, wrong every time.


My new routine—the brown cobwebs on the small ceilings in the downstairs' rooms. The ones I start getting down with a stick like I'm making candy-floss. Her, not the least bit concerned with me being up on chairs and windowsills and the dining table, in June, with the paper christmas tablecloth and its little faded green trees and all that red that's gone pink.

My new routine—walking along the ridge of that place from the cottage and back with bags and bags of black toffee. Me, this little donkey to sadness and her confection. The women in the shops asking where my mother is because a boy my age is too young to be out on his own. I'm thinking she's back in the cottage smoking and being anxious and eating this shit and looking a fucking-hundred-and-fucking-three. That's where she is. The Fucks in big endless waves, because, since my dad deserted me, I feel the fucking need to use language he'd have called profane.

My new friends' mothers that don't look like mine.

Who arrive at school and get out of cars and talk to one another. Even maybe run through the playground when they're in a hurry. I'm not able to imagine them sitting at home, in the same chair, saying the same things over and over, always on the end of a cigarette while spiders you never see run amok on the ceilings making webs for nicotine and tar and dry, empty air. *They* haven't been made to look like Rameses The Third by a dehumidifier going full-tilt in July.

Not being like my mother at all.

My mother that *isn't*.

Things always seeming to be like that. Appearing to be one thing while all along being something different. Like her not being my real mother for one. The old woman who only ever takes a break from fixating on the health of her dog to fixate on the crossword puzzle or the deaths being no more a blood relation to Little Manny than the dehumidifier's a fucking aunt.

# FINDING NUMBER 5

I'm outside an apartment block by the Thames, looking through big glass doors at a vase of flowers on a table. Everything here plush but for my reflection. I stare at it. Push some hair from my face. Notice some dried paint under my forearm. I stand in the doorway and pick at that.

I watch my fingers trace a row of numbered buttons.

I press number 5.

'Hello, darling. Come on up. Second floor.'

I climb the stairs. Watching myself. Feeling that everything that happens on a daily basis has a place in my head to put it. That this doesn't. Just white noise where a normal consciousness should be.

Not knowing whether she's a maid, a madam or a prostitute when this girl opens the door to number 5 before I reach it.

She smiles really nicely.

The hall's like a strange garment as I stand there, smiling at her and saying nothing. Holding on to the Australian? girl maid/madam's smile like a buoy out at sea.

'She'll be ten minutes, darling.'

I follow her into a room.

'You can wait in here, darling,' she says. 'You like a drink?'

'No,' I say, watching her as she leaves the room. Wondering at the protocol of this place. Knowing nothing of it. Deciding this girl must be a maid or a madam. Like that's the first foot on the first rung of the ladder that's this big new mystery.

Trying to throw down an anchor by concentrating on this room.

It's clean. Like a hotel bedroom. There's a long dressing table with an open book on it.

There's a long mirror above the long dressing table. I glance at myself. There's a small television in the corner. It's on. I turn it off. I open the drawer of the bedside table to a steel vibrator on top of a bank statement. Open the wardrobe and look at neatly put away clothes. There's a bookshelf with a line of airport fiction on it. I read the titles of some of the books. Try to imagine someone sitting in this room, reading, casually.

I go back to the dressing table and flick through the book. I'm assuming that this is the room in which I'm going to get reacquainted with sex. I look at a photograph of a beautiful Latin woman and put my hand down my pants. I feel as though I'm holding another man's penis as I hold mine and look perplexed and try to gauge its potential in an environment like this.

There are moaning noises from another room.

A woman moaning—Miki who's pretty and a size eight.

Who has long hair.

I try to strike up a connection between my brain and my penis for Miki. I collage together an oriental size eight from nowhere, bite my lip and persist.

The Miki in my head, she falls apart.

I look up towards the ceiling and mouth 'Fuck off,' really slowly. Vaguely aware that the moaning noises have stopped.

The door opens. The maid/madam looks at me. She lifts her head and follows my gaze to the ceiling. She looks down to where my missing hand should be. I'm at this table set for a feast, with fifteen strange Knives, as many peculiar forks, and, knowing nothing of the etiquette, I'm holding the wrong cutlery.

She gives me a nice smile as I let it go.

'Come on through, darling,' she says.

I follow her while dividing my average weekly wage by straight sex. Hal from 2001 singing Daisy Daisy a long way off.

She shows me into another room. It's like the first, only smaller and with more evident signs of what's about to happen.

Miki's nowhere.

There's a ruched towel on the bed like an enormous, fancily folded napkin in a restaurant.

There's an electric fan and a bedside table with a tube of lube, baby wipes and a can of air freshener on it. There's a green hand written menu encased in plastic on the bed.

The room smells sweet and hot and musty, like the air in it might fertilise the wallpaper.

I stare at the wallpaper closely. Run a hand across it.

She comes in dancing, like an oriental clock automaton above a street in Austria.

The Daisy Daisy thing disappears.

'Darling,' she says, and glances at the wallpaper.

She's wearing a flimsy slip and a smile.

'Darling,' she says.

She goes around and round, smiling, saying darling and glancing at the wallpaper.

I smile, stupidly. 'Hi,' I say. 'Miki,' I say. 'Hi.'

'Hi,' she says. 'What you called?' she asks.

'Manny,' I say.

'Me not Miki,' she says.

'Oh,' I say.

She slides her hand under my shirt and moves her head towards the bed and looks at the menu and nods her head slightly towards it and smiles. 'What you want, Manny darling?' she asks.

'I want to remember where things are on a woman,' I tell her and smile.

She looks past me towards the wall.

'What?' she says.

## ZIP-THING

She asks me if I want anything. If I'm OK sitting there, where I am. I say yes and thank you and clench my fists and look across at my father as this woman in a uniform walks away.

I don't like seeing him lying there looking like that.

Me, Little Manny. A ten year old boy. I don't like it at all.

Him with a long straight dry brown cut down his chest as if some monster had come in during the night and stolen his heart.

It looks like a zip.

I'm sitting there, in an orange padded chair, a knee close to the thing like a handbag that's hanging off the rail which runs along the side of his bed.

The translucent thing like a handbag that's full of my father's urine.

A man walks past with the same zip thing and another long one down the inside of his leg. Two nurses are carrying things attached to that man as the man walks past my father's bed.

They look like they're heading off for a day at the beach

or something.

I noticed this bad smell as soon as I sat down but I'm thinking I have to be brave and I'm thinking that maybe all places like this smell of shit.

I notice I'm hardly thinking the word FUCK at all. The word FUCK's not running around in my head. I'm having to find it and prize it out like any other word. And then its only coming quietly.

I'm kind of wishing it was there for company.

Even my fuck's gone wrong.

My dad's giving me this strange look.

I've never seen him with a bare chest like this in a public place except for swimming.

If you look, carefully, you can see that everybody in bed, they've all the same zip thing. I wonder if my father has a long one on the inside of one of his legs as well. Like the beach man.

A nurse smiles as she takes readings from all the machines attached to my father. She looks at the handbag thing and lifts the tube attached to it that disappears into my father's bed. She peers in.

She doesn't look happy when she does that.

Another nurse comes along and says lots of cruel things to my father. Him, lying there, with this look on his face. A look that makes me find I have no muscles in my body and my skeleton's made of thin paper and my lungs can hardly move to take in any air.

Me, like that, and him this fleshy bit of plumbing, with things going in and things coming out.

The nurse lifts my father's bedclothes and crinkles his face up and shakes his head and looks like a big angry animal on TV and says, 'Really, that's disgusting. Do you soil yourself like this at home?'

The nurse saying this makes time stop.

I go completely rigid in the padded orange chair. I hold my breath. I can't move my head. I can only move my eyes, slowly.

My father's right there, next to me: this boy with no muscles and a paper skeleton who can't breathe.

He's looking down at his hands.

There're tears in his eyes.

There's his face, and then his chin, then the top of the dry brown cut which makes a straight line down to his hands.

Two weeks later he's killed by complications.


With a personal history like that, sooner or later, you're bound to hit complications.

# THE PHOENIX THING

It's just a small daily miracle. A giant compensation for the night before.

A neurological penance.

Every night incinerating yourself with drink to wake up a small pile of ash and do the Phoenix Thing. To get it washed, brush its teeth, take its pills, put its clothes on, look in the mirror and say 'Fuck.'

Scraping the ash together to call it Manny and get it down the stairs.

Or, wake as ash on the stairs already (having been too well incinerated the night before to understand the complexities of a door) and, in a position that even ash finds it difficult to comprehend, be woken by the builder who lives upstairs as he tries to get to work around you in his big boots.

You, losing any first-person narrative in this mashed up, degraded state. The percentage of 'I' in ash being far too small. The 'Me' amongst it, at the moment, negligible.

Fuck.

You smile at the builder from the floor as if everything is OK.

Be surprised that some part of you bothers to read the label on one of his boots.

Get down the horribly echoing stairs, out the door that's loud and into the car that's quiet.

Reconstitute.

Being vaguely grateful that ash, apparently, feels no shame.

You drive to work in the quiet car and picture a Petri dish containing a culture in which anything will grow. Picture every night prising the lid off. Every morning forcing it back down against a forest of phantoms grown from thoughts.

You squeeze it down.

You drive to work. Smoke cigarettes. Listen to the radio and do the Phoenix Thing.

A man on the radio says 'Don't talk to your neighbours, don't talk to your friends—if you're signing on and working *we know* who you are.' Then a woman says, 'It's no use hiding your car, *we know* you haven't got a tax disc.'

Feel paranoid.

Hold onto the steering wheel like the machinations of this road are as complicated as an asteroid belt to one of Jabba's Sci-fi TV heroes.

Fuck.

Wonder what else they know.

Glance in the rear-view mirror and notice the subtle imprint of some stripes and some backward writing across the side of your face from the metal-edge-tread thing on the stairs.

Inhale largely on a cigarette as the radio-man with throat cancer posthumously gargles the dangers of smoking.

Stare at the radio.

Be convinced that it's talking to you, personally.

Yawn and blink.

Gurn with your mouth because it does make a difference.

It does.

It does.

It does.

Keep picturing yourself as others might see you. At this time in the morning that being difficult. At this time in the morning there being nobody most everywhere out there. Just a lot of illuminated business that is London. Dart your eyes around to find an other who could be looking at you to get the correct vantage point in your head for a vision you know is going to be terrifying.

Suspect that this is a symptom of something.

On rewind, try to remember the night before, saying 'Fuck off!' to the radio, nonetheless.

Fill with trepidation at the sight of the first, big roundabout. Never knowing with clarity whether it should be left, right or straight ahead.

Remembering that you work in lots of different places.

It could be left. It could be right. It could be straight ahead.

Poor ash, being shit at navigation.

But liking little Edward Hoppers all the way to work.

A woman sitting at the back of a two-tone cafe. All on her own. Burgundy under the dado, cream above. The tables and chairs black. The woman over a big white cup of something. Then a small Thai shop. An oriental woman on the way in. No big colours in there—just small fragments of brightness like hundreds and thousands.

And big lit up billboards advertising TV and new films.

Say 'Fuck.'

Drive at 40mph past a speed camera.

Say 'Fuck.'

Always say Fuck a lot in the morning.

Say, 'Fuck, I missed it,' to a huge illuminated billboard being beautiful TV women languishing by a picket fence, like so much small washing blowing away. On... the night before when You'd missed *everything*.

Say 'Fuck,' again.

Think they looked *great*.

Meet the eyes of a woman who's crossing the road in front of you on faded black and white stripes. Do that scratch-card thing with her expression and yours—*looking for love in everyone*.

Try to Forget you thought that.

Still be saying, 'Fuck, I *missed* it,' ten minutes later.

Know you're part of something because you still know you have a penis.

As ash waiting
to become
Manny.

Fuck.

Or, say, Shit. For variety.

'Shit.'

## PALM TREES IN BARKING

Heights Are Bad.

Heights are a direct challenge to throw yourself off them and see if they work.

There's no doubt that heights are bad.

Gravity will take absolutely no convincing that it should do anything other than let you mercilessly fall. Gravity's mean— heights prove it. Gravity's a gauntlet thrown down by God to those with the slightest inclination to jump. Or those with poor proprioception who can't be sure what their right leg is doing while instructing their left leg to do something different.

I feel I fail on both counts as far as God's immediate gauntlet's concerned.

I feel I've got a relationship to heights like a Tourette's sufferer to the word *Cunt*.

Except my relationship to heights is much more dangerous.

It being possible to leap into the word *Cunt* and come back as often as you like.

Heights not being so forgiving.

The sky-lift's here, its big arm, on the end of which I'll soon be, bisecting the sky as the physical embodiment of God's challenge to me: an I'll-take-you-up-*you*-throw-yourself-off-thing.

The carpenters are in a cage on its extended arm. They're preparing to erect a sign saying something in Thai, high up on the side of a derelict factory in Barking. They don't look in the least bit concerned. The only challenge they seem to feel God's setting them is how to get to breakfast as soon as possible. Them, being able to do that easily, any morning of the week. I feel that God's incredibly unfair with the different gauntlets he's throwing down: death for me/breakfast for them.

It doesn't make any sense.

The good coffee shops end in Whitechapel, in Barking the best you can get's what I'm drinking, although I'm unaware of drinking anything, everything being so totally eclipsed by this ballooning fear that's belittling any sensory pleasure as a pathetic irrelevance when faced with the little springboard trip/the bold definitive jump into the unforgiving, murderous, downward-hurtling arms of gravity.

I'm noticing, with increasing chagrin, that God has a tendency to embolden his chosen recipients of the death gauntlet—not the breakfast gauntlet—The *Death* gauntlet, with the added disadvantage of that *fuck-what's-happening-to-my-knees?* thing.

I'm aware I'm judging God by the apparent laws of the universe as I might a regular person by the clothes they choose to wear.

I'm finding God wanting in every conceivable way.

I blink.

'Hey, Manny,' shouts this carpenter.

I look up and blink.

'Which way up should this thing go?'

I watch him, this carpenter. And the other one. I blink. They

21

gesture with open palms. I look down towards the sign. It's some distance below them.

'I don't know,' I shout. 'How the fuck should I? How *should* I know? It's totally impenetrable. I don't read Thai.'

The sign rests on a low roof below the face of the building on which it's to be fixed.

'Try it the other way round,' I suggest.

They finish securing the baton on which the sign's to sit. The operator lowers the cage. The carpenters get out onto the low roof. They flip the sign.

They look at me. 'Well?'

I tell them, 'Fuck knows,' aggressively, not feeling too inclined to be helpful. Thinking why should I be helpful? I'm going up there in the I'll-take-you-up-*you*-throw-yourself-off-thing. They'll be eating breakfast as I'm trying to not oblige.

I swallow. My mouth's dry.

On the other side of a wall a hundred yards away prop men are positioning fibreglass palm trees. I notice the art director walking towards us.

'Hey, Greg,' I say. 'What do you reckon?'

Greg looks up at the sign. He doesn't know either. He hasn't the faintest idea. He appears to know as little or even less than anyone else.

'Try it the other way around so I can take a look,' he says. The carpenters are standing on an ancient concave concrete roof that's friable and full of holes. The sign's twelve feet high. It looks really heavy. One says, 'Fucking hell.' The other says, 'We just done that already.'

They flip the sign.

Greg still doesn't know.

He phones the man who made the sign.

'That's fine,' he says.

I finish my coffee.

22

'I couldn't see anywhere selling good coffee on the way in,' says Greg.

'It's not available this far out,' I tell him. 'The rate of good coffee shops per mile, it just dies after Whitechapel. It's a kind of demarcation line to civilized London—this far out you're too conspicuous holding a Starbucks' latte. This far out you want to be holding a polystyrene cup, wearing a shaved head and the England strip in nylon, have tattoos and be able to say Fuck 'n Cunt in front of your children.'

Greg says something I can't make out.

He walks back towards the palm trees.

I transfer some gear from my car to the sky-lift cage so Stuart, the operator, might take me up to lay my cards down with God. The carpenters go to breakfast. The *fuck-what's-happening-to-my-knees?* thing betrays me to Stuart immediately. It's difficult to ignore the dancing mixtures of paint in my buckets and the way my long garden wand with a hose—a device for spraying diluted down paint—is wandering in my hand as if it were gripped by a sufferer of Parkinson's divining water above an artesian basin. Stuart, he's looking at me with the merciless disregard of the completely disinterested in testing gravity, oblivious to an alternative reality where everything's viewed as some kind of gauntlet, and possessing perfect proprioception type; a type that in itself is another gauntlet to me. I notice Stuart opening his mouth. I know that what's coming is born out of, at best, courtesy, or at worst, Stuart's inclination that should he be with a jumper, it's wise to be pacifying the jumper, just in case the jumper feels the need to take the operator with him.

Stuart's read about people like me in training manuals.

'Are you OK?'

'That rather depends.'

'On what?'

'On the state of my credit.'

'On the state of your credit with who?'

Stuart doesn't like the way I'm looking up at the sky. He doesn't like the way I say 'God,' as if he should've known. I don't like the way Stuart tries to surreptitiously clip himself to the cage with his safety harness, as if I'm some kind of madman and not to be trusted. It's then I make a mistake in referring to the sky-lift in a way that, in retrospect, I can see might be easily misinterpreted. All Stuart hears is the 'I'll-take-you-up-*you-throw-yourself-off*' bit. The psychology of it's weird. As soon as Stuart starts looking as terrified as anybody I've ever seen, I feel much better. Stuart's somehow managed to steal the mantle of jumper. I feel that if God has any bad intent as far as gravity and falling is concerned, Stuart's somehow volunteered himself for the part and left me in the clear.

I dirty down the sign.

Make it look as though it belongs to an old, derelict factory.

I catch glimpses of a different London. It occurs to me that down there on the street, everything's seen from far too close up; like having your eyes pressed up against the bare breast of a woman and seeing only flesh. Where from up here, from this vantage point, you can actually see the shape and curve of the woman that's London.

I think she's beautiful.

I smile at Stuart in the way a very relaxed man without a care in the world might smile at anybody. I think it strange that Stuart should have stolen my *fuck-what's-happening-to-my-knees?-thing* as well.

'It's odd. Don't you think?'

'What's odd?'

'Life. You never can tell.'

He just looks at me.

'How things will turn out. What will happen next.'

I smile and look at Stuart with the merciless disregard of

someone completely disinterested in testing gravity.

Stuart attempts to bring the cage down, as though whatever repository of fear he's built up in all the easy hours he's spent as master of this cage is suddenly unleashed. He's operating the machine with faltering indecision and timidity.

The carpenters return from breakfast just in time to witness Stuart on his hands and knees kissing the ground like the Pope.

They've never seen anything like that before.

'Very *fucking* peculiar,' one carpenter's saying to the other as I skip into the factory.

There are props lying around: large wooden crates, ammunition boxes and machine parts. A rigger is up a scissor-lift attaching lights to the ceiling.

'Manny, we need you to do some graffiti on the walls,' says Greg. '*Thai* graffiti.'

'Oh, yeah?' I say. 'What's the reference?'

He offers a crumpled page from a Thai newspaper.

'Anything from that,' he says.

'Anything?' I ask, '—doesn't matter what it actually says?'

'No,' he says.

I paint a selection of Thai graffiti onto three of the walls he's indicated. I just pick random groups of words from the newspaper. The unknown Thai being:

AGEING SKIN TYPES
SIXTEEN SESSIONS IS HIGHLY RECOMMENDED
CHICKENS ARE

Then I phone Nadia from number 5. I tell her what I'd like to write next. She photo-messages me an approximation.

Greg says that the graffiti's fine. He really likes it.

I pack my gear back into the car and leave.

Opposite CHICKENS ARE is the last graffiti. It says,

approximately:

GOD – THE QUEEN – THE PRESIDENT – THE PRIME
MINISTER
A SUCCESSION OF CUNTS


The next location's across Town. I drive through central London.
Past designer shops. I watch women glide by on the pavement
as if God were running the pavement on a different timeline.

I picture God dragging a finger along the edge of reality for
these women.

Who look sublime.

Who're drifting elegantly into sublime shops.

I catch the illuminated, aspic interior of a shop selling monogrammed luggage. Full of sublime women. Sublime women of
27. Sublime women of 64. I'm thinking that even for all their
platinum cards, they look so desperately sad, with their modern
woman's knowledge that the great beyond's an infinity of nothing.

I look up at the sky.

That's when I hit the Irishman.

I see him ever so briefly: he's digging a hole in the middle
of the road with a jackhammer, an horrific wide-eyed stare, a
fluorescent green waistcoat and ear protectors.

He's *really* old.

Must be 76.

At least.

There are no bollards between the two of us.

Nothing.

The sublime women don't look.

Everybody else forms a crowd.

They witness the Irishman lying under his jackhammer like
a knight on a tomb in an old church.

The police arrive.

I take a breathalyser test. I feel very animated. My head keeps snapping to the Irishman. Maybe this is standard behaviour for people in my position. The police, they don't seem in the least bit concerned.


The Irishman, he's very much dead.

I pass the breathalyser test.

The police take me away nonetheless.


Luckily, the Irishman turns out to be somewhat of a Council vigilante; he's often been setting up shop, where he shouldn't have been, with far too few bollards. He *was* 76, but had managed, somehow, to evade retirement. His eagerness, or most likely the necessity for him to keep making money, had combined with a bureaucratic Council loophole through which he'd fallen to meet his fate with me.

I picture him underneath his jackhammer.

This dead old Irishman.

My first real victim.

I sense a certain hostility from the police. I believe them to be very much in allegiance with the dead Irishman. The overriding feeling seems to be that I've publicised an anomaly in the employment practice of the Council by killing their oldest employee. They would have far rather I hadn't. That's how it appears to me.


The Irishman's been dead for a day.

I'm surprisingly unmoved. I put this down to the fact that the pills I've been taking for months enable me to view some significant elements of my life in a pleasantly distant and distracted way. I appear to be able to cope with big things; things of a certain enormity. It's all the minutiae that I find insurmountable.

Anything with a delicate nuance.


I arrive at a garage-set in a rugby club car park—the next location—36 hours late. The same Manny but people seem to be reacting very differently to me. The carpenters are very deferential. Very polite. They're hanging about as though I'm some porn film on a loop.

Even The Cloud and Invisible Nick look at me strangely.

The fact that I don't look in the least bit traumatised only seems to increase the strangeness of their behaviour.

I keep saying '*What?*'

They just smile.

It takes me three hours to realise that the respect I've never managed to gain by the quality of my work has been afforded me, in the blink of an eye, by the merciless killing of an old Irishman.

It's a beautiful morning.

We work on the interior the carpenters have built full square in the middle of the gravel-covered car park like a doll's house in the middle of a carpet. We paint the walls to make them look like breeze-block. There's no roof. We're under the shadows of the carpenters who're attaching timber batons to the top of the set while working like a curious poultice; pulling out the mechanics of something big—the slaying of an ancient Irishman.

I feel that it was one thing to witness myself running over this old man who should've been sitting on a couch somewhere but was out and about in a fluorescent jacket and ear defenders—I feel it's quite another to barter with the details.

I barter, nonetheless.

The amount of the story they manage to be getting from me seems to be running in direct correlation with a downward turn in the weather.

The carpenters' shadows disappear as thick black clouds slide overhead.

They notice what's happening. This transition. The eerie nature of it.

They start attaching plastic tarpaulins to the batons like medieval farmers protecting a hay-rick. Their shadows come back fitfully as an electrical storm runs cheap, flat strobes of light parallel to the earth. Below, standing amongst brief silhouettes of them struggling, with the rain coming down as though it's been saving itself up all summer, we, the painters, read one another's faces. We're holding our roller-poles like three chiefs in the back of beyond.

A cold wind flaps the tarpaulin.

'*What*?' I ask.

I wonder if maybe the stuff on the walls in Barking was some strange, Thai, talismanic, Satanic shit.

I wonder if maybe God, the Queen, The President, The Prime Minister and the dead Old Irishman are out to get me.

# M&Ms

I'm sitting in traffic when I catch sight of a fat woman on the pavement who's dragging along a fat boy who's eating from a bag of M&Ms. He, in turn, pulls a worn out fragment of a personal jigsaw back to me in the form of Eddy Michaelheimmer's fat mother's M&M covered breasts.

Eddy Michaelheimmer, who'd always been OK about visiting my mother's house when everyone else had known better. The hilltop town being small enough for them all to have heard about the noises my mother's fucking dog made and everything else.

Eddy Michaelheimmer's head was full of the suffering of the Jewish people. For as long as he could remember his father had clearly and graphically indicated the plight of the Jewish people with the aid of a small book filled with horrific black and white photographs that threw a big bad light out into a dark empty space in little Eddy's head. A space he might have populated with something different of his own volition years later. Eddy Michaelheimmer, whose mother was the fattest

Jewish woman in town. With the saddest eyes. A big, spectacular vision to barter for Eddy's friends: her, watching TV from bed all day long. A giant packet of M&Ms on her enormous breasts. A remote control balanced on an enormous thigh, like that's what thighs like that were made for. Her big sad soulful eyes traversing her breasts to the TV and back again. She, attempting to forget the plight of the Jewish people like that.

Eddy and I trading visions of our parents as though we were stuck in the back-end of a zoo populated by monsters.

Pointing and being amazed.

I sit in traffic thinking how you're like a bit-part player in your own peculiar past. The Manny from way back then, sometimes I can only witness him as a stranger.

This Little Manny Marbas.

Little Eddy, who knew the most peculiar facts from each year's issue of The Guinness Book Of Records, verbatim, and was desperate to witness a family that was more monstrous than his own.

He couldn't wait to get to Little Manny's house and hear the noises that his mother's fucking dog made and everything else.

He'd take in the disarray in the winter gloom with the bulbs nearly all gone. He never knew whether he preferred the winter gloom and imagining the half-seen indications of all that filth and squalor, or the full-on summer illuminated revelations of how little Little Manny and his mother could cope with being human.

They'd steal some of Little Manny's mother's liquorice toffees and get themselves comfortable in the dinning room like they were at the cinema or something.

It always took the dog longer to get going when there was company.

Eddy Michaelheimmer, he'd go into the front room and look for the black ring of liquorice around Manny's mother's mouth and smile towards that and ask her, so politely, to please start talking *all-Coochy-Coochy-coo* to her dog. Please. Her sitting off there in the gloom somewhere with the dog on her lap. It staring at her. Mesmerised.

And then he'd come back and sit next to Manny.

Going *Coochy-Coochy-coo* turned the dog into something that sounded like a whale and made people stop in the street outside. They'd hang about in the cloud beyond the rigid, smoked-orange net curtains and the filthy glass of the small window and listen to the eerie whale noise too.

Little Manny and Little Eddy's weekly show.

Sitting and waiting for the *Coochy-Coochy-coo*.

The dog starting on the long peculiar whale noise and Manny's mum saying words in a way that she knew would make the whale noise worse and the whale noise from the dog building and building and her moaning back something similar and Eddy's eyes widening and his big smile taking up more and more of his face like he just knew all this was the best thing ever.

Little Manny would get up and distract the fucking dog when it all started sounding too much like sex on TV. Eddy Michaelheimmer sitting there in an ecstatic state like he was being fed ice-cream with a long spoon by a girl with tits.

After a few weeks of whale noises Eddy and Manny added some little moans of their own to the big aquatic ones coming from the next room. It seemed important to be able to make a new thing in your life that was something other than fat mothers with M&Ms or dogs with delicate veins or the death of millions of black and white jews or the death of your father, as Manny found some kind of solace in his fat Jewish friend Eddy.

That was about the time that Manny realised he could draw and the others were blind as they told their hands holding pencils to go left a bit and they went right a lot. Manny couldn't understand how the others couldn't see what was in front of them when they had their eyes wide open and all they had to do was look.

It was kind of fetching in Eddy but pathetic in the others.

Three weeks later everything about Eddy stopped being fetching. Little Manny discovered Eddy's sister Kate and took solace in a preferred physical under-the-dining-table sexual topography.

Eddy'd cried and played with himself at the other end of the dusty green trees and the faded pink. Him, alone, casting glances at Little Manny and his sister drawing the best possible pleasure through their fingertips from one another and acting like Eddy was invisible.

Afterwards they both smiled at him and that was even worse.

Foreign travel, years later, always reminding Manny of Kate.

As familiar material thrown together in a wonderfully different way.


I'm sitting in London traffic picturing it like that...

Because that's more like the reality of it.

This bad bad fiction.

My past.

# THE NEEDLE

Dear Mr. Lipman,

On recent visits to Elijah I have made some worrying observations. He is still as slow as a snail and still sometimes rational, but the rational times worry me now too. He will keep talking about the "Needle". When pressed he says the "Needle" is what you get if you don't go quietly. When pressed as to who exactly is going to give him the needle, he says the nurses; that he's seen it done before— they did it, apparently, to Mrs. Jenkins down the hall. She wasn't going to go quietly, so, she got the needle. After that, Elijah says, one of the nurses winked at him in the day room and said, 'Better for everyone.'

Elijah is petrified that he won't go quietly and that he'll get the needle. That they'll "quieten him for good and proper"—so that he doesn't upset the others.

*Last week I took him out to a tea-room we've been going to for forty years. Everybody was being so kind and helpful, but after eating a lardy cake that he'd soaked in tea, Elijah stood up and non-chalantly urinated over the back of his chair, sat down—without paying any attention to whether it was tucked back in or not—and preceded to rifle through my handbag. At this point I said, 'Elijah what are you doing?' and Elijah, in front of everyone, as if he hadn't done enough already said, 'I'm looking for the needle you something something.'*

*Honestly, Mr. Lipman, how does one go on? I shall never be able to show myself in the rectory rooms again.*

*Even the squirrels are becoming an irritation!*

*Love Beatrice.*

## VLADIMIR'S PENCHANT

The Hoover thing's different.

I know my mistake's in trying to explain the logic of it to the woman across the road. The woman who witnessed me naked at three in the morning, trying to find out what the Hoover thing was all about.

The Latvian/Polish/Czech woman.

Me, all backlit in my kitchen window like a disgusting oriental paper puppet.

I know by the way she keeps saying 'Yes,' that she isn't following me at all.

For two days I'd been conscious of a growing sensation in my left ear. I put it down to urine, faeces and chlorinated water. I'd taken to swimming again. I'd spent a good part of the previous week in the local pool.

Years before, Italian food had driven me to swimming shortly before swimming had nearly killed me.

I'd met this Italian exchange-student with poor English.

We struck up a relationship based on sex, carbohydrates,

hand gestures and post-coital cigarettes. She, Bella, was proficient at three but hapless and dangerous with the fourth. She was more than contentedly soporific after sex, she was catatonic—a tendency which I (with a then less acute but soon to be burgeoning sense of self-doubt) quite rightly put down to a genetic abnormality. According to Bella, two of her relatives had suffered adversely from the same problem: a luckless baby cousin suffocated by an overweight, penniless aunt with a voracious sexual appetite, a drink problem and only one bed; and an ancient grandfather with a predilection for smoking and wearing antique, highly flammable celluloid collars and an outrageously large beard. The severity of the old man's death having immolated his name from my memory as successfully as he'd immolated himself from his own front-room.

I was never sure whether the surreal quality of her relatives' deaths was due to my misunderstanding of her poor English or whether I was actually nightly putting my life into her hands in the form of a last shared cigarette.

She was a big girl. I'd lie dreamily beside her, amongst the pillows, picturing hideous deaths in Italy while paying close attention to her closing eyes and falling hands and wondering at the size of her breasts.

When she wasn't attempting to murder us both in our sleep she methodically taught me how to cook.

I enjoyed rolling meat balls while watching her in the kitchen.

I watched her while we made love.

She had a way of looking at me during and after sex. That was enough.

I started to approach sex with Bella the same way I expect an anorexic might approach a plate of food: at worst never, at best with trepidation. I found myself to be filled with trepidation around a naked and conscious Bella. She stopped being my sexual partner the moment I realised she was such an accurate meter to the fucked up nature of Me. That's what she thought, anyway. However, there was something about her catatonic, sleeping self, her complete lack of awareness, that nightly turned trepidation into sexual frenzy.

I couldn't wait to position her prone amongst the pillows, to compose this wonderful, inert draped sleeping Venus.

To abuse it repeatedly.

Every which way.

It was the lack of any kind of judgement of my performance on her behalf that was so completely liberating.

It was sublime.

Perfect.

I'd walk around the bedroom having solitary post-coital between-bouts cigarettes. I'd catch glimpses of her patient, beautiful, sublimely awaiting nocturnally-white arse raised up on a bolster. A serene island rising from the trashed contours of my bed.

I'd never felt so close to a woman.

She left for Italy.

I drove her to the airport and waved at her plane as it was flatish, before it did that big lurching thing.

Her big white arse wrenched out of my life just like that to leave me two stone heavier and uncomfortably closer to a Manny that I'd been oblivious to before.

I stopped eating Italian food and started haunting a local gym. I befriended a local shop keeper with a shoe shop, early closing on Wednesdays, a penchant for swimming in the sea, a fast car and an enormous, jealous wife. His name was Vladimir. He had a speech impediment: everything he said, he said inaudibly at the end of a long gasping breath at the beginning of which he was struck dumb and incapable of saying anything.

That was OK with me.

He had a thing about the sea. He had a thing about black women. And he hated shoes.

All this was evident in his shop.

Vladimir was not.

He employed two large white women to sell his shoes. Vladimir hid in a room at the back as the large white women cheerfully greeted customers with their smiles, big breasts and heavy perfumes—customers, who were desperate to be shocked by the shop's lacklustre presentation and the unavailability of the latest ranges; Vladimir's trade in the town being based solely upon his unrelenting ability to provide the townspeople with fresh and different stories of inept calamity and un-tradesman like behaviour. The shop always being full of people intent on prompting disaster while reluctant to buy anything. That was OK with Vladimir. Vladimir had more than plenty of money. He ran the shop solely to escape his enormous, jealous wife who was not black and who was the bane of his life because of it.

On that quiet, monotonous street, Vladimir's well-known and much discussed plight stood out like a disgustingly real ruby on a string of paste, as Vladimir, in his back room, thought about the sea and fixated on the two black carved ebony breasts which protruded from the only artwork he'd ever possessed and the big smiling women who were renowned for their reliable clumsiness as much as their girth brought down high piles of boxed shoes like fast glaciers upon customers all too willing to be insulted by such another valued and barterable offence against the values of good tradesmanship.

The shop was a totem to the town.

It was full of wonderfully totemic vignettes, like the never changing display of camouflaged platform-heels from the 1970s. The green-flash trainers that had overstayed their welcome long enough to temporarily disgust the townspeople by having the audacity to come back into style as retro-designer-label-foot-wear. Any small, albeit unwitting success for Vladimir being a huge festering insult to the town.

The most valuable, least-known truths about Vladimir's shop hid in his back-room along with Vladimir. They swelled magnificently in the town's imaginings, like some giant fungus in the dark. At the pinnacle of the town's curiosity was an imagined, shining, black ebony sculpture of a beautiful negress. She had been witnessed by a plumber thirty years before. He was a timid man full of an irrational fear when faced with anything other than that which had been familiar to him in the first dull years of his life. He had run to The Olde Ship Inn, on the crest of the hill that cradled this hilltop town, like a man on fire with an unwanted, foreign knowledge. Before he extinguished it with beer he planted a black spectre into the rich, fertile loam of the town's curiosity. Each generation fashioned it larger, blacker and shinier, more wondrously endowed than the last. Night or day she could be witnessed over Vladimir's shop: a colossal black nimbus with shining conical breasts and a face too black to behold.

I walked under her on the first Wednesday of my acquaintance with Vladimir. Vladimir's wife was just leaving. She didn't know me but she treated me the same way she treated everyone else—as someone who potentially represented a threat to her sole handling of the strings that dictated the fixed direction of Vladimir's life.

She looked at me as though she wanted to rip my head off.

I offered her my hand, 'Hello,' I said, 'I'm Manny.' The enormous woman who wasn't black swelled in front of me. I felt myself to be clinging like a luckless mountaineer under a giant heaving promontory of aggressive rock. 'I'm a friend of Vladimir's,' I said. The word Friend acted like a trigger to her metabolism. She blanched. She changed colour like a large, extraordinary sea-creature with a limitless capacity for anger.

She detached herself and strode away without saying a word. I watched her go. A lot of people on the street were watching the enormous woman and smiling from a safe distance.

Only I knew nothing of her history of violence.

Vladimir was blighted by his past. By his family's wealth. Generation after generation, successive sons had received bountiful inheritance and systematically showed not the slightest inclination to squander it in any way. The family were Quakers and proud of it. They clung to Quaker values like limpets to a clean rock in a polluted sea. Every successive Quaker son dutifully multiplied his inheritance and led a blameless life; they were all unremittingly good and faithful servants. It was evident the day Vladimir was born that something had gone horribly wrong; whatever gift of retail it was that had shone so brightly from the new-born eyes of all his forebears was plainly dormant now. The caretakers of the family fortune even thought they recognised a profligate will and a proclivity to squander in the early smiles and hesitant exclamations of the new-born baby. Lest anybody should forget the threat they felt him to be, they named him Vladimir and made the very contemporary decision that the management of the company should fall into the hands of his sister; she had been born, as expected, with a genetic predisposition to retail and the right look in her eyes.

Vladimir not only forfeited his inheritance, his ocular deficiency acted like a passport to a land devoid of love.

He was shunned with the same remorseless efficiency with which his Quaker family bore down on anything they found to be ineffective and wanted to be shot of.

The first few words he uttered were to an empty room— some mashed up syllables at the end of a halting breath.

Hyacinth Le-Grand filled the vacuum for Vladimir.

She was Vladimir's nanny. She was black and beautiful and loved Vladimir.

He loved her back with a vengeance.

He left on the spring tide of his life for Australia. He felt himself to be an anomaly and was looking to be washed up, wasted and insignificant far away. He tried his hand at opal mining. He was just another opal miner with a strange name and a penchant for swimming and black women. He took up with an Aboriginal girl called Peckum Desiree and was happy until he had to return on a different tide to bury a complete stranger with no more of a glint of any description in his eyes—Vladimir's father. It was too late for Vladimir to be the happy, returning prodigal son. He'd left for the wilderness, willing to obliterate himself with the loosest of women and the strongest of drink and drugs, without any kind of dowry to this marriage of sin from his father.

Vladimir stared at his father's eyes.

There was no chance now that this dead man might show his son any affection.

Vladimir found a drab little English town and the nearest thing to a white, black woman he could. He settled down, and, knowing little else, opened an independent shoe-shop. The two large white women started selling camouflaged platform heels and green-flash trainers as Vladimir began his long, languishing, solitary, self-imposed exile in a room in which the only concessions made to comfort were emotional ones. He was a big man sitting on a schoolroom chair at a schoolroom desk from where he daily confronted a giant wallpaper seascape, and, on top of his desk, a small, black, ebony sculpture of a beautiful negress. On its ebony base, in small, scratched letters, he'd inscribed one word:

*HYACINTH*

I was one of only a handful of people to have entered the room in thirty-five years.

Vladimir's chosen form of communication was monopolised

by facial expressions and physical gestures. He was practised at it. I followed him on our first outing; it was like following a benign and strangely casual SAS sergeant through enemy lines. That day we set the template for a weekly occurrence that two months later nearly occasioned me to lose my life.

Our wordless friendship blossomed each Wednesday as we left the hilltop town, found a distant beach, abandoned our clothes and confronted the sea. This was very cathartic. My fear of the sea was complete. The sea, to me, being like a horrifying on-button to the deepest, blackest parts of my imagination:

It was a big wet bully employed by death.

I'd had dealings with the sea before. It had nearly killed me as a child because of my fixation with the number fourteen. For a while, before I'd said a small good-bye to childhood neuroses, only to say a surprisingly immediate big hello to their adult equivalent, I'd been completely fixated by the number fourteen. If I ever became conscious of touching something while aware of this conundrum, I was driven to touch that thing fourteen times. Everything depended upon it, from the safety of my father to the legs of my cat. Thinking of the number fourteen while analysing a sea creature at the bottom of a deep rock pool had nearly killed me.

As a baby I'd screamed at the sight of the sea.

As a small boy I'd neurotically sealed the fate of the sea for Manny as an adult.

It couldn't be messed with.

It was like height.

Liquid height.

You took any shipping away, and the odd buoy, and it was completely, terrifyingly timeless. Behind you, the land—with all its obvious signs of human endeavour, its history of being coped with by humans—in front of you, the sea, a big blank declaration to your own fallibility. A *jump-in-me-and-let-me-*

*fucking-drown-you* thing. Full of faceless wet monsters and forces desperate to grab you by the ankles. To pull you off somewhere until the spark that drives you to want anything at all has been extinguished.

Swimming close to Vladimir was salutary.

Every week saying hello to the sea felt slightly less like playing Russian-roulette with a fully loaded gun.

Every week saying good-bye to the sea seemed slightly more poignant.

I looked forward to these therapeutic sessions with Vladimir.

The session that I had with Vladimir's enormous wife was completely different.

It happened outside Vladimir's shop, much to the delight of the crowd that witnessed it. I felt as though I were trying to argue with some giant piece of agricultural equipment. The fact that I wasn't having a sexual relationship with Vladimir plainly made no difference. In the arms of Vladimir's wife, I rode the equivalent of a liberated medieval ducking stool in the high street of a small gloomy country town with the certainty that I was damned if I had and damned if I hadn't.

When she'd finished I was on the ground, unconscious and in need of an ambulance.

The town was a-buzz for weeks.

I didn't care for that kind of exposure. I'd always craved anonymity.

My experience with Vladimir's enormous wife was left subconsciously standing in a queue that was then short but would soon become long—a queue of reasons to leave the country and move to London.

It was Russia that made the queue too long to bear.

I thought of Vladimir as I lay on my back in my local London pool. I stared up at the ceiling and smiled as the infection that would wake me in agony two nights later swam into my ear.

Waking up with a pain like that in my ear was bad. Getting up, at three in the morning, to walk naked into my kitchen, put the light on, find the hoover, remove it from its cupboard and applying its cold steel tube to my ear, to switch it on, all of this fulfilled a notion that at three in the morning, in complete agony, had seemed strangely logical.

I was only made conscious of how absurd this all might appear when a light came on in the kitchen of the flat immediately opposite: Me, the late night freak show, creased up and naked with an ear funnelled into a hoover. Smiling at the beautiful Latvian/Polish/Czech? woman opposite.

Before she'd looked so astonished, she'd looked very lovely, standing there, pouring a glass of water at her sink.

'Yes?' she's saying, standing there with a bag of groceries and a grimace.

'I'm very sorry. About last night. It was just... I've been doing a lot of swimming.'

'Yes.'

'And I woke up with the most terrible pain in my ear.'

The beautiful Latvian/Polish/Czech woman just looks at me.

'And I know I shouldn't have had the light on.'

I notice the Latvian/Polish/Czech woman sneak a glance at her watch.

'Or at least have been wearing some clothes.'

I'm longing for her to say Yes again. The yeses, they hadn't been much but they were better than the just looking and the glances. I know that first impressions count. I know she's probably not going to get beyond this. The one she's got of me.

'Yes,' she says.

She's a very beautiful Latvian/Polish/Czech woman.

The information from her face, her body and her posture, it's hitting my brain the same way alcohol and cigarettes hit the back of your throat.

I stand there inhaling her.

Drinking her in.

She walks off and takes it all with her.

I'm starting to look for God in my head because I've got this post-party washed out grievance coming on. I picture that expression you see on people's faces when they're walking around with a plastic bag of dog-faeces.

I think I'm wearing that same expression as I look to deposit this grievance.

I go back into the flat. Into the mess of the kitchen. Desperately trying to feel more optimistic about the Latvian/Polish/Czech woman.

A wall of noise is coming from Jabba's room: screeching tyres, howling engines and crashing cars all careering off a heavy-metal soundtrack.

There's a refrain: a tap-tap-tap-tap-tap-tap-tap and a slide of metal on glass.

I'm thinking I need advice about the Latvian/Polish/Czech woman.

That anyone will do.

Everything in Jabba's room's opaque and non-reflective with dust except for his skin. He's prone on the couch. Only the most minimal movement of his torso and the slightest lean of his head towards the TV. The furthest eye from the TV shut. The other just a slit. The speedometer on the TV, it's saying 185 mph.

'The Latvian/Polish/Czech woman opposite?' I'm shouting. 'Do you know anything about her?'

There's only this slightest movement of Jabba's nearest eye.

# JABBA

Jabba's like an air traffic controller. His aeroplanes: pleasures. With consummate skill, one night after the next, he guides them in: big curries, big joints, cocaine, cream cakes and endless TV.

He's a constant fucking revelation.

The simple pleasures in life, to me, they seem completely inaccessible. He's no such problem. He doesn't need help from anyone. He locates them easily with money and a telephone. His endless epiphanies of pleasure only ever a languid stretch of a slow arm away.

Jabba, he's into conspiracy theories: The Prime Minister eats babies. The Queen's a lizard. The President of America's related to lizards. All the big banks are run by lizards.

There are a lot of lizards.

As much as Jabba hates and despises lizards, he loves and admires aliens. His room is a homage to this intergalactic, un-requited love. Aliens litter every flat surface. Under a settled chiffon of dust they've long since slumped into one of his two favourite positions:

the recline

the catatonic.

They lie about like victims of some high-tech Lilliputian gas attack.

Any night—his raised finger pursuing a lazy semicircle of air as he takes in the latest arrangement of TV pixels.

Any night—'See,' he says. 'It's nothing to do with whether she's on fucking wide-screen or not.' Him being fixated with the way TV women let themselves go. The way they so quickly get to be the wrong side of slim.

His circling finger, the ongoing radar to his conning-tower head, it means *let's not get into talking when there's something on TV.*

TV being everything.

His circling finger with its Ghee sheen. Same as the rest of him.

I drink some wine, look from the TV woman to Jabba.

I screw up my eyes and scrutinise all the dead little prone aliens.

Jabba's entourage.

His small audience to the ongoing enlightenment of Jabba and the ongoing exposé of the naiveté of me. His congregation as he expounds his theories pertaining to the fucked-up nature of human beings from a horizontal position on his couch. From behind his coffee-table lectern and his remote control bibles comes his fire and brimstone space-theology with lazy horizontal gestures slowly punctuating hideous descriptions of alien intervention.

Amidst the steady onslaught of TV and pastries and first-press pollen hash. Behind drawn curtains, in the constantly pixilated gloom, he's living for alien intervention. He's awaiting the day he's totally convinced will come: when his enemies will be routed by unimagined instruments of death and he'll be sucked up in a beam of light.

I blink as I picture that.

In the meantime we hold weird discourses in the three minutes afforded us by commercial breaks to all the programmes he's so desperate not to miss.

Him being more practised at the art of TV than anyone I've ever known.

I watch him finger his five remote controls with the dexterity of a concert pianist.

I gaze at his massive bulk and fantasise about bludgeoning him to death with whatever dust-covered large blunt instrument might come to hand.

I think:

Not that I want to.

Not that I would.

It's just easy and accessible and only almost real because:

I do it every night.

Bludgeon Jabba.

I wonder about us. Him and me.

I remember a man in the country who had a pig which became sick. The man called the vet, the vet took a look at the pig and said that the pig was fine but that it was lonely. The vet said that the pig needed company—anything would do.

I'm sitting in this chair, part-ways pleasantly drunk, picturing this pig.

The pig that had a chicken put into its pigpen, got its appetite back and became fat and happy.

I'm staring at Jabba.

His head being permanently engaged with the largest pillow at the furthest end of the couch, leaving his feet always to be waving a big hello to me.

The feet emerging from the loose fitting TV trousers.

The big brown ascent of his belly.

Two intertwined sets of fingers like so many reclining figures on Hampstead Heath.

Beyond that, the brown chins—the foothills to Jabba's taught, oily face, inclined ever-so slightly to the right to better accept the nightly offering from the land of TV.

Somewhere in there a big drug-coshed sun of a consciousness, slowly, nightly, closing down on Jabba.

The couch, like the end of some mad paper-trail to self-indulgence, surrounded by the debris of his pleasures: cocaine paraphernalia, crashed cream cakes, macerated joints, fallen korma and ash.

I think how the position he spends as many hours in as he possibly can bears no relation whatsoever to the proximity of any cleaning tool or the kitchen sink. I think he's like a shameless incontinent with his own history of indulgence and neglect.

His subconscious defence seems to be based upon the premise that there's a limit to how seriously you can expect a man waiting on imminent alien intervention to take housekeeping. Him not taking it seriously at all. Whatever measure of merit an alien judgement of worth's likely to be based upon in Jabba's mind it's definitely not determined upon a predilection to housekeeping.

I know I believe myself to be the chicken.

His detritus, it's backed up through the flat and come into conflict with my already fragile, delicate susceptibility to perceiving injustice everywhere.

And I believe Jabba to be the pig.

I'm convinced that Jabba's all-consuming interest in aliens is based upon an innate laziness and absolute disinclination to involve himself in anything bereft of an immediate sensory pleasure.

I stare at a livid plastic alien with big green eyes and blink.

I think of Jabba's big advantage when it comes to detachment—him having so many more hours in the day to work towards it than me. Him always already being on the couch in his TV trousers and completely detached by the time I get home.

I fill my glass in the kitchen, try not to look, but take an image of the parlous state of the kitchen back to the collapsed chair that's my station next to Jabba's feet.

Still in these paint covered clothes but having had sufficient wine already to be in some confusion as to what was actually said in the last commercial break. Regarding all I'm thinking.

I can't remember.

But the spaceship people with the ridged plastic looking faces and the shoulder pads have gone and the commercials are on.

My three minutes to commune with Jabba:

'What makes you think that they're going to like you because of it?' I ask him.

I'm throwing this in like a piece of wasted artillery. Just to get some range.

He's obviously quite at a loss as to my thought process.

'What makes me think *who's* going to like me because of *what?*' he asks.

'*They're* not.'

'Who?'

'The aliens,' I say.

'What about them?'

'And housekeeping.'

'What?'

'Do you imagine they might have to urinate or defecate or eat or anything?' I say.

'Don't be ridiculous,' he tells me.

'Well, if they don't... where are they going to get the fucking strength from?'

'To what?'

'To annihilate your enemies and suck you up in a beam of light. I take it that *might* necessitate some nutrition, which *might* cause some unsavoury fucking alien by-product, which would probably be left to the only alien with a mind not permanently occupied by high alien ideals to fucking deal with.'

'What?'

'The alien faeces and the alien urine and the fucking alien fucking eating utensils. All that shit. Or do they just have disposable bags and plates and cutlery?

'As in some geriatric birthday party in space?'

I can tell he doesn't like being confronted by the notion of alien genitalia.

And faeces.

And such.

I can tell he thinks that this is in some way insulting to his friends, the aliens, who, in his mind, I'm convinced, have no genitalia at all; they're as neatly devoid of all that as intergalactic Kens and Barbies.

I smile as it occurs to me that I wouldn't know what to do with a proper friend anymore than a real mother.

'You get really *aggressive* when you're drunk,' Jabba tells me.

'No,' I hear myself say, '...*You* get *really* fucking *par-an-oid* when you've been smoking.'

His concern that the commercial break's about to end's manifesting itself in a wobbling foot and the finger.

'We're at different altitudes the whole time,' I persist. His brown chins have cranked his head minutely back to allow his face to engage the returning spaceship people. 'I'm too up, too airborne, too divorced from reality,' I continue. 'I'm after a fucking nightly ride to bring me down.

'I'm after subjugating myself with alcohol.'

Jabba, he's curled himself onto his side.

'*You're* looking to get high.

52

'It's like a fucked-up sensory airport.'

He holds a flat palm towards me and assumes a look of utmost concentration as he attempts to unpick the ridged-faced aliens' words from amongst mine.

'One of us is always destined to be landing while the other's fucking taking off.'

'Urck,' he moans.

I think: I did all this to get to the Urck.

The *Urck* that always comes after the foot, the finger and the palm.

Before the Fuck-off-this-is-my-room.

'It's the altitude thing, the take-off-and-landing thing,' I say. 'I shouldn't think we've known one another for more than a few milliseconds in three years. Altitudefuckingwise.'

That's how it goes. From space to Jabba's couch, getting white hot on re-entry like a tile on the nose of a space-shuttle.

I clash with him later by the fridge as he's looking for something gourmet and I'm after chilled white wine.

We've got this addictive Muslim and Hindu thing going on.

It's Jabba's love of aliens that's going to seal his fate.

I know it.

I know that much.

The same way I knew from the beginning about my mother's dog that never came back. The same way I knew from the beginning that that dog's days were numbered just solely on account of the look on its face. It's a kind of scenario I've been playing out but am desperately hoping is just an idea-slash-nightmare from the niggling seed of all that noise. From Jabba's huge TV with *surround-sound,* that takes a noise and hurls it around the room like it's a monster riding the skirting board. The ultimate never-ending nightly rumble of awe-inspiring alien spaceships, that come and come, because the more awe-inspiring alien spaceships there are for Jabba, the better he can envisage the day he most eagerly awaits—the day when alien intervention will come:

Judgement Day for the human-race.

Jabba's speakers being always set at optimal levels for his alien friends.

Every time a spaceship goes by the contents of the flat, they oscillate, shake and hum. The epicentre of these endless invasions always seeming in too close a proximity to my head. Most of the time this doesn't matter. Me being too drunk to care. But sometimes I imagine a fleet of passing spaceships, months on, when I'm *way* out of sight of land, angry and still conscious.

And everything'll change.

And I think of the gun.

Picture it perfectly.

And I know I'm going to convince myself that it's all on account of Jabba's arteries.

I know that because that's how this story always ends.

Me shut down completely. Only the Daisy Daisy Thing. And I can see the final look on that dog's face and it's floating over everything as in my mind Jabba's blocked arteries stop on the information that's pounding way too much blood through him way too fast. And that being nothing to do whatever with a beam of fucking light.

It being to do with me and the gun pointed at his head.

# BLING BLING FRANKY'S NOTORIOUS BOY

Having killed one of them, it's easy to imagine the others know all about it. OK, so it might not be a Mexican hairless. It's not. It isn't. It's something else. A different kind but a similar sort of size.

The woman at a table across from us is looking so beautiful.

The dog's lying upside down in-between her open legs as she feeds it her lunch. Its tongue coming out and its little chin going up and down. Her, sitting astride a bench seat in a short skirt in dappled sunshine and pampering that dog. The pair of them oblivious to anyone else. A composition doubtless contrived to prove quite how easy it is to get in-between the legs of a beautiful woman.

The pub garden in dappled sunlight. A little Renoir vignette in West London.

The dog's noticing nothing.

The beautiful woman with the short skirt and the casually open legs talking to it in a coochy-coo voice.

I drink some beer, smoke a cigarette and continue staring

at the dog.

The job we're working on, it's not going well. Our breaks are easily sliding into post-mortems. Everybody's holding up bits of the job to one another and looking amazed. It's to do with the Crazy Horse thing—The *Crazy Horse* being the one we've all chosen to ride as an occupation and continually discuss the antics of. As if they were actually unexpected, these antics, the kind of which you'd obviously get from a crazy horse.

We've all been acting surprised for years.

The dog's hairy head, in my mind it's bathed in a heavenly gilded light that's shining from the confluence of the two sublime legs under the tiny pelmet skirt. I feel like I'm attempting to charge a pair of psychic cylinders with something beautiful and unfamiliar to sustain me on the Crazy Horse and the mundane template I'll be riding later with Vince and Traffic's Appalling and Xav and Bling Bling Franky and The Cloud.

I witness an alien, beautiful, long caricature of an afternoon. Hers. I build her home environment in my head the same way an ignorant 18th century palaeontologist might have recreated an entirely fictitious animal from one strange bone. With the paint still wet she's naked, draped across some fancy furniture and masturbating. This woman and her sunlight dappled shaved vagina, all built on not even a micron of vacant lot in my brain. I'm so gone with the notion until some phantom curiosity of the small dog's whereabouts in all this brings down my daydream with the ease of an elephant walking through a cobweb.

I can almost hear its toenails on the parquet floor.

I run a hand through my hair, blink and turn my body back towards the Crazy Horse normal template.

Everybody's familiar attitude and stance and foible just waiting.

Traffic's Appalling's glaring at a menu. He's running one of his big hands around his face, as though his face were some kind of braille message.

Bling Bling Franky's looking benign.

Xav's in his head for Lob being dead from drinking too much methadone. Lob, having died only last week. Lob "All bloated out like something from the sea" Lob.

And Vince, not drinking alcohol, drinking an orange juice and looking only marginally more amazed than he ever had when he'd been drinking alcohol and was about to be going through the Crazy-Horse motions of deciding who was being a cunt.

'He's a fucking cunt,' he pronounces. '*Could you lose these fucking side-pieces and move the fucking set back ten feet,*' he mimics.

The Cloud drinks his beer, smokes his cigarette, stares through his newspaper; forever in a private cubicle with the engaged sign showing.

'I don't get it... fifteen pounds for some fucking chicken. Jesus-fucking-christ.'

'So? Who cares? You don't eat lunch.'

'That's not the point... it's still fifteen pounds for a piece of chicken.' Traffic's Appalling rubs his big hand around his face some more and contemplates the price of chicken as earnestly as he might a complicated piece of carpentry. Traffic's Appalling, who, on a German building site, witnessed eight Turkish workers fall to their deaths having had their gantry attached by crane to a section of green concrete one hundred and fifty feet up.

Every time I see Traffic's Appalling there's falling Turks.

'It's just the part of London we're in, Traffic,' says Vince, indicating the casual diners with his eyebrows as he sucks on a cigarette and squints through smoke. 'These people, they don't want to buy a chicken dinner for under fifteen pounds. They'd assume some fuck was poisoning them with some substandard chicken. They'd be imagining some chicken breast with more antibiotics about it than a pill you'd get from the fucking doctor.'

Traffic's Appalling doesn't look convinced. His big hand's

about the constant conundrum of his face and his eyes are on the menu.

I'm looking back towards the beautiful woman as though I'm way below the surface of the sea and she's air.

'I don't know,' says Xav. 'What's going on? We go to bed every night, we *know* what the world's like. What the score is. We know not to expect *too* much. But something happens in our sleep. We wake up the next morning expecting everyone to be so reasonable and kind. So considerate. And everything's such a fucking surprising affront as we start afresh, remembering that, Oh yeah, that's what people are like—They're cunts. As far as the people at work, them, as far as they're concerned it's an us and a them thing. We're not expected to use our brains and they're not expected to use their bodies.'

'Who?'

'*Them*. They're the biggest part of the problem. But the whole system's just a fuck-up waiting to happen.'

Xav notices me staring at the woman's dog.

He looks at the dog too.

'Who?'

'Them—the people in the clean clothes that come in at six pm and say Ohh-*back-a-bit, Up-fucking-a-bit. No. Warmer-Cooler-Pinker-Greener-Shinier-yes-fucking-no-yes-**no***. You know, the ones that come in late, can't look us in the eye and move through the set in a group looking for something vertical to piss on.'

'To *piss* on?'

'Yeah, verbally. Like dogs. They get their bearings and then the serious fucking pissing starts—"*Have we got enough height? No, the height's fine, it's the…*" Bla-Bla-Bla, all that shit.'

'Higher, lower, cooler, warmer—Fucking Cunts,' says Vince.

'And what did the fucking art director say to the fucking clients?' asks Franky.

The Cloud fleetingly couples himself to this train by momentarily putting down his newspaper.

'The clients were worried that the set was looking *too butch*,' says Vince. 'He said we'll Feminininise the set. *Feminininise* for fuck-sake.'

'Fucking Cunts.'

The Us And The Them Thing's just masochistic, bad maths. With all the chalk in the world you won't get to the end of it. It just runs its course and peters out leaving a fifteen pound chicken dinner hanging in the air. I look at The Cloud and put an end to the enigma/riddle of the crazy-horse-us-and-them-thing by handing the conversation to Bling Bling Franky like a bad baton in a relay race. 'How's the boy, Franky?' I ask.

Bling Bling Franky's a rigger, you don't call him "Bling Bling" to his face.

'The boy's *fine,* Manny. Thank you.'

'Who is the boy?' asks Traffic's Appalling.

Bling Bling takes the baton.

'—Well, we were striking the Raiders Of The Lost Ark set up at Pinewood,' Bling-Bling starts. He's arranging his jewellery with tiny movements like he's a well prepared linen tablecloth and his jewellery's the solid-silver cruets. 'And the props boys, *the cunts*, they were chucking all this stuff into skips—bones and skulls and the like. And I saw him—this *small skull*—and thought *I'll have that.* It was coming up to Halloween, see, and I thought it would be good to have a skull, like—stick it on the garden wall with a candle in it for the kids. And the skull, *the boy,* he stayed in the garden, here and there, about the place. And the years went by. And then one day the neighbour's fucking dog fucking went off with his fucking jawbone.'

'Fuck,' says Vince.

'Yeah, fucking right. The fucking dog, little bastard, took it into their Kitchen next door and started chewing it on the fucking lino. And when I got back that night my gaf was crawling with the filth. And I didn't know what to fucking think. So, I go into the pub opposite. And I have a drink and watch the filth through the window. Fucking flashing lights and my gaff all taped up. And I think...it must be the fucking gas meter—'cause I like had a brick under it that stopped it reading gas. So, I have a couple more drinks, walk across the road, jump the fucking wall, kick the fucking brick away and confront the nearest filth. Anyway it isn't the fucking gas after all. It's *the boy*. They take me down the station thinking I'm FredfuckingWest, send the boy for analysis and start digging up my garden to find the fucking others.

'And I say you're going to look like a right load of fucking cunts when you find out he's only fucking fibreglass. Anyway, the analysis comes back and Fuck Me if the boy isn't fucking fibreglass at all; he's fucking real two hundred year old fucking Per*uv*ian. Fuck. Fuck knows what the prop buyer had done. Stupid cunt. Anyway, well, the fucking filth *loved* it that it was real but were really fucking *pissed* they couldn't do me for *mur*der—what with the boy being two fucking hundred.'

'Yeah?'

'Fuck.'

'And?'

'Well, they rang me the next month, didn't they, and said he was legally mine and what did I want to do with him. And I said: *send the fucking boy home.*'

Bling-Bling's back to fiddling with the cruet. Addressing himself like that. 'They did,' he says, distractedly. 'He came back in a polystyrene box the following week. All wrapped up.'

We all mutter various oaths to the memory of Bling-Bling Franky's notorious boy.

It's nearly two o'clock.

We move to get back to work.

I look across at the beautiful woman with the short skirt and the dog. I wrap up what I can of her beauty to take it with me.

On the way back to the studio The Cloud and I stop off at a hardware shop. A very old shopkeeper helps The Cloud find what he wants while I stand back to one side in her tiny cluttered shop, pick up what appears to be a blade in a colourful plastic mechanism and try to make some sense of it. The ancient woman's beige legs and the end of her nylon hem reappear under the knife just in time for her to witness me liberate the blade from its colourful plastic mechanism and slide it into the palm of my hand.

'For God's sake, dear,' she says. 'What on earth did you go and do that for?'

She jostles her feet in a strange way on the faded linoleum. I remember the woman from the TV the night before. From the Sumatran jungle. A scientist studying the courtship dance of a small, colourful bird whose courtship dance is so beguilingly fast and complicated that it can't be properly witnessed by the naked eye. The TV woman had mimicked the bird's dance on the jungle floor, in a clearing, for the camera. I'm thinking how it was one of the most beautiful things I've ever seen. The TV woman in the jungle clearing, she's overlaid amongst the clutter of this old woman's shop.

As we leave, I look at the cut on my hand. I'm holding my wrist. I think about the woman in that Sumatran jungle.

Through some random hardware the ancient shopkeeper's watching me go.

She's wondering what a poor, lost, hapless looking boy like me's doing in a job that necessitates the use of tools.

# THE GUN

When you push your boat out every night, not through drink alone, but chemically, you start getting numbers stored on your phone for people who can get you more than drugs.

That's how The Cloud and I got the gun.

The quiet time had come. There was no work. A quiet time like that's far worse than doing a job you don't enjoy. The multiple of sixty thing, killing me completely. The other stuff too. That's what happens when you start doing what you instinctively know you shouldn't—pushing your boat out with alcohol and then blowing it up way out of sight of land with the other stuff.

Phooom.

Even I can see the maths is bad:

sex + sex = 120 per week
+ drink + cigarettes = 240
+ rent = 360
+ other stuff = 420

I tried to economise:

sex = 60 per week
+ drink + cigarettes = 120
+ rent = 240
+ other stuff = 310

It didn't work. It doesn't work. Of course it doesn't. More other stuff keeps on coming:

+ viagra

Even I can see what's happening in a quiet time.

no work + cigarettes + sex problem + drink problem + drugs problem + gun =

# YOU'RE ALL OVER THE PLACE MANNY

Once a week, I'd go on the District line to a small room and sit with a woman. I'd talk and cry and talk some more and she'd listen.

I didn't like her.

She said things that irritated me. She once said: 'I'm very good at my job, Manny.' I didn't like that. It reminded me of being in my studio in the country, years ago, before I'd fallen into the business and London. A woman had walked in, unannounced. She looked very composed. I didn't know her—she was a friend of my big Italian girlfriend with the gorgeous arse who'd gone.

'I'm very highly spiritually evolved,' she said as some kind of hello.

I told her to fuck off.

I didn't like people like that. I don't like people like that.

There are, obviously, a lot of people like that to not like.

I'd been renting rooms in an Old Rectory in the country. Using a converted garage in a courtyard as a studio. In it I painted pictures that I'd later burn at the end of the walled garden.

I used to burn them with Charlie the gardener.

I liked Charlie.

When I moved in, we acknowledged one another with a smile but we didn't talk for weeks.

One sunny day I was preparing canvases on the front lawn. Charlie approached. He asked me what I was doing. 'Well,' I said. 'I'm stretching canvases.' Charlie indicated with a shrug that I should maybe elaborate. 'Well, first,' I continued, 'First, you stretch the canvas onto stretchers, then you wet the canvas, that kind of stretches it, gets the wrinkles out the cloth. Then you size the canvas. With glue,' I told him, 'Rabbit-skin glue. Then you sand it down, then you prime it. And sand it again.'

'Then you let the monkey out of the cupboard,' said Charlie. That's what he said. Out of nowhere that's what he said.

I liked that.

I'd hung a piece of muslin at my studio window to defuse the light. In the mornings Charlie'd arrive on his bike, move the piece of muslin aside and say things like: 'One ticket to Bombay please.'

That's what he was like.

He'd always come up when I was burning paintings at the bottom of the garden. He liked to witness that. We'd stand together and watch months of work burn. The canvases would catch slowly. The topmost receding in a fringe of small flames. Charlie always said the same thing: 'They're no good as paintings and they don't even burn.'

To me he was like something out of a Russian folk tale.

He was solitary as I was solitary. There were certain things that neither of us would put up with. One of them arrived on a summer's evening—the local Liberal candidate.

I remember Charlie was watching.

He watched me pursue the old Liberal candidate towards the front of the house, where a younger Liberal was waiting in a car. He watched the old Liberal get into the car and me get half in behind him. He watched the car speeding off up the drive.

I remember he was smiling.

Neither Charlie nor I liked being disturbed by people like that.


The analyst had asked me about my dreams. What I could remember? I recounted a dream in which I'd witnessed a big fish in a shallow pool of water in a basement.

'What were you doing in the dream, Manny?' she asked.

'I was trying to get out of this small window,' I answered.

She told me I was all over the place. That I was vulnerable and needed to build a vessel to keep myself safe in.

The following week she changed. There was no more bravado. No more bluster. She was nervous. Her voice was different. The way she moved was different. Everything.

I never went back.

## THE CLOUD

The Cloud would say, 'If they don't kill us, we can retrain in jail.'

I knew he meant it.

The Cloud, he has no anchors. Nothing to attach him to the real world. What I have might be frayed and fucked and thin and fast unravelling but The Cloud has less. He's the only person I've ever met that I feel's more vulnerable than myself.

The Cloud, up there, in the air somewhere, detached and changing shape.

It's his mother's fault.

His mother was born in Halifax. She hated Halifax with a quiet, intelligent precision. She wanted to reinvent herself in London, in a big house, full of fine, tasteful things, without her father's name.

For some time before The Cloud was born his mother had already possessed all she desired. She tended what she had like a fire warden in a small, arid National Park. The two things she feared most were heat and the subsequent loss of all she had. The most significant threat being the prospect of fire—Fire,

The Cloud's mother knew, would incinerate everything.

Fire would take it all from her.

It would run screaming through her herbaceous borders, shave her lawn off to blackened earth, fly through her French-windows, grip its red-hot teeth into her Persian rugs. Her old oak boards. It would engulf everything. It would leave her only what she'd always been—the daughter of an electrical engineer from Halifax.

That's why she hated The Cloud.

She could see the prospect of fire in his face at Queen Mary's. She saw a significant and resolute, artistically emotional, dreamy baby. She could see it in his gaze. He terrified her from the start. She brought him home from the hospital as though she were carrying a burning lump of coal into the dry brittle centre of everything beautiful that wasn't Halifax. The Cloud soon surpassed her most quietly pessimistic expectations of him. By the time he was three hours old, his relationship with his mother had established a pattern which would never change: the more she denied him love, the more peculiar and upsetting to her his behaviour became. She watched his gaze mature into a terrifyingly distant soulful wonder that ate up her house like a laser beam.

There's a limit to what you need ask. Regarding all this. The evidence, it's about him in profusion like DNA at the crime scene of a fucked-up bloody murder.

The worst thing for his mother was The Cloud's resemblance to her father.

It was complete.

She'd escaped Halifax and realised her goals in London just in time to bring into the heart of her ordered world a small disordered virus; with its grandfather's face, its grandfather's dreamy eyes and its grandfather's completely destructive lack of ambition.

She watched The Cloud for sixteen years.

On his sixteenth birthday he did what was expected of him. He left.

Under the auspices of going to art college in Liverpool, he systematically and resolutely let everything, except a compulsion to fall in love with women who treated him badly, go. Women who wanted to treat The Cloud badly found him irresistible; there was something so open about his expression that perfectly advertised a vulnerable, innocent man. His lack of artifice drove them to distraction.

His sublime nature was a big glass window to smash again and again.

He painted fat people incased in small houses. Stylised. For three years he did that.

He moved back to London and met a construction manager in the film business.

He was surprised when people liked him.

He was The Cloud.

He is The Cloud.

If he has the thinnest thread to hold him
it's
his work.

# MIRAGES

You casually nurse a lack of respect for your body; so much so, before you know it, your whole life's constructed around all the various different ways you might disrespect yourself. Getting to any one of them, it's like staggering towards a mirage.

In the morning you waver through work towards the lunch-time mirage. It's there in the shimmering distance:

a l c o h o l.

In the afternoons you crawl towards the evening mirage— the real oasis; a bigger incandescent anticipation of cold bottles / hard drugs / number 5 and the multiple of 60 thing. The oases being thoroughly predictable. The analogies symptomatic of your confusion.

Soon enough, you're this wayward Captain Cook. Charting a nowhere-land of vice, plotting a course from London public house to oriental prostitute, slowing every circumnavigation only for somebody willing to paddle alongside and proffer small parcels of immediate release.

Captain Cook. Doing the carrot and stick thing all day long

for England. A place charted in your head for number 5, a place in your head for drink and a place for the other stuff. Pulling out an image from one, fixating on it and keeping going.

All Out at sea.

A tiny little flame left that's you.

The wick and the wax seriously undermined. You, a guttering-flame, cupped hand exponent of how to do things badly.

In a dark place.

Discovering an alternative world of dangerous distractions and analogies instead of continents—looking for analogies to sum things up better than the word AUSTRALIA might a fucking unknown land mass.

You're holding onto this world you neither like nor understand with an analogy.

That's pretty much how it seems to me.

But then again, The Cloud would tell you. He'd tell you how I inflate everything out of all proportion.

Caricature it.

Worry it to death.

Even a fucking sentence like this.

# HUMAN ARCHAEOLOGY

An electrician walks past. He's enormous. So wide his footsteps look ridiculously small. Like they're in competition with his girth and all the physical rules of the universe. He's passing in silhouette; looking all wrong; looking like a big old dinosaur-torso grafted onto the legs of a bird with a long beak, a timid attitude and an appetite for fish.

It turns out he's not an electrician at all.

He's the soundman.

That makes more sense; him, being sedentary like that; doing his slow metabolic act and gradually invading the immediate air with more of himself.

A big accusation to his lack of self-control's standing nearby; a beautiful young Indian woman who's a client at the shoot and a lithe exclamation mark to the obese. I'm thinking she doesn't need any significant archaeology to get to the real her. Being as it is, right there, under her elegant, expensive clothes.

I fixate on her beautiful hips as she stands talking quietly to a colleague.

There's the Indian woman and her hips and now a production-runner and her dimples. She's casually bending down to look at a newspaper. Her jumper riding up behind her to let God orchestrate the beautiful dimples above her arse. The only urgent thing about her, God's intent for the dimples above her arse.

God, choreographing all this shit just to spite.

And Traffic's Appalling, he's looking *really* bad. Hunched over his saw bench in his standby position. Reading his newspaper like that. Like he can do for hours and hours. Traffic's Appalling, hiding in there somewhere under years of beer—inside his rock solid beer geology like the air inside a Russian doll.

I look from Traffic's Appalling to the Indian woman, from the Indian woman to the production runner's dimples—still right there—and back again.

It's all too much. No way is it logical but I've got a really strong desire to climb to the top of a big hill, a mountain even, drink whiskey and repeatedly shoot a gun in the air.

The man with the girth and the birdy legs who's the soundman, I think he's just responded to the director's request for playback. He's not the soundman. He's definitely the video-play-back-man.


The big man with the birdy legs is the only one to not take lunch. He doesn't seem in the least bit interested. He must have been big when he was little. That's what I'm thinking as the stage clears, and there's only the big man, him, sitting in the middle of the mechanics of the job. Amongst monitors and banks of buttons and snaking thick rubber cables. He's enormous in his foldaway chair. It's got to be to do with his metabolism. I smile at him and walk out into the sunshine with Traffic's Appalling. I hold on to a large section of Traffic's Appalling's consolidated

73

beer as we leave with urgency for the pub by the canal on Traffic's Appalling's motorbike.

I remember painting a landscape years before. I'd been standing in a field, staring into another distant field, looking at something regular shaped that was a particular colour. I was looking at it, mixing that colour when the regular shaped thing started up and drove off. I'd packed my gear up then and walked home. It seemed ridiculous to be standing there painting something you believed to be one thing when all along it was something else.

That being an early indication that my judgement as to the nature of things couldn't be trusted.

A specific incident that soon became something of a general law to being Manny. The big man with the little legs, just the latest addition to the pile at the bottom of which was this rectangular thing that wasn't organic and had up and driven away.

Traffic's Appalling's pretty much convincing though.

What he's wearing's definitely beer.

We sit, drink beer, smoke. Watch the pub clock. Watch its minute hand accelerate towards 2. Greenwich meantime fast throwing the country back to work and two unwilling disciples onto Traffic's Appalling's bike and back to the studio.

The video–play–back–man's inert in his small chair. He's got his eyes closed and his fingers linked on his massive belly. You can't help but think if you walked round behind him he'd have the same slingshot effect on your mass as the moon's had on several American space-missions.

I set myself down as though I'm on a beach and the camera crew are the sun. Pleasantly anticipate the production-runner's dimples and the Indian woman's hips. Whatever's available. Float there in a proxy sea breeze.

I ruminate amongst the recent past. Head down amongst it like an urban fox amongst so much rubbish. Rooting about in a collage of oriental erotica. Considering that in order to successfully bury my past I need to keep events coming / in lieu of earth / as raw material.

I need to urinate.

I sway out of the studio that's dark and into the white corridor that runs alongside it. This cold corridor. I remember that the studio today's a mess of anomalies as I stare at the white door I've just shut behind myself and note how easily it's confused with the cupboard doors surrounding it. I attempt to heighten its identity as though with a 4B pencil over a faint sketch:

White.

No architrave.

Boot marks at its base.

I feel dully intimidated by this white rectangle.

The studio's cold.

The corridor's cold.

The toilet's warm.

I'm into a cubicle and shutting the door. I've been in there for a few minutes when a door opens. A man's at the urinal. I'm looking at the grouting in-between the tiles next to my head. I notice a line someone's drawn with a pencil as if driving down a skinny road with regular right-angle intersections. There's a tiny pencilled message at the end of the line:

LOOK LEFT

I do. There's another wandering line in the grouting, at the end of it there's another tiny pencilled message:

LOOK STRAIGHT AHEAD

I look at the door in front of me; at eye level there's a miniscule grey aberration. I lean closer: a word. I lean closer. I'm screwing up my eyes to accommodate whatever this word says when a door opens.

Another man's at the urinal.

I can hear him urinating as I receive the second rebuke from a door in ten minutes:

ARSEHOLE!

I'm wondering how a man who's so little affronted by a flying Irishman and jackhammer can be so easily fucking defeated by two doors.

The man at the urinal lets out a few big sighs. He says 'Fuck,' a couple of times. There's a missing section of formica on the cubicle door. 'Fuck,' says the man at the urinal. He says it in a kind of tired, defeated way. 'Fuck. I'm really fucked-up,' he says. The man at the urinal shakes his penis. I look beyond the formica and blink. The fucked-up man's penis, Jesus, it sounds enormous. I'm surprised at the sound of it. The man at the urinal says, 'Fuck. *What a life.*'

Silence.

I stare at the message on the door. I listen to myself intently. In this vacuum of a cubicle. In this epicentre of nothing as far as sound's concerned. Around me in this cubicle, it's completely silent: Nothing.

I turn my head slightly. Raise my eyebrows:

Nothing.

I appear to have no sound to me.

I'm frightened enough by the prospect of that to cough.

The man at the urinal is humming now. At the sink.

He leaves.

I wait a few more minutes and then go back into the studio, remembering the white door with no architrave and the boot marks as though unimaginable fucking monsters are in the cupboards all around it.

I stand in front of this white door subconsciously checking it for pencilled abuse.

The crew's migrating down to the next set. Leaving the kitchen set and moving to the hall set. The big man with the birdy legs is pushing his gear on a trolley that's festooned with bad food: bags of chocolates, crisps and sweets.

I stand there watching him, like I'm lost and he's this fat compass. I think that maybe he wasn't born big after all. Maybe he didn't go to lunch because he couldn't cope with the stairs. The more I see of this man, the less I feel I know about anything.

I'm wondering who's most likely to be the individual with the big sounding penis that feels like shit.

I can't decide.

I go and sit back down with Traffic's Appalling.

I'm thinking at least you know where you are with Traffic's Appalling.

The production-runner's talking to a producer. He's a long thin man in a crombie coat. She's making coquettish, quick movements and ends up with her hands on top of her head. She somehow makes this look natural. Her standing like that, it's made her jumper ride up. Her beautiful belly's showing. I'm wondering two things:

1. if the long, thin man in the crombie coat's the one who was shaking his penis in such an aggressive way earlier.

2. whether the production-runner was letting her jumper ride up like that—first at the back for me, now at the front for him—on purpose.

I don't know about the long, thin man. He doesn't look like he feels like shit. I don't know about the production-runner and her jumper either. I think that apart from what I believe I know about Traffic's Appalling I can't be sure of knowing anything about anybody else.

I think about the rectangle in the landscape that drove off.

I'm holding onto my knowledge of Traffic's Appalling in the same way a mountaineer might hold on to a rope secured to a piton driven into solid rock amongst so much friable shit.

I look at the three inches of denim below the buckle of the production-runner's belt. The way it dives into her crotch.

A kind of visual balm to everything.

I just look.

Eventually, her eyes appear through a haze like two hostile Arabs with patronage and a gun.

Goddamn.

The long, thin producer follows her gaze. She takes her hands down from the top of her head and her jumper comes down like a curtain on something sublime. She cranks her hips back to horizontal.

They're both staring now.

I feel like a pathologist to everything. I inspect my psyche as though it were a wall of compressed sediments relating to my personal history of confusion.

Gauging the chronology.

Realising that the rectangle in the landscape that drove off wasn't / isn't at the bottom of everything.

My mother's at the fucking bottom of everything.

She's the one that made me really understand how things could seem to be one thing while all along being something completely different. My mind attaches itself to her cottage. Looking for love. Finds my father's car from the only time I remember it as being there. Attaches itself to my father's car like a limpet. To travel off with him. The back of my head, finally right there, where it might have been all those years ago, in that car / next to him. My father / him and me.

My father / him and me.

My father / him and me.

Driving back to the place that he and I had called home. With him never having to drive off to any hospital.

Like the one from which he'd never return two weeks later.

My memory, stomping about in this old small stream. Lifting sediment.

Little Manny still in there so confused. Never understanding how you could just drive up to a hospital and have a heart operation like that. Like it were a drive-in movie or a fucking takeaway.

I'm telling Eddy Michaelheimmer the Grim Reaper's a cunt.

'The Grim Reaper's a cunt.'

Eddy Michaelheimmer, collapsing around the video-play-back-man, close by now. Rising to stretch himself.

I watch him.

'Fuck,' says the video-play-back-man. I get this jump running through my body. He looks at me. 'I'm really fucked up,' he says.

The video-play-back-man-/birdy-man's holding the butt end of a pencil and a clipboard on which a piece of A4 paper holds miniature pencil notations relating to his work.

My eyes start bouncing up and down the length of the birdy-man's torso like he's a vertical Wimbledon. This ongoing rally between his face and crotch. The video-play-back-birdy-man not minding at all. Him just staring straight back with his big arms raised, his clipboard hovering and his huge, slack stomach on wide screen.

I settle my head into my shoulders. Slide the wide-eyed amazement I'm feeling away from the video-play-back-man and towards the agency people and the clients. The transition's disgustingly segued by the sound of a big flapping penis.

The one that must have been the birdy-man's.

His big flapping penis.

I can hear myself breathing with puffing cheeks as though about to vomit.

The agency people and the clients are standing around an actress.

I focus in on these people, hopefully to the detriment of everything relating to the birdy-man. The actress is practising taking the lid off a jar of coffee. The agency and the clients are

79

talking. They're discussing the optimum way she might take the lid off the jar of coffee. They're attempting to find some gesture in the removal of that lid that might incite people to buy coffee as never before.

Anything's got to be better than the noises.

'Synergy through the idea,' one of them proposes.

'Like on the super-sized poster for the bus.'

'Yeah, synergy. Like on the bus.'

'Yeah.'

'Yeah. Synergy through precise movement.'

'Less is more.'

'That's right. Less is more.'

'Minimal but definitive movement,' one of them says.

The actress smiles and nods.

The others sit back down in front of the monitor.

The macro lens on the camera shows a tight shot of a cup.

A cup with coffee in it.

The agency and the clients discuss the arrangement of bubbles on the surface of the coffee.

They wonder if maybe the bubbles would be enhanced by a bit more separation. They indicate to the director that they feel a degree of separation in the bubbles would be preferable. It would improve the shot, compositionally. They ask that, also, if, when the coffee spins, it might spin slightly faster. Ever so slightly faster.

The coffee spinning as if just stirred, that seems really important.

They all stare into the monitor and wait.

The food technology woman minutely separates bubbles on the coffee.

The prop man tweaks a machine under the work-surface. Somehow, by way of a magnetic bean in the coffee cup, this determines the speed with which the coffee spins.

The group in front of the monitor wait. They look like the figures following the gaze of Doctor Tulp in The Anatomy Lesson of Doctor Tulp by Rembrandt.

My mother's cottage is still there in my imagining.

Like a badly made model in a low budget horror film.

A pall of cloud diving in the slightly opened front window.

As in films where something truly evil's just died and its spirit rushes away like smoke backwards.

I follow the cloud into her house to get ensnared in all those memories.

The nothing getting done because of her dogs. Her and Little Manny failing to get on top of anything as the cottage slid into greater and greater disorder.

All on account of the veins in his mother's dogs' heads.

This miniaturised, dolls-housed mess still there.

Me, as Little Manny, amongst it. I'm attempting to defeat an early symptom of that disorder by sitting up at three in the morning, I'm replaying this significant memory, back there, hoping against hope that my hamster's still alive. That there might be a logical explanation for it not being in its cage.

Me. This boy.

Hoping that maybe he might hear a scratching noise. Might find the hamster somewhere in the middle of the night.

Because that's what hamsters did.

Stuff, in the middle of the night.

Sitting in the gloomy front room with the bulbs all blown. With the one lamp on that worked and his Disney torch shining into corners. It being really so important, then, that his hamster should be alive, with his dad having just died and everything.

He'd wanted to be able to rely on something. Like a hamster being in its cage. Where you might expect a fucking hamster to be.

He had a suspicion that his friends from school weren't sitting up in *their* homes doing shit like this. They would've been in bed hours ago without having to worry about their fucking hamsters. They'd have known their fucking hamsters would have been in their fucking cages.

Where Manny's should have been.

He must have gone to sleep but have still been listening in the back of his mind.

Little Manny.

There was definitely a scratching noise coming from the kitchen.

It was nice, creeping in there, full of expectancy. About to save his hamster from staying lost. Slowly picking through all that garbage studded with cigarette ends. So much rubbish before the hamster.

His heart beating in anticipation.

The look of his hamster.

Caught in the beam of his Disney torch.

Soaking wet and looking like an earthquake victim from TV.

Saving it from a fate worse than death because whatever day it was, it was the day before the bin men came with their big truck and its hydraulic crusher.

It was like a miracle for Little Manny. That his father, a big strong man, was dead. And his hamster wasn't.

But in a house like that anything could happen.

He stood there drying his hamster with the sleeve of his pyjamas, picturing his mother lying asleep in bed and trying not to be hurt by her only caring for veins in her dog's head.

Looking at his hamster.

The one his dad had bought for him.

Little Manny looking at the hamster.

The hamster looking at Little Manny.

Little Manny putting the hamster back in its cage and giving it a bit of food and watching it for ten minutes with his Disney torch.

And thinking.

And going back to bed.

His mother's dog was outside her bedroom door, sitting there, staring, as though it weren't the middle of the night at all.

The dog and the Birdy man, they're vying for position in my head as I drive home to Jabba.

# MANNY'S JACKET

To be tightly ensconced with Jabba in our council block below the flight path to Heathrow.

Drunkenly aware of weird, layered geometry. Of international flights bisecting the sky. Of Aztec-desert lines of cocaine on Jabba's coffee table. A threaded-spun-sugar topping to all that—the fly-like zigzag of local moped riders bringing Jabba his gourmet food. Invisible lines of passage, criss-crossing everywhere; flights to London and food and drugs and TV to Jabba's face.

Most of Jabba's gourmet food swims in a cream or ghee sauce.

Living amongst the remnants of his dictated diet I slowly put on pounds.

As though I were assimilating some horrendous local dialect.

I grow larger but somehow fail to notice.

The mirages seeming more real to me than the real things. I collate the mirages while systematically failing to see what's evident to others. The recipient of the chants of, "Hey, fat-cunt," that echo around the estate, he looks dreamily up at balconies and windows and wonders who's being so horribly mocked.

It hadn't always been like that.

I'd been a portrait painter in the beginning. Being solitary, I painted myself a lot. Solely with the intent of accurately witnessing what was in front of me.

I found I didn't like it. What was in front of me. Replicating that. I didn't like it at all.

I began acting like a self-operating back street abortionist— for three years I despatched all I created down the bottom of the garden by repeatedly sending my own image up to God in the form of smoke.

The first self-portrait I refused to burn won a prize at The National Portrait Gallery.

Being accustomed to finding myself wanting, I was amazed to see my own image looking back at me from broadsheet newspapers. The fact that other people found me less than wanting struck me as being very odd.

The National Portrait Gallery received enquiries about Emmanuel Marbas.

The stunning new talent.

They gave out my telephone number.

There was an insurmountable problem in this; being so quickly propelled into the company of people desperate to be flattered, while not having adequately thought the portrait-painting thing through. Having followed a natural talent without anticipating that any degree of success would force me to sit for hours with people I only wanted to assault. My refined pathological hatred for people in a position of authority encroaching upon a delicately-nuanced sensibility which, like some vile gagging-reflex, recoiled.

Balked.

I gagged at the people in a position of authority who began

expressing an interest in my services.

I did retrospective-belated maths:

Deep seated anger + hatred of authority + portrait commissions =

## PORTRAIT NUMBER 1: Mr. and Mrs. Business

A black granite worktop ran down the middle of their kitchen. It was twenty feet long and could have comfortably borne the dead from a small battle.

Their enormous living-room afforded all manner of receding vistas to grab your attention and send it reeling towards distant chalk hills. Inside, the sprung ballroom floor, the two gigantic marble fireplaces, the giant windows against which giant cranked shutters were nightly cranked shut, the full size snooker table, the shot silk on the walls and the massive overabundance of hysterically ornamental plasterwork offered a revolting aperitif to the madness to come.

It was the type of environment in which a sensitive, observant child might be driven to suicide.

Years before, late, drunk and with no expectation, I'd been filled in about the tragi–comic–drama of the cuckoo-chick. I discovered that cuckoos are much maligned because of the predetermined antics of the hapless cuckoo chick. I sat with a glass-clutching wide-eyed stare as an horrendously ugly naked goose-pimpled cuckoo-chick fell about the parameters of my miniature black and white TV. With a sardonic BBC voice over artist proclaiming the demonic reputation of the cuckoo-chick as a cold-blooded pathological killer. The scene with the small, oven-ready monster stumbling, it went on and on. God's predetermination of the lot accorded to cuckoos was, to me, another unmistakable stain on the bit of litmus I was forever holding up to God. I didn't find God having turned the cuckoo chick into an involuntary catapult in the least bit funny. The fact that he'd also contrived to make the cuckoo chick hideously ugly didn't help. It only increased the volume of water down the drunken well of compassion building in me that night for the cuckoo. I recognised a surging feeling. I'd felt it before, as a child, while watching Indians being slaughtered by all those fucking cowboys. The Indians with spears, arrows, implacable dignity, painted handprints on their horses' flanks and feathers everywhere. And then the rampaging cowboys firing off Remmingtons from a safe distance while looking so-*far*-too-fucking conscious of how handsome you could remain while slaughtering savages.

Poor Indians.

And Fucking bastard cowboys.

And poor cuckoo chicks plainly without a clue.

The macro lens pointing this out as it homed in on where God had seen fit to sculpt a hideous, goose-pimpled hollow at the base of the cuckoo chick's neck. The oleaginous voice-over actor, with unnecessarily comic tone, had described how disgustingly sensitive this hollow was, is and always fucking shall be to the cuckoo chick. He continued to horribly embellish the gauntlet God had seen fit to throw down to cuckoo chicks. I thought about God as I learned that the disgusting goose-pimpled hollow is just the right size to accommodate the eggs which are destined to fall into it "One by *fucking* one". This cuckoo chick, being born monstrously large in a small nest leaving the hollow in-between its scrotum-skinned shoulder blades the only end to every small journey ever made in this twiggy fucking Barnardo's; the goose pimples in that disgusting hollow the trigger to its foul huge drumstick-thighed legs. I thought more about God as the macro lens got close up on the little chick's agony.

As I watched its ugly little face distort and its foul huge legs straighten.

Just as God had intended.

You don't need litmus for a God like that.

My empathy for the cuckoo chick was complete.

From that moment, I started to feel strangely imbued with the cuckoo chick's authority to balk at and eject the unacceptable.

In the big front-room of the revolting mansion I felt that same urge to balk.

I felt I was being confronted by a lot of things that were definitely unacceptable.

Mr. and Mrs. Business' gawping, wondering at my expression, as I stared through the shot-silk walls and thought of cuckoos and said nothing. It was obviously the kind of room which most people would feel the need to pass comment on—to look around and walk about and smile and say something.

I left a big gaping silence where that something might have been.

I demanded to be shown my room.

Mr. and Mrs. Business appeared to believe this a typical form of artistic behaviour. Through some mute facial communication, some kind of eyebrow semaphore, they agreed to make nothing of it.

I lay spread-eagled on my bed, stared at the ceiling and let my mind critically rein about the confines of this, my chosen career.

Small, foul words rising.

I moved my head about on the pillows and ran my arms up and down on the expensive bedding beneath me. I was surprised at the noise that made. At how luxurious the pillows and the bedding were. I began wondering quite what kind of bird it was, the feathers of which were so very comfortable.

Me, with this big ongoing empathy for birds.

I tried to envisage an eider-duck.

Nothing.

I filled the biggest bath I'd ever seen. The tap was like a fire hydrant. The plug, a long cylinder of steel.

I persisted with the eider-duck in my head. I concentrated.

It just looked increasingly ridiculous.

I wondered how many eider-ducks it had taken to stuff the contents of my bed. I decided you wouldn't be able to denude a duck, like a sheep, while it was still alive.

The duck would have to be dead.

Definitely.

For some reason, as soon as my mind proffered the notion of a *dead* eider-duck, a multitude of entirely convincing eider-ducks appeared in my head.

Mr. and Mrs. Business' soap looked beautiful.

Like a big block of amber.

I put my face close up to it. I stared through it. I imagined a fly stuck in the soap. A millions of years old fly. As in an ancient block of amber. I made a moaning noise and said the word *Fly, fly, fly*. Again and again. Slowly. In a strange croaky voice.

I started stroking my cock and moaning and saying *Fly*, intermittently.

I felt myself to be in a very luxurious, comfortable cocoon. What with the expensive bedding, the beautiful soap and the deep, warm bath.

I remorselessly homed in on my pleasure.

With wonderful relish and watery abandon.

There was a shuffling noise from the other side of the door.

I became silent.

The bath water became still and silent.

There was no noise in the bathroom.

The slightest noise came from the other side of the door.


Mrs. Business crept quietly away.

With a weird stiff gait.

She'd intended to knock and announce that dinner was ready. She'd succeeded only in becoming poleaxed and frozen just outside the painter's bathroom door. Her right hand raised as a tiny, manicured fist. She'd stood like that for what must have been five minutes. With her heart in her throat and the frantic splashing and moaning and the growling and the drawn out ghastly repetition of the word "Fly" from within. She was searching for an innocent explanation as to what this extraordinary painter might possibly be doing. She couldn't find it. The innocent explanation. She couldn't stop looking at her wedding ring. She felt as though a giant perversion were coming through the door and tainting the metal and the jewels of her wedding ring and by way of that somehow horribly sullying her.


Mr. Business was occupying the smallest percentage part of the black granite worktop. Finishing the preparations for dinner. Carving a joint of meat. Purposefully. As if it were the physical embodiment of problems-relating-to-the-portrait-painter who'd been in the house for three hours but whose presence was already eliciting questions. Questions which were multiplying like replicating cancer cells:

'What would he have been doing?'

'I don't know what he would've been doing.'

'What do you think?'

'I don't know. I've absolutely no idea.'

'Well.'

'Yes?'

'Well... It's just the noises. The moaning. And the "Fly Fly Fly". And the splashing.'

'So?'

'Well, maybe he's a——?'

'Maybe he's a *what*?'

'I don't know.'

'He's a very unsettling sort of man. Don't you think?'

Mr. Business earnestly carved another slice of meat. He watched it fall against the plate while picturing his wife's face in his mind's eye. She had her eyebrows raised. She had her nostrils flared. Twitching slightly. God. She had that transparent look in her eyes which let the panic in her brain shine right on through.

'Let's agree to make nothing of it.'

'Yes? But wh——'

'No. Don't. Please.'

'But——'

'No.'

'But what if——?'

'What if *what*?'

Mr. Business looked frustrated. He didn't like finding himself in the sort of position that left him asking questions like that. He didn't like losing control of his electric carving knife and hear it clatter against the plate.

The word C U N T swam through his mind like an exotic, small, colourful fish.

I broached the subject of the eider-duck over dinner:

'The quilt and the pillows on my bed are *very* comfortable,' I said.

Mr. Business looked up from his food. 'Good, Manny.'

'You can tell, as you lie down—just from the sound of them, that what's in them is *very* good. The *feathers*. *Very* good. Very, very good.'

Mr. Business smiled. Mrs. Business looked at Mr. Business.

Mrs. Business was thinking about the profound value of etiquette. The way etiquette enabled you to relax in the knowledge that you knew what was likely to be coming next. Conversationally speaking. Looking at Mrs. Business, Mr. Business knew, with a profound misery, that that was what she was thinking.

He woke the dormant CUNT-fish in his head. He projected it down the table towards her.

'Do you think it's necessary to kill the eider-ducks to get them. The lovely feathers?' I asked. I noticed a jolting stop to the noise of the Business' knives and forks. Only their careful chewing continued, sporadically, as they watched me.

I felt I was steadfastly hunting the Businesses.

As though following their clumsy trail through newly fallen snow.

'I don't know, Manny. I expect so.'

I looked at Mrs. Business. She said nothing. She only swallowed.

'Do you think, if they *are* killed,' I persisted, 'that they are eaten afterwards or just, I don't know, thrown away? Do you think?'

The Business' knives and forks were suspended in mid-air.

I was a puppeteer to the Business' cutlery.

Mr. Business said, 'I really don't know,' and looked at his wife.

I said that I was convinced they were. And that it seemed a dreadful waste that what must be such a fine bird should have something as precious as that, something it so obviously prized itself—what with it being entirely necessary to survive in such a cold climate—taken forcibly away, to stuff the pillows which enabled wealthy people to sleep well at night. Especially, as then, in all probability, this *fine bird* wasn't even eaten.

The three of us sat in silence, each picturing the plight of wildly imagined eider-ducks. Mrs. Business looked as though she felt personally responsible for the death of every eider-duck, eaten or not. Her eyes moved miserably about in-between her knife and fork.

I ate and drank and stared into the distance as if I could see the landscape beyond the walls and it were strewn with corpses.

Mrs. Business believed the moment to have passed.

'A terrible vision,' I said.

'What's that?' tentatively enquired Mrs. Business; in the way, I thought, a cowardly person might ask a potential murderer: 'Are you *really* going to kill me?' While all the while desperate not to know.

'The vision of a naked eider-duck standing on some God-forsaken, freezing tundra.'

Mrs. Business left the room quickly.

Mr. Business poured me a glass of port and lit himself a cigar while repeatedly looking off towards the door she'd just walked through.

We ended the evening in the enormous room with the sprung ballroom-floor. We sat together on a large couch in front of one of the huge marble fireplaces as the Businesses exuded small personal facts in a transparent attempt to build a wall in-between the three of us on the couch and the memory of the eider-duck.

The facts built up around the duck.

Mr. and Mrs. Business had met in a Bookies' Shop in East

London.

They were both good at maths.

Mr. Business now ran a Swiss bank on the Stock Exchange.

One of their mothers came from a Scottish island.

The other didn't.

The one that didn't or the other one or someone one of them knew had a bull-mastif or a pug or a peke, fuck knows, which had won best of breed at Crufts in 19' whatever.

The two of them offered up information like that as a balm to Mrs. Business.

I noticed the way Mr. Business kept checking his wife's eyes as though they were partners in a tightrope walking act and only Mrs. Business could register an accurate appraisal of the degree of danger.

Her eyes radiating danger like two fucking cliff-top-beacons before the Armada.

'I knew when we saw your painting in the "National", that you were the one for us, Manny,' said Mr. Business. 'So intense, so detailed.' He checked his wife's eyes.

'Yes,' said Mrs. Business.

Mrs. Business looked giddy and sick.

'Yes,' she repeated.

Mr. Business had asked me to bring my portfolio. He'd suggested it might be nice to see some of my previous work. He'd imagined there might be a lot of it. He'd imagined many beautifully wrought two-dimensional military, clergy and brothers in high-finance. But I didn't have a portfolio. All I had was a large pile of ash at the bottom of the garden. I'd anticipated this deficit, however, and had had the foresight to bring something to placate Mr. Business.

'It would be very interesting to see your portfolio, Manny. Wouldn't it darling?'

'Yes.' said Mrs. Business.

I took from my pocket the object I'd had the foresight to bring. A small battered tin. I offered it to Mr. Business.

'I don't understand, Manny,' said Mr. Business, peering into the tin. 'It's full of ash.'

'I know,' I said.

'It's the remnants of me,' I said. '*The likenesses of which have only been witnessed by God in the form of smoke.*'


I was snowed in with Mrs. Business for nine days.

The light that bounced off acres of snow outside made Mrs. Business look to be completely devoid of blood. She'd chosen to wear an old-fashioned, heavy black dress with a strange convoluted ruffle at the neck. She had a terrified rigidity to her posture. She looked like a life-size porcelain doll.

For nine days I wanted to run screaming to the bottom of the garden with the two-dimensional Mrs. Business and a box of matches.

Things got worse.

The roads reopened. Mr. Business returned from London. He chose to wear a black suit and stood, as I instructed him, in a pompous, old-fashioned, positively Victorian way behind Mrs. Business; who now looked as though she were attempting to elbow Mr. Business in the testicles.

The painting was almost as devoid of colour as Mrs. Business appeared to be devoid of blood. With two exceptions: a solitary turquoise stripe in Mr. Business's tie and Mr. Business's head rising—his face florid, his hair ginger—like a red-hot-blown-glass-orb from a fucking furnace.

Being business people, Mr. and Mrs. Business felt they should have been able to see a portfolio. They plainly felt betrayed by the offering up of a small pile of ash, the relevance of which was upsettingly absent, and they were visibly stunned by the emerging rendition of themselves. The huge canvas looking like some joke scene from a fairground through which the public might poke their heads and grimace. But they were decent, well-mannered business people, the only adverse comment made was by Mr. Business, saying, one evening, in a deferential, light hearted way, 'Manny, you've made me look like a square-headed child-murderer.'

I completed their betrayal that night, at 3am—with a box of matches and a pint of accelerant, I tangoed with the enormous two-dimensional Businesses through the huge, quiet house. A strange tactile revelation coming through the crossbars of the painting's stretchers, the rub of the canvas against my shoulder, igniting a sensual anticipation that the next transition of this material was to be sublime.

Wide-eyed and stumbling, me and the Businesses waltzed across a back garden to which I couldn't find an end.

We tangoed back.

Me and the Businesses.

I burnt them in the middle of their own front lawn.


I returned to the country.

That morning I gathered the few possessions I had and found other accommodation, using as deposit the one thousand pound down-payment I'd received from Mr. Business for the now non-existent painting.

A few weeks later I was burning paintings with Charlie.

The National Portrait Gallery tracked me down. I was surprised. I'd been expecting the police or a legal letter. What I got was notification of a growing interest in Emmanuel Marbas.

The stunning new talent.

The new, dangerous, fractious kid on the block.

I assumed the Businesses must have been too ashamed to

pursue the loss of their down payment and the damage to their lawn.

The commissions rolled in.

# MANNY'S JACKET 2

On days like these, it's necessary to put a bit of distance between yourself and your perception of things.

Things that on days like these seem far too abhorrent to bear.

The real fucking world for instance.

It seeming easier to walk through life being one step removed. Easier to have a narrative running through your head referring to a *You* instead of an I.

Just a subtle distancing of yourself and it, the real fucking world.

You're in a department store. Holding onto an image of Angel's arse. Trying to forget the Spade, Wooden Planks and Metal Bars.

Feeling vulnerable enough anyway.

Never really wanting to have known anything much about alternative uses for implements like that, as you parked your car in the store's basement car park and the reception on the radio finally gave out amidst all that bad information about the brutal murder of a Chinese restaurateur.

With implements.

You fixate on Angel's arse.

Hold it out in front of you like Moses' staff to part a swathe through late-night shoppers, all too willing to part for you anyway solely on account of the look on your face.

The conviction that your clothes are shrinking has driven you here.

Only going shopping at quiet times of the day.

Hating crowds.

You force your way towards the vile voluminous clothes in the distance. Colours, like pennants above an Olympic village. Towards the quiet of a changing room. In this low-budget zombie classic, a witness to consecutive horrible catatonic late-night-shopper stares. You can't help but imagine yourself, in extremis, dispatching them with spades and planks and metal bars.

You project Angel's arse into a distant quiet corner and stride towards it.

Forgetting the Chinese restaurateur.

Picturing something friable travelling at great speed; feeling your perception of things fragmenting like that.

Thinking of your mother that wasn't and her dogs systematically killed by smoke—until the one that never came back from the walk it took on a day when it was destined not to die of cancer but something far more brutally immediate.

The empty lead just dangling an exclamation to that.

Try to banish everything with thoughts of number 5.

As though it were bleach.

You remember the dancing girl.

Getting to your knees and kissing her arse. Having half an hour. Asking her the time. Wanting to make it last. Being unaware of the etiquette. A while away from knowing for sure that most girls who fuck strangers all week, most girls like that, all they prefer is for their clients to be as quick as possible

100

and then leave.

It taking the second girl at number 5 to clarify that.

The obvious, to you, always a stranger.

With the dancing girl it'd felt like Christmas Day.

Just a bit of chiffon and then her.

You approach this rack of clothes. Your mind elsewhere and your hands cupped in remembrance of the dancing girl.

Everything about your psyche a mashed up collage of oriental sex and death.

A dapper man watches you from a distance. Watches you blunder about with Hawaiian shirts in strangely kneading hands.

He believes you to be a *Level Three*. A level three, in his mind, being the ultimate offering / a most highly-prized sacrifice. The only real sop to his gaping lack of self worth.

*A level three.*

He smiles. He speaks into his sleeve. It's something to do with your eyes. *Level Threes* always having that look about them. He announces the presence of a *Level Three* in Gentlemen's outfitting to his sleeve. He looks about and gently brushes at his lapels as if he were being rained upon by gently falling poisonous particles. The general fallout he daily perceives to be coming from the foul British public. He twists his neck in his pristine collar and fixes his eyes on you.

He is Maxwell Homison-Forbes, the deputy head of security.

And you're a Level Three, for sure.



When you'd left number 5, you'd thought it strange that The Dancing Girl had stuck her arse out at you and said: 'You fuck my cunt, OK? pull out – OK – Pull out and come on my arse.' You thought that was really weird.

You weren't wearing a condom at the time.

You wanted to wear a condom.

You didn't believe that the girls at number 5 would have unprotected sex. You couldn't see any reason why it might be volunteered. In retrospect, you thought that maybe you were underestimating the combined properties of latex and friction. Constant friction. You imagined that combination initiating a dreadful ongoing equation between submitting to unbearable soreness or risking a potentially fatal sexually transmitted disease.

But you couldn't be sure.

You'd felt like an animal dying of thirst while having found a water-hole you suspected might be poisoned.

Three nights later you phoned number 5.

'Hi,' you said.

And waited.

'Hi, darling,' said the Australian? girl/maid/madam.

'Who's working tonight?'

'Tabi, darling. She's five-four, very slim, very beautiful. Small breasts. She does all services except A.'

'OK,' you said, tentatively. And how much *is* it for full service?'

'Sixty pounds, darling.'

You liked the *darlings*. You felt emboldened by them.

'And is that *with* or *without* a condom?' you asked.

There was a pause. 'With.'

'*With*?'

'Yes. *With*.'

You didn't like it that the Australian? girl/maid/madam was sounding so irritated. 'It's just that I was there the other night,' you said. 'And the girl, well, she didn't seem to expect me to use one.'

There was a big pause at that.

'Which night are we talking about?'

And another big pause in which you quantified your desire

102

to drink+your fear of poison+your concern for the well-being of the dancing girl. All of that tinged by the Australian? girl/maid/madam's refusal to keep calling you *darling*.

You remember hating it that the *darlings* had gone.

You were pathetically holding onto the hope that there might be more.

'I don't want to get anyone into trouble,' you said.

'I need to know which night,' said the Australian? girl/maid/madam.

The maths and the lack of darlings got all mashed up in your head.

You told her.

You remember the Dancing Girl.

You remember feeling like Judas. Having kissed the Dancing Girl's arse and betrayed her. Your sense of guilt had wavered and bobbed, barely connected to your sense of self.

You worried for the Dancing Girl nonetheless:

*The dancing girl would be fine.*

*The dancing girl would be dead.*

*Nothing would change for the dancing girl.*

*Everything would change for the dancing girl.*

You had to stop thinking about it. Anything seemed possible.

There'd been this drawn out silence between you and the Australian? girl/maid/madam. You'd rolled your eyes as if it might help.

There were no more *darlings*.

She said nothing.

She just hung up.

You take another brightly coloured shirt from the rack. You feel your resilience to this place fading. You gather up most of what's to hand and looking large in a great bundle like washing from a line before a deluge.

The dapper man watches you stumble into a changing room

with an amount of clothing that's well in excess of the stated boundaries of company policy. Boundaries that are clearly indicated on a white plastic plaque by the curtain through which you've just fallen.

The dapper man updates the movements of the Level Three by way of his sleeve and approaches the changing room. Everything he says into his sleeve is said for Cristine, the Head of Security.

Cristine without an H.

The love of his life.

She, always impressed by his unwavering ability to spot a Level Three.

You, to the dapper man, the latest in a long line of offerings to Cristine. He follows her name through the air, as though it were stretched out and attached to the curtain between you.

He's momentarily stunned as the culmination of his daily enterprise, his every waking moment, his every night-time dream, speaks softly into his left ear.

Cristine.

Without an H.

Talking.

Everything he's ever wanted behind that sweet voice. He closes his eyes and experiences one short moment of extreme bliss.

As you attempt to try on a colourful shirt by removing your own.

That's when this big foul fucking revelation comes.

The changing room's mirrored on three sides. What you see's so closely linked to a surprising day from your childhood. The day your mother saw fit to leave her chair, the deaths and her bewildered dog, and enter the kitchen. To find bowls you'd never known the existence of before. To proceed to make the only thing she ever had that hadn't already been made by somebody else in a factory before her:

A loaf of bread.

That thing had been so surprising to you.

That loaf of bread.

The bit with the tea-towel and her unveiling of whatever she'd been pummelling earlier. Its weird growth under there'd been really wonderful and strange.

You drop your shirt to the floor. In your mind it's the tea-towel from years before.

You release this new, disgusting miracle:

Fat

Fucking

You.

That's when the moment of bliss ends for the dapper man beyond the curtain with this otherworldly howl the foul miracle-you's emitting. The dapper man doesn't like it when level Ones Twos and Threes behave in a way that belies their classification. His practised reckoning of them. He doesn't want to have to reassess you. He doesn't want to acknowledge any lack of judgement with Cristine / right there / in his left ear.

Beautiful Cristine.

He doesn't want to lose his unsullied reputation for complete accuracy in quantifying the levels of lunacy all too prevalent in this great store.

Maxwell Homison-Forbes' eyes scan the curtain like two aimless flies.

His already dead moment of bliss is buried now by your first real communication. A gale of profanity.

The dapper man wonders if there's someone else in there with you. And, if so, he wonders how that's happened. He feels that in his job he stands or falls on his powers of observation.

With each successive expletive from you he feels more undermined, wrecked and wretched. He feels as though his legs, which he'd always believed to be adequately powerful and reasonably strong, have been suddenly diagnosed as diseased and in need of amputation, as, in his mind, you burst from Level Three, ransack Level Two and proceed with great velocity straight through Level One. With no signs of stopping.

This, the *Coup de Grace* for Maxwell Homison-Forbes. There being absolutely nowhere above Level One to accommodate an obese madman with Hawaiian Shirts or anybody else.

'You fucker. You Fucker. You fucking, fucking cunt.' Maxwell Homison-Forbes receives these words as dumbly as a Spanish bull barbs from a Picador.

With this mindless bull-like stoicism.

'*God?... Indeed.* Hahhh. Cunting Shit and Bollock-Piss!' This dreadful sentence, through the loose weave of the curtain to envelop the dapper man who sees profanities adhering themselves to his suit as though they were a particular kind of veracious insect and he their only source of nourishment. He abstractly holds a finger from his left hand against his left ear and relays to Cristine that the Level *he-isn't-quite-sure-what?* is going berserk in changing-room six of Gentlemen's Outfitting. And might he please, if it's not too much trouble, have some help.

Maxwell Homison-Forbes, the dapper man—who's dapper at St. Mary's on a Sunday, as he adjusts the neat lie of his trousers, the immaculate knot of his tie and kneels to politely beg God for Cristine—he's being eroded by profanity:

'Fucking/fucking/fucking/Jesus/Fucking/Cunting/Cunting/Christ.'

All those fat yous. Three-mirrored and stretching into infinity. Coming from nowhere just like the thing in your mother's bowl.

Determined to witness the full extent of this betrayal, you undress. You stand naked in front of this host of Fat Dough-Boy-Manny angry Yous.

You knead your love handles.

Poke your index finger into cloned-into-infinity stage-frightened screaming fat babies.

Conscious of fat for the first time.

You watch the horrors move in unison and howl.

The dapper man retreats with the dreadful surprise of that.

He seeks refuge in another cubicle and worries at the flimsy nature of the curtain as he closes it quickly behind him. He stares nervously at his sleeve. His conduit to Cristine.

There's you, screaming.

And then nothing.

And then another dreadful, protracted animal howl.

The dapper man, as much in the corner of his cubicle as he could possibly be, vaguely tries to remember your eyes, so—in the future (if there is a future)—he might avoid making such a mistaken classification ever again. He bounces badly upon this new dilemma of what category the obese lunatic with the Hawaiian shirts might possibly inhabit.

He returns to there being nothing above Level One.

He thinks that wherever he puts you he must be vigilant—vigilantly watchful should there be any more out there amongst the general public like you.

He can't believe that can be likely.

He mutters, 'Without an H, without an H,' vacantly. He stares at the the curtain. He collates himself for anything on which he might get some small purchase. He loses the *"without an"* and just repeats the 'H.' And makes do with that:

'H.

'H.

'H.'

You, the naked hub to three endlessly horizontal lines of fat dancing spectaculars, feel over your shoulders to the top of your back. Half expecting to find a zip. You blanch at the dreadful, synchronised fat-you-nightmare choreography this incurs.

You stare at the three nearest Yous:

*'Dough-ball!*

*'Judas!*

*'Jacket of fat!'* you scream. Snapping your head to three points of the compass—the only tidy thing in your mind being the neat arrangement of these three exclamations.

You fall about the cubicle loudly as you dress yourself in enormous, colourful clothes. You feel like this big, fat entity that's just entered the earth's atmosphere and come to ground.

The Three repellent yous rolling around your psyche like bingo balls.

Floating there as you confront a check-out girl with a pile of your old clothes and force her to scan the labels of the new ones in situ on the fat you've got off with in that singles' bar of a changing room.

You leave this garden of Gethsemane.

You pass through the big glass doors.

You gaze backwards towards a dapper man who looks like some shack in a hurricane and appears to be eating his right sleeve while shaking uncontrollably.

He gives you a strange, nervous, faltering smile.

You, a fat man, growl and approximate running off.

## TUNNELS

I've two tunnels and one vague notion:

The Blue paintings.

The illustrated children's books.

And Cloud and The Gun.

The French Ultramarine paintings I've done for years. They're of blurred, hardly discernible faces on a field of blue. The eyes always shut. They're contemplative, quiet paintings. Way-a-way from portraiture. The faces being generic; representing no one in particular. They sell in a gallery in London and through that gallery a gallery in America.

The London gallery specialises in postimpressionist work—they sell big name, dead artists. I'm their umbilical to the present.

The bargain bucket on their pavement.

I believe the gallery only exhibits my paintings when it's necessary for them to make a loss; when they've sold too many Picassos and Mondrians and Moores and backed up too vast a weight of currency.

I'm some kind of artistic sphincter through which the gallery might achieve a foul, immediate drastic loss.

That's how it seems to me.

The dealer's very tall. He's very awkward when he's with me. His name's Austin De Kramboline. I feel myself to be too conspicuous with Austin simply by being vertical.

Being Austin's only vertical artist.

All the others being dead.

I attempt to dumb myself down.

I believe that if I were less obviously alive I might somehow become more valuable.

I'm a hogtied, lachrymose shadow of myself. Capable of conversing on equal terms with Austin De Kramboline only in drunken dreams, horizontally inclined in a pine box.

I feel like a flea, clinging to the back of a dog, trying to get a purchase and find some blood. I'd always suspected the dog was sick.

I begin to realise the dog's most likely been dead all along.

# DOG-BINARY

Even if I'm identifying with the flea and not the dog, it's not auspicious to be thinking about dogs in any context. It's not a good idea. I'm leaving the flat to buy some cigarettes and some drink, what with not working today and my not-working-today-reward-system extending to my rewarding myself with most anything I fancy at any time of day after a day like yesterday.

It's walking to the car that I see it.

The thing.

It's just sitting there and staring.

I feel myself rock back on my heels as though I've just stepped out on deck into a howling fucking gale. I just *know* the thing with the watery brown eyes, the rickety body and the leer has read my vulnerability as surely as if it were a mixture of some pheromone rich urine sample and some stagnant meat on the end of a filthy bone.

That's the way it's looking at me.

With complete fucking authority.

I smile at it pathetically.

It's just sitting there with its head cocked. Reading everything I think in some dog-fucking-binary:

URINE-MEAT-MEAT-URINE-URINE

I'm thinking a mixture of things.

I'm picturing myself drinking the cold beer and rolling the nice cigarette and smoking it but I'm conscious of some deep meaningful undercurrent of powerful emotion—like I'm a flimsily constructed house on stilts and this emotion is the subtle sound of a big swell of water which is right now undermining my foundations. I picture the base of the stilts supporting my house like they're some loosely fitting teeth-roots in a jaw with rampant gum disease. I'm wondering what a Mexican-hairless is doing sitting on its own outside my block of flats staring at me with its little head cocked over like that:

URINE-MEAT-URINE-URINE-URINE

I've never seen a Mexican-hairless around here before.

URINE-URINE-URINE-URINE-MEAT

I'm standing completely still. As though mesmerised. Closing my hands into fists and opening them extravagantly, as though loosening a slipping glove of honey from both.

URINE-MEAT-MEAT-MEAT-URINE

God.

I make a slow, sideways break for my car while nervously smiling at the dog. The Polish/Latvian/Czech woman opposite, as beautiful as ever, she's standing at her kitchen sink, pretending to not notice.

Gross insults to my already whittled self-esteem raining down.

My puckered-up face, looking at that dog, I'm a TV kidnap victim pathetically gazing at a TV kidnapper, who, in this victim's mind, shows all the signs of being capable of horrendous brutality.

I've got the TV face of some pathetic loser on a TV reality

programme.

T fucking V.

The motherandfuckingfather to us all.

I look at the evil little bald head and hairy ears on the skew:

MEAT-MEAT-MEAT-MEAT-MEAT-MEAT

I have a horrible feeling that the Mexican-hairless is projecting this telepathic dog-binary at me. That it's not just my idea of what it might be thinking.

I look up.

The beautiful Polish/Latvian/Czech woman has disappeared.

I look down at the brutal kidnapper Mexican-hairless.

It turns its head surprisingly quickly on the skew. I feel like in doing that it's taken an invisible fine tube of air and twisted it into my psyche.

Like a corkscrew.

I drive to the arcade of shops twice as fast as I ever have before. I keep checking the rear-view mirror. As if a tiny Mexican-hairless might actually be capable of competing with this car's 0-to-60.

No matter how shit this car is. It can't be possible.

That's what I'm hoping.

I sit in my car outside the arcade of shops and smoke a cigarette from the ashtray until I consider that it's safe because it's more than likely that that dog wouldn't actually follow me all the way to the shops. I'm a little bit concerned to notice that I only consider it to *be* safe when there's a sudden surge, an influx, of pensioners; maybe arriving at the pub for the discounted pensioners' lunch advertised outside.

I picture the pensioners being able to pull a small dog off someone as though they were practised at it.

As though they're members of some ancient Olympic squad who train just for this eventuality.

I check the vicinity for Mexican-hairlesses.

I smile at the pensioners as though I'm making a small deposit in some strange little bank that only needs exist for five minutes.

I make a dash for the shop before they're in the pub and eating something with mince. And the mince makes me think of meat and the meat makes me think of the way the Nepalese honey-hunters stroked the liver of the sheep who's head they'd just cut off for that purpose on TV last night. Killing the sheep to stroke its liver. The purpose seemingly being to stroke the liver and check it for blemishes, blemishes which might indicate whether they were likely to die that day if they climbed that sheer cliff to steal the inaccessible honey belonging to those wild and angry bees. I'm holding onto that image. Holding onto that image so as to keep the really big image out:

MEAT/MEAT/MEAT/MEAT/MEAT/MEAT

The image of me MEAT/MEAT as a small boy MEAT/MEAT murdering my mother's Mexican-hairless instead of just taking it for an itsy ickle walk like I said I would.

It, like some small mottled bag filled with snapable sticks and blood.

I remember feeling like Tarzan Lord of The Jungle.

I'm standing in front of my mother, later, holding onto the retractable lead that had retracted two dogs before the Mexican-hairless. The lead on the end of which for as long as you could remember at this time of day there'd always been a dog. A dog attached to you, having just got back from its fucking cunting itsy ickle walk. Your mother looking up from the crossword or the deaths. You, looking at the black ring around her mouth as she opens it to its O shape, that's bigger than most ever it's always been before, and takes in the unusual sight of there just being air where the Mexican-hairless should be. And she's reading your face and coming up with all kinds of heavily embossed signals of death and disappearance and already saying a little subconscious good-bye to the empty space on her lap which will no longer be the bed for a Mexican-hairless.

Ever.

Ever.

Ever.

Ad-infi-fucking-nitum.

And you, laughing so loudly you surprise yourself.

You, who found out only the day before that this woman was not only *not your mother* but *not your mother* and being paid to have you around to walk her dogs and clean her filthy house and sit up until all hours to save *your* pets from being crushed the very next morning by the fucking bin men. Her, so ready to chuck your hamster in the bin like so much rubbish.

The hamster given to you by your real 100% dad.

The one whose head you can see the back of now as he drives off into the fog and leaves you with this woman on the first day of your acquaintance with your mother who wasn't and never cunting would be.

Red lights glowing and the back of your dad's head.

Your Dad.

Your dad lying in bed in hospital having soiled himself under the sheets and with the handbag thing full of urine in close proximity:

*Your dad*

*Your dad*

*Your dad*

And *this* woman, who you're now witnessing crying for the first time ever.

You, surprised enough to stop laughing and start crying without so much as the slightest pause in between. You, on the floor and hugging this woman (who's all you've actually got) because your real 100% dad who loved you and was kind and funny and nice is dead. You, telling this woman not to worry, that the dog is only most likely lost. Like the mottled leather handbag with pulverised bones and blood in a shallow grave might actually *be* only lost. And the woman calms down and says that she's probably been overreacting but it was just the look on your face.

You, watching the black ring around her mouth wobble into a shut position.

Like it was some kind of radar to every kind of madness.

You, back in the field, knowing there's just *no way* you're going to bump into a lost Mexican-hairless which looks just like the one you've recently slaughtered.

Not until years later when you least fucking expect it anyway.

You think how you only have to look down for two seconds and then look back up again to find two decades gone—Two:

Whish

Whish

Just like that.

Like you're in an express train travelling through a flat landscape passing two insignificant trees tight together:

Whish

fucking

Whish.


I pay for the whiskey (the beer and wine alone today seeming no way near enough), the beer, the wine, the cigarettes and a small piece of fish.

I look at the man giving me my change without seeing anyone, my consciousness is just so entirely full of the small dog that in my mind's staring at the door to my flat with its head cranked on its stupid little handbag body as it waits for me to come back into its field of vision.

## GIVING MY FAT BACK TO JESUS

No mail comes to the flat for Jabba.

Ever.

He has to remain invisible for business reasons.

He collects his mail from another address. Jabba's Albanians are invisible too. They start being invisible as they physically commit themselves to jumping from the backs of ferries approaching Dover. That, being as regular a means of arrival in England for them as stepping off a plane for someone with a passport.

I picture them becoming invisible shortly before they hit the water.

These falling Albanians coming to London for Jabba.

Being young and capable and not long before having been carrying armalite rifles.

They don't mind jumping, falling or being invisible at all.

All that being a walk in the park to them.

I'm the human face for Jabba's flat. I exist. My being sentient, perversely as much a benefit to Jabba as it's a hindrance to

Austin De Kramboline.

The utility bills that come are addressed to me. Any council communication. Money from my work mostly comes by post. Apart from that I receive little else. Occasionally, mail arrives for the previous tenant, Mr. Lipman. From this mail I know he'd been a blood donor, liked old-fashioned roses and had an acquaintance up North. Three or so times a year a letter in a hand written envelope arrives for Mr. Lipman, with a Northern postmark. The ink always turquoise. From a fountain pen. I'd been throwing these letters away for three years.

The one I opened by mistake made me mourn the ones I'd lost. I stood holding that letter in the kitchen, looking at the bin as though it might be able to give the lost letters back. From that time on I've always opened and read Beatrice's letters.

They're like messages in a bottle. Washing up for me. Always special.

I dread the day they'll stop.

I suppose that Beatrice must be just writing into a peculiar void that's the man who'd liked old roses and had been a blood donor.

Apart from work, number 5 and Jabba, I see no one. I've stopped getting newspapers. I only watch documentaries on TV. I've been eating nothing but fish, salad and fruit for three months. I'm doing two hundred stomach crunches a day. Occasionally, I go back to the changing room in the department store to confront the mirrored battalions of Me. Each time they offer slightly more resistance to my prodding finger. Each time they swing me flags to a small victory for us in our ongoing battle with God. The changing room's become something of an optimistic crystal ball in which I can foresee an increasingly svelte and sensual self.

I feel in a constant, diminishing, curiously-larval stage of re-invention; shedding pounds and dropping clothes sizes. I believe

118

that whatever I'm yielding by my own discipline's being forc-ibly reinstated back to God:

I'm giving my fat back to Jesus.

I continue swimming at odd hours when the pool's most likely to be empty. Enjoying the hot showers there, bending my head down, looking past a fringe of falling water, watching reflections fragmenting on the surface of the pool.

Watching the movement of the trees through the big win-dows.

Feeling that, maybe, somewhere, deep down, there's a big smile coming.

Once a month I drive to a deserted spot and practice using the gun.

I talk to The Cloud on the phone.

Neither of us likes making arrangements.

But we do something difficult:

We make a date for the Gun Thing.

## ELIJAH GOES BERSERK

Dear Mr. Lipman,

I'm afraid to say that things are quite bad.

I was telephoned the other night, at a late hour, by a nurse at Elijah's home. A nurse who I've become quite friendly with. She surprised me with her tone and informed me that Elijah had gone berserk. She said I should get to the home as soon as possible. Whatever I expected, I don't know, but what I saw was ten times worse.

An ambulance and two police cars were outside—a very large nurse was being stretchered onto the ambulance. I didn't recognise her but I suppose I must have been staring (she had a very bad long straight burn across her face and a bloody mouth and obviously some missing teeth). As I passed she shouted, 'That something husband of yours did this to me you something something.' I can't be one hundred percent because of the teeth, but I'm pretty sure that's what she said. I'm definite about the somethings though, and, as you know, I can't stand language. It was a bad beginning to what was soon to become much worse. And the taxi driver witnessed it all; it will be all over the village as I write.

A policeman escorted me to a glass fronted room down a passage. And, Mr. Lipman, it was just too bad. Elijah had taken hostage a much smaller nurse. He had her round the neck and had one of those gas jet things that you start fires with held up in the air beside her. That in itself was odd. I thought technology like that went out with the stone-age. I think it speaks volumes and is a general castigation of the home that anything like that might be to hand! Anyway, the poor thin girl had already lost most of her hair. And all the time Elijah was screaming like a wild animal about the needle thing from before, screaming how he wasn't going to let the somethings give him the something needle. It took two and a half hours for the gas-supply to be sabotaged successfully and for Elijah to then be safely rushed by the police (who were, I thought, unnecessarily brutal with someone who'd so plainly lost his mind).

They took him to St Catherine's that night and administered a Thorazine lobotomy. (I think.)

He just lies there looking completely blank. We were married when we were eighteen, he doesn't recognise me from the wallpaper now.

And to think I used to worry about him pouring tea over his dinner.

It seems pointless (and something of an insult to Elijah) to make any comment about the squirrels.

*Or the garden.*
*Love*
*Beatrice*

*Ps. Elijah is in room 6 Churchill ward, if you want to write.*

*(Not that the poor dear would understand it if you did.)*

# STEPPING STONES TO ELIJAH

Prostitutes and drugs and guns; a growing proclivity to strange things, with everything a package of a lesson to be learnt, and each lesson a stepping stone towards Elijah.

Now, the police, in this big London gallery; the wrecked installation upstairs having gained their attention as easily as women on the streets outside are eliciting glances.

I'm smiling. I feel fine. I check my heartbeat the same way I might have stared through the bars of my hamster's cage when I was a boy, to check that my 100% hamster was OK.

My heartbeat seems really slow and regular.

'You've been banned. OK? Like from a public house. OK? You've been banned.

'OK?'

I think the happier I seem, the more necessary this policeman finds it to repeatedly say, 'OK?' Like I must be nuts for smiling or something.

I like the attention of the police and the gallery guards and the gallery head of security.

I remember the woman who came to do my mother's hair; somehow, there's the faintest ghost of her in my head. The woman who liked Dean Martin. The woman for whom my mother would put on some old LPs. The small, dark house being full of American happiness as my mother smiled and had her messy hair fluffed up into something large and unnatural looking. Her being cosseted like that.

Her and her smile. The one she kept for her dogs and that hairdresser.

I'm thinking it's good to feel valued and recognised, even for all the wrong reasons.

They're watching me like I'm some unclassifiable animal at the zoo. Like they're nervous as to whether these teeth belong to a carnivore or a vegetarian. This is while they still think I'm just Manny, before all the confusion sets in.

Everything being still a bit of a revelation for me: this saying a big 'Boo!' to fears and watching them scatter, like all along they were nothing more than falling dust; falling dust I've been mistaking in magnitude for a mountain.

Taboos being just an imagined plague of bad expectations.

Obviously.

Braking taboos in reality being no trouble at all.

Whatever's happening here, the logic of it's leading straight to Elijah. Everything being just a dress rehearsal to that. Like I'm familiarising myself with the psychology of all this the same way you'd familiarise yourself with a machine you intended to fly or ride or drive on a journey later.

I think that I mightn't realistically be able to save myself but I can at least maybe save him.

Poor Elijah.

I take in the reality of all this.

The reality of it being a complete farce.

'Bloody serene, with this horrible smile,' says the fat guard.

He's fixing a stare to the wall ahead of him and clawing at his shirt front as he watches a hideous mental replay of us, him and me, about the exhibit earlier. He draws in big lungfuls of air until his wrecked constitution finally allows him to verbalise some more thoughts: 'The smile. The f-fucking smile. And those f-fucking eyes. Christ-f-fucking-Jesus-F-Fuck.'

He'd looked fine, back up in the gallery, before he'd had to start shouting into his radio and calling for assistance.

Before he'd been started on this journey of how a fat man attempts to hold onto a runaway metabolism.

With all this clawing and these big breaths.

He looks, now, like a big old washing machine on the back end of a spin cycle that's proving too much.

It's at this point that I stop being Manny and start being the Disembowler From The Gorbels. The police, in and out because their radios aren't functioning in this basement room. Every time they're in they're looking at me with more concern—like dismantling an exhibit actually is some heinous crime. I remember the old Irishman in ear defenders and think that maybe that's what they've discovered on whatever kind of machine passes for their database. They're in and out some more as I have endless collisions with the council worker who should have been on a couch somewhere but's still available to be bounced off my bonnet.

'Are you, or have you ever been a resident of Glasgow?' the "OK" policeman finally asks.

I smile at him.

'We need an answer, *Sir*,' he says.

I smile. I say, 'No.'

'Have you, at any time, had dealings with a Miss Daisy Penfold? Of 63 Fenwick Court, Sauchihall Street, Glasgow?'

Apart from the fat guard, everyone's on the balls of their feet.

'I, *Sir*,'—he's saying the *Sir* in a tremulous way. Not at all like he was the "Sirs" at the start of all this—'have reason to believe that you are, in fact, Thomas Anderson-Kildair—of 69 Fenwick Gardens, Sauchihall Street, Glasgow—and not Emmanuel Marbas.' He peers at me intently at this, as though he's just hurled a few insults into a monster's lair. He's looking into my eyes like that's where the big bad monster's likely to be leaping from. 'Not *Emmanuel Marbas,*' he continues, 'but Manny Minorbas. Manny Minorbas being your previous active alias—you fucking, deviant bastard cunt—and that you are wanted for the brutal murder and disembowelment of Daisy Penfold.' He licks his lips like he's just finished a donut.

I think two things:

That Scottish psychopaths are bound to be destroying works of art in London after their latest foul event north of the border.

That it's somehow strangely pleasing to be thought capable of disembowelling Daisy Penfold.

That's when they jump me. Everyone plainly empowered by the vision of ancient, steaming intestines on a pissy floor in the Gorbels.

Everything goes up a gear into major disorder.

'She was eighty-fucking-nine, you degenerate cunt,' screams the OK policeman, simultaneously throwing me to the ground and landing an elbow in my face. And the fat guard, who's off the peak oscillation of his spin cycle, he starts screaming: 'Christ, I fucking knew it,' and aims a dainty kick by way of completion as everyone else just piles right on in.

Two hours later, restrained by all manner of straps and metalwork, this me, the dead-ringer of a Scottish madman, has left the impression of his teeth on two of the OK policeman's colleagues. He's assured them in a thick Scottish accent that he carries the fucking HIV virus, and they would soon too, for fucking sure, the fucking cunting-cunts.

Brought to this room like badly packaged recalcitrant shopping from hell, faces above uniforms are staring. Staring at me, this Thomas Anderson-Fucking-Kildair.

This epitome of evil.

I smile right back at them; a big fat top lip of a stranger to my face, riding slug-like up over teeth and bleeding gums.

The uniforms are all being very deferential to the OK policeman. The hero of the hour. The rounder up of this foul Scottish fugitive from justice.

I'm saying something which isn't easily heard from beneath my restraints and my swollen face. One of the uniforms approaches tentatively. He's holding his hands as though flapping them fast would be his best means of retreat. I think I must be suffering some kind of stress-induced Tourrette's. I can't help myself as I relate garbled, fictitious, disgusting ghosts of what I might have done to Daisy Penfold—the old pissy bitch—other than just the disembowelling.

The close uniform says, 'Fuck.'

He looks like he might vomit.

I'm thinking The Cloud will never believe all this.

'What?' another uniform asks, the trail of an ambulance leaving with the latest bite victim spreading today's madness yet further afield.

'He said,' says the close uniform, 'that. I can't say what he first said. He said first. Then he. He said he anally raped her. Daisy Penfold. And killed her cat with a fucking mallet.'

I mumble something else which induces more 'Whats?'

'I don't know,' says the close policeman. 'Something about a Mexican Hairless.'

'A Mexican Hairless what?'

I figure it's taken all these years to finally be able to confess about the Mexican hairless.

'I don't know, I don't know. Twigs and blood. Twigs and fucking blood. How am I supposed to get inside the head of

some fucking animal–madman like this?'

Me, this animal, I notice through a badly swollen eye, some kind of literature being passed around the room.

The low–down on Thomas Anderson-Kildair.

There's a big slice of awed silence as they read the 'Previous' they believe to be mine.

They all back off about three feet.

All this two pages of hideous, disgusting detail before they discover Thomas Anderson-Kildair's passion for Chinese drag-ons. That he's a regular walking gallery of Chinese dragons. Them being liberally spread about his person as every manner of dancing tattoo.

They home in on that piece of information with genuine terror.

Them, now being able to prove my authenticity as easily as if I were labelled up like an item on a supermarket shelf with Chinese bar-codes under the packaging of my shirt. This is the meat–eater / vegetarian moment. They all look excited and ter-rified at the same time.

I watch the OK policeman's smiling face as he approaches, eager to reveal my Granny-rapist's torso that's the final proof of his worth as a detective.

I smile.

He smiles like maybe the Queen of England did once whilst launching a ship.

I can hear a circus drum-roll.

He unveils my torso like he's playing Scissors/Paper/Stone with knives and guns and dynamite.

They're all looking confused and staring with intent; as though if they were to stare hard enough I might somehow generate Chinese dragons from the inside.

My pristinely naked torso being devoid of dragons.

There being no dragons.

Zilch.

The OK policeman's face falls like a suicide victim from a cliff.

The lack of dragons sending him straight back to being less than he was this morning and me straight back to being just Manny.

As before, with the ancient council worker, I'm the culmination of an embarrassment that two men in suits are eager to do paperwork to release. The upshot, again, a kind of playground policing based on the premise that

they won't pursue mine

if I don't pursue theirs:

my antics /

their brutality.

We do a deal. At no stage do I request a solicitor. I make no mention of compensation. I feel compensated enough by my new found liberating perception of things.

All I want is for them to let me walk my swollen face out into the beautiful London evening to begin violently rectifying things for Elijah.

Every paving stone in London being a step closer to that.


Out of nowhere, I'm thinking that masturbation, it's *so* unlike the real thing.

Like mimicking a moon landing with nothing more substantial than a tea-tray and a couple of fucking sticks.

## 60+60+60+60

I ring the number of the man from whom I'd bought the gun and order a silencer.

Picking up the silencer, it's just going to somebody's flat and doing a transaction for cash. I'm struck by the multiple of 60 thing as I hand the money over:

Silencer = 60+60+60+60 = Nadia+Miki+Nikki+Angel.

I put it to the back of my mind, attach the silencer to the gun and drive to Birmingham.

I stop at a motorway services for a coffee and a cigarette. I've got the gun in a plastic bag on the table in front of me as a challenge to my new found theory as to how things actually are. I'm thinking it looks very much like a gun in a carrier bag:

It's a gun in a carrier bag.

It's as though all my life I've been living under the misapprehension that people know or care what I'm doing. In the motorway services I realise I don't have thought bubbles over my head saying: "I'm going to kill Elijah and the fucking gun's *right here.*"

There're no thought bubbles above my head.
Nothing.
There never had been.
That's how things are.

# KILLING ELIJAH

I'm feeling fine. Feeling of no interest to anybody.

I've got flowers and the carrier bag.

I'm feeling calm.

Being Thomas Anderson-Kildair.

I walk up some stairs and down a long corridor.

Half way down the corridor there's an old man in normal clothes. He's leaning up against a wall, bent over, rubbing the back of his right leg and grimacing. There's nobody in uniform about. I stop beside him.

'Are you OK?' I ask.

'I've just got this ball of cramp,' he says. 'At the back of my thigh.'

I touch the old man's shoulder. I stick out my right leg and move my right foot up and down in a way I believe might be beneficial for cramp. 'Try doing that with your foot,' I say. 'You need to stretch the muscles a bit.'

The old man mimics what I'm doing with my leg. He nods his head towards the entrance of a ward. 'My wife's in there,' he says. 'There's no way I could go in there limping with a ball of cramp in the back of my leg like this.' We look towards the door to the ward. I keep choreographing something good for cramp until someone in uniform comes along.

As I walk up the corridor I hear the old man telling the person in uniform how there's no way he'd be letting his wife see him with a ball of cramp like that.

There's a tea-room sign posted off the corridor. I go in. Two old women are behind a bank of bad pastries and cheap chocolate. They're staying close to an enormous teapot as if it were something dangerous they'd been put in charge of and a war was on. Asking for a cup of tea's like swinging a switch in them. I'm surprised by the amount of separate physical actions two people can devote to one cup of tea.

I sit and drink tea and imagine Elijah being imminently dead.

I can only imagine a B-film version of Elijah's death.

I finish my tea.

The two women are trying to work out a problem with the till as I leave.

At the end of the next corridor there's a multiple choice of corridors and ward signs. There's a man coming out of a toilet.

I read:

CHURCHILL WARD

LADY CHURCHILL WARD

CHAMBERLAIN WARD

And I meet the man's eyes. The expression he gives me's odd; the way he holds his head to one side and cranes his neck. I turn right, walk up a corridor and stop outside the door that's marked 6.

Apart from me the corridor's empty.

I'm aware of feeling the same way I did when approaching Number 5 for the first time. Standing here, a minute away from being a murderer.

I knock and enter.

Smile and look about.

I'm alone with Elijah.

I put the flowers on the end of Elijah's bed.

The room smells sweet and bad.

Elijah's all plumbed in to machines the same way I remember my dad being from when I was ten. I wonder why he's linked up to all these machines. I imagine it must be a drastic way to mollify Elijah.

I take out the gun.

I stroke Elijah's head, which is completely bald.

'It's all right, Elijah,' I say.

I'm surprised by his features. I find it difficult to imagine him going berserk. I'm going through the motions in this room like there's a dance that I've been practising in my head for some time and I'm on the stage now. Going through the steps. I'm aware I'm not taking in obvious things around me in the way I normally might. I stare at Elijah's head. I feel the look of him's trying to communicate something to me but I just don't know what.

'Everything's going to be fine,' I tell Elijah.

I squeeze the trigger.

He opens his eyes and gives me a very strange look.

I shoot him twice in the head.

## NADIA

On the way back to London I listen to Arabic music and re-peatedly play back the last minute in the life of Elijah.

No matter how used I've become to strange things, killing Elijah was odd. The look of him for a start: his bald head and his fine features. He looked jaundiced. And all the equipment he was joined to, that was weird.

The two pops into his taught yellow forehead.

The sweet smell in the room mixed up with a nutty smell from the bullets being fired.

There being hardly any blood at all. Just basically one hole at the front and nothing at the back whatsoever. The ridged black bindi at the front and nothing under his head as I'd lifted it to check like I might've been looking for bugs under a rock.

The bullets lodged in there somewhere.

As in the past I've smelt my bed to better remember a woman that's just left it by her scent, now I'm trying to stimulate my synapses to tell me more about killing Elijah by remembering the nutty smell and the sweet smell of his room.

They're not.

I feel completely divorced and separate from the unbelievable death of Elijah.

I keep checking myself in the mirror to see what a killer like me looks like.

Maybe you've got to kill a whole lot of people before you stop doing stuff like pouting into the nearest mirror and screwing up your eyes like everything's such a big joke.

I've no idea.


Coming into London I decide to drive to number 5.

Somehow I reckon fucking, it'll be dropping more earth onto dead Elijah and that can only be a good thing.

Friday at number 5 means Nadia. She's like a surly waitress: she gives you sex the same way she might throw a plate of food in front of you in a restaurant.

I like her technique.

The dancing girl had kept saying, 'I love you darling. I love you.' I hadn't liked that. It'd seemed ridiculous.

The surly waitress thing seems OK.

My hands and my mouth start relaying information about the beautiful physical truth of Nadia; the beautiful atomic dance that's the end of everything else and the beginning of her.

She's got a small fine silver chain around one ankle. Its joined by a flat inch of silver. There's writing on that. Tiny letters spell one word:

l o v e

Any small pretence at playing a part for me leaves her when she realises why I'm repeatedly asking her the time.

'No way,' she says. 'I remember you,' she says. 'You no fuck me for half an hour.'

'Why not?' I ask.

She watches me holding her by the ankles and smiling.

'No way,' she says.

We keep talking over our genitals like we're discussing something over a dog eating its dinner.

She looks really fed up.

'What you laughing at?'

'You,' I say.

'Why you laughing at me?'

'Because of your face.'

'What's wrong with my face?'

She's completely oblivious to what I'm doing to her.

I look down at her vagina. At my cock sliding into it. I let out a long bovine moan as I stroke the soft concave area at the top of her thighs.

The only thing in the whole world's the information coming from her.

Elijah's just some bad movie on another channel that ended five hours ago.

'There's nothing wrong with your face. You're beautiful.' I tell her. 'You've got a beautiful face.'

Just as I think I'm molifying her with my thin body and my easy going manner, I'm let down by my metabolism. All the alcoholic toxins inside me, by some sort of common arrangement, they start escaping in the form of sweat from my head like people abandoning a burning building from the roof. There's a regular concerted exodus of toxins. I watch them fall onto Nadia's thighs. Each drop makes her flinch. She brushes every single one away with a tissue and an exhalation.

'Twaa,' she says.

'Twaa.'

'I never seen nothing like it,' she says.

I imagine a cartoon hot country full of oriental people who can do anything they choose in extreme heat without sweating onto their neighbours.

I feel all colonial.

She won't let me kiss her.

She grimaces and shakes her head and says, 'Cigarettes,' and nods towards my tobacco which's next to the lube and the tissues and the air-freshner and she exhales another big humph of disgust and looks at her watch as she goes up and down horizontally, telling me to hurry up with her angry oriental eyes.

I think she looks really pretty and lovely like that.

I get into being mesmerised by her hips.

I close my eyes and send information about her hips back to my brain with a small caressing movement of my thumbs; I'm holding up all other stimuli and waving this small procession right on through; a big whole party just queuing up behind and waiting to join in.

There's a radio on in the background. The music's stopped. The man with throat cancer's gargling his warning about the dangers of smoking; he's segued amongst the delicate information about Nadia's hips before a woman says the same thing she's been saying for months: 'Sydney died three months after recording this heartfelt message,' she says.

I'm saying, 'Fuck, Fuck, Fuck,' as a little metronome to my movements as Dead Sydney stalks the room.

'Yeah,' says Nadia, using his fate like a club. 'That what happens to smokers.'

I smile at her and she smiles back. Afterwards I think that that was my and her only nearly tender moment.

I try to magnify the information that's Nadia by repeatedly telling myself I'm fucking a beautiful woman, as if it isn't evident enough. I collate her body to throw anything about her as fuel into this overheating engine that's me. To get it to the station. To pull it up at the fucking platform and let out the spunking multitude.

I lean backwards to turn the radio off but I can't find the switch, so I turn the volume down instead.

The fan hums.

Nadia's complaining.

I miss the item on the news about the mystery killing of a pensioner in Birmingham.

# VERNON PRENDERGAST

Vernon Prendergast sits amongst the confines of his pristine first-floor flat in his favoured silk kimono. The one with the flowers and the bees. The cream one. The one in which he can think calmly.

He pictures the patient going 'that way'; with bullets, instead of all the more regular ways they invariably did.

Looking as peaceful as any he had ever seen regardless.

Vernon sets to manicuring his fingernails as he contemplates the man languidly strolling down the corridor and into Vernon's life. The man, stopping. Looking at the ward signs. Maybe even smiling.

The killer.

The murderer.

The man who looked so familiar.

The man he failed to mention to the police.

Not that they'd have thought to ask much of Vernon anyway—his history, his past setting him anti-clockwise in a clockwise world and almost invisible for that.

Vernon watches the killer in his mind's eye. His expression had been benign, easy. Almost completely convincing. Just that shaft, that slant of artifice, though. Unmissable to Vernon. Artifice being Vernon's forte.

His métier.

Vernon holds up his left hand. Moves five fingernails in front of his eyes as a small perfect parade.

He puts the black emery board amongst the silk bees on his right knee, slips his right hand under the lapel of his kimono and cups his heart to feel it beating.

He witnesses the man moving towards the man's goal. (Vernon's psyche hovering as a moth in that room waiting for the holes to be impacted into the patient's head.)

Vernon feels his heart quicken. He pulls his psyche back to keep a distance lest he be squashed, scuppered and defeated.

Pushed into the blackness.

He ruminates gently amongst the brutal serenity of an abstract solace.

About the periphery of that.

The whole event so precious he's determined not to wear it out by holding it too close.

He'll keep it at one step removed.

He'll keep it to himself.

APOTHEOSIS

Ten letters drifting about his fingernails.

This man, out of nowhere

Showing

Vernon

The

Way.

## PORTRAIT NUMBER 2—The Bishop of W.

The Idiot is very strongly lit from below. There's an odd arrangement of cut white card and felt hat upon his head, a kindly, bemused expression upon his face and a hideous leather jerkin upon his body. He leans forward slightly, his right hand pointing out. He appears to be proffering a strangely dignified yet sly accusation.

'The Idiot,' the Bishop concludes, reading from his exhibition catalogue, feeling a dull empathy towards this gormless unfortunate. 'A very odd marriage,' he thinks, taking one step backward on an ancient, unworn heel, adjusting his purple raiment, '—between delicate, Italian Renaissance style and stunning, heartrending contemporary angst.'

He sips at his white wine.

Moisture in his eye, almost a tear, minutely fragmenting the leather jerkin and the white card, the felt hat and the pointing finger. The Bishop is happily moved by the poignant, distant plight of this Idiot. He lazily considers the Christian merit of the tear forming in his eye. He lazily considers the doubtless artistic merit of the highly skilled portraitist; who, according to the curator of the exhibition, is a most unusual young man: "an intense, confirmed recluse with a growing, if enigmatic reputation."

The catalogued details of each exhibit include a small photograph of each exhibitor.

The Bishop cranes his neck.

He offers his chins for the consideration of The Idiot.

He looks down his nose.

Blinks.

*Emmanuel Marbas.*

My goodness.

The look of the man is *extraordinary*.

The Bishop stares into the eyes of Emmanuel Marbas.

'Something of John The Baptist?' he wonders.

Definitely.

Completely terrifying.

But *so* right.

The Bishop inspects the painting carefully to better appreciate the skills of the intimidating Emmanuel Marbas.

The intense recluse.

He believes that an artist talented enough to render this handicapped, gormless fool with such gravitas and serenity would, surely, when faced with a subject such as himself: a *Bishop* nonetheless (a man who'd studied the classics, achieved a glorious 1st and become *The youngest ever Bishop of any diocese. Anywhere. Ever.* A man with undeniable physical charms; who, at one time, with the flash of his golden locks and his stunning physique had on several occasions been reliably noted as reminiscent of a particular Greek God)—

...Well, surely, in those circumstances, this artist might produce

'...A masterpiece?' the Bishop muses.

A tear finally fully graces his right eye. It signals to the Bishop the smooth running of his soul. Its passage down his cheek offers such an irresistible Godly frisson that he can't help but oddly slope his eyebrows and pucker his eyes to better eke the pleasure of it out.

Above his white wine, he morosely contemplates his imminent retirement. Only the premonition of a magnificently wrought, beautifully conceived portrait acts as a sop to his extraordinary sadness.

He dabs this sop like soft bread amongst rich gravy as the idiosyncratic peculiar curve of his mouth slowly accommodates a ghastly breaking smile.

He's determined that his diocese shall have something startlingly original to remember him by.

/

'The Bishop of W. has asked me to contact you,' says The Bishop of W.'s private secretary.

I say nothing.

'He is *most* impressed by your extraordinary technique and by your obvious compassion towards the handicapped gentleman in the painting.'

'Is he?' I ask.

'Yes,' says The Bishop of W.'s private secretary. 'Most definitely. He's very touched by the handicapped gentleman. By his plight. He'd like to know more about it.'

I say nothing.

'Is he hospitalised?'

I think of Charlie.

'No,' I say. 'He's a gardener.'

There's silence on the other end of the line.

I can hear The Bishop of W.'s private secretary thinking.

The hatred I feel for this man, I try to push it into that silence.

/

The Bishop of W.'s mouth is like a little puckered wave; he's holding it in a shape he believes to be beneficent; a whole army of artifice in there's waving flags, blowing bugles and banging fucking tambourines.

I picture stabbing him in the eyes with a long handled filbert.

'I believe that God would not approve of the debasement of style and content prevalent in clerical portraiture today,' I hear myself say.

'Really?' asks The Bishop of W., with a coquettish smile.

A pleasant light drifts into the room by way of the well-tended acres of the Bishop's garden.

'Definitely,' I say. 'The contemporary style is grandiose in the extreme. Completely abhorrent. An abomination to everything humble and decent. I believe that what is called for, is...' I rub my chin and gaze about, '...a portrait that denies the frivolous intrusion of finery...' My movements are lavish, flowery. Theatrical. The Bishop of W. sits silently smiling. '...

That *glorifies* the humble, natural, *naked* dignity of man. I believe I can instigate a *new* renaissance; a resurgence of…of what is more appropriate to the teachings of Christ, with my portrait of *you*, your eminence.'

The Bishop of W.'s staring past the ornate contents of his room towards some imagined, disgusting beatific flaccid rendition of himself.

'That would be a most flattering and wonderful thing to behold,' he says.


The next morning I confront The Bishop of W. in his well lit, oak-panelled front reception. I undo the clasp of a small wooden box, remove a small stuffed bird and attach it by means of a wire and a strap to the outstretched index-finger of The Bishop of W.'s right hand.

I stand back and manufacture a look I believe a disciple might have adopted for Christ himself.

'You look…*divine*,' I say.

I busy myself with small preparations. All so familiar. Preparations, until the Businesses, undertaken with great care and optimistic artistic inclination. I vaguely contemplate my recent portraiture back-catalogue as though it were a series of disgusting sexual trysts. I'm hit by three waves: self-pity, self-disgust and self-loathing. I think this Bishop is hobbling more than my spirit as I begin to conjoin myself with the foul information that's him.

I angrily look from him to the canvas and back again.

The Bishop of W. is, apart from one small ragged cloth, completely naked as instructed.

'*Divine*,' I repeat.

'Really?' he asks, attempting to cover his withered breasts with the small stuffed bird, doubtless worrying as to how far from his imagined vision of an immortalized self mine appears to be straying. 'Do you *truly* think so?' he asks.

I say nothing.

I start to delicately translate the physical reality of The Bishop of W. onto the canvas by means of a small piece of charcoal that had only recently been a conduit to far more profound emotions in the privacy of my studio. I'm thinking that this poisonous old Bishop, he's even tainting my stick of fucking charcoal.

I hate him for it.

Somewhere in the building I can hear his retinue creak.

It's listening at the walls.

I tell him it can't be expected that a venture such as this should be easily achieved. That what we're attempting is altogether *new*. I stare out past his small, leaded windows and let my gaze wander about his wonderfully manicured lawn and ancient cedars. In the middle distance a man drifts past on a lawn mower. 'Like setting off under canvas,' I say. 'In a wooden boat,' I say, 'to discover an unknown land.'

'Yes… Maybe… I suppose so,' says the Bishop of W.

'Un*questionably*,' I say.

I'm thinking that I'm riding a wave that's only limited in height, as far as my scope to be anything I choose is concerned, by the Bishop's vanity. I believe the Bishop to be very vain. I trace the bulging line of his stomach. I sense that I have absolutely nothing to lose, anyway. What have I to lose? Plainly despising portraiture as I so obviously do.

I picture a life without portraiture:

Nothing.

I attempt to revel in the moment. The authority of it.

The horrible similarity of it to the instant of realisation that a new lover's willing to comply with any foul order or request, no matter how degrading or perverse.

The desire in me to be anything I wish in relation to The Bishop of W., I determine to harbour it as no more than a notion.

/

Two days later I can't help myself.

It's something to do with the look on his face.

'Bishop,' I say, with a slow flourish of the tainted charcoal, 'I think it would *very* much *fucking-**advantage*** our venture if you were to consolidate your fucking fears, shitting trepidation and irrelevant cunting-conceits and incinerate them promptly on the altar to this fucking masterpiece which I am going to be fucking exhausting myself creating.'

This sentence, it's the equivalent of watersporting as a sexual hello. It's said with a look of such bravado and conviction, such positive artistic flamboyance, that The Bishop of W. is forced to concede to my expertise. Which, unknown to him, consists solely of immolating one disgusting, large portrait in the dead of night in the middle of The Business' lawn.

He wriggles his hips and shivers.

Now I've set sail, in the right boat, I'm free to be any kind of captain I wish. That's all I'm thinking.

His insufficient protest being a green light to any amount

of profanity:

'You must be fucking steadfast and take instruction without complaint,' I pontificate. 'You must heave on the fucking rigging and shin up the fuck-cunting mast. So to fucking speak. Jesus-fucking-christ-all-cunting-mighty. Do you or don't you under-cunting stand?'

'Yes,' replies The Bishop of W.

I think you must never underestimate quite how quickly weird shit can become familiar.

'You must eat the fucking weevil biscuits.'

'Yes,' replies The Bishop of W.. 'I must eat the *humhum* weevil biscuits,' he intones, as though it were a canticle. The cunting humhum some kind of high-church screen to profanity.

'You must man this and swob the fucking other.'

There's a lot of troubled creaking in every direction from beyond the oak panelling. What sounds like an entire tea-set falls to the floor somewhere.

'Yes,' the Bishop mutters with a stagnant little grin. 'I must man this and humhum the humhum other.' This Hum-Hum sliding around him like some badly controlled feathers attempting to conceal his gone-to-seed-Rubenesque nakedness.

At no time in my life have I had the occasion to use the word Cunting with such relish and abandon.

'Or, by cunting-christ...' I persevere, 'I'll shackle my cunting wrath to your pathetic fucking ankles and keelhaul your repulsive, ancient cunting-arse against the razor fucking sharp barnacles of this fuck-cunting renaissance,' I say.

'Yes,' submits the Bishop, and he repeats all of the aforesaid threats in a monotone nasal drone with humhums cleaving to everything.

'In the meantime,' I say, 'It would far better advantage the portrayal of your *path-et-ic* gland, if it were to be facing somewhat more in a northerly direction.'

'Pardon me?' requests The Bishop of W., looking down at his rag, which, owing to the prominence of his belly conceals his nudity as well as a stick-on moustache or party-hat.

'Upwards?'

'*No*, your fucking eminence,' I scream, 'not *Northerly* as in upward pointing *Northerly*—God-for-fucking-bid. *Northerly* as in more inclined to the *Northern* light you cunt.'

I manufacture a voice full of mimsy and foolishness: '*Maybe the Bishop could tilt his bovine hips towards the fucking window slightly?*'

'Certainly. Sorry,' says The Bishop of W..

I've a horrible feeling he's enjoying all this.

I leave the room, suddenly. I have to think things through. In the large echoing hall I pace around a giant, wooden, highly polished figure of the crucified christ. I smoke a cigarette and march about it. Every now and then I dart a little look at the slanted head of Jesus.

At his sorrowful little face.

/

Each day, the Bishop of W.'s perpetual state of confused, compliant, naked obedience hovers like a yet-more gay, tragic, suicidally inclined moth about the burning flame of my anger and hatred. I treat this foul gay moth (my tattered, leprous, solitary congregation) with complete disdain. I manipulate it casually at will. I conduct its every revolting, lassitudinous movement.

The word cunt, it assumes a position behind everything. Like the stoical, rigid tock of a metronome:

*Cunt*

*Cunt*

*Cunt*

'Your *Fucking-Holiness*,' I say, 'it is a thing of great importance for the success of our painting.

*Cunt*

*Cunt*

*Cunt*

'...that there should be a figure about you representative of the cunting-suffering of all mankind.'

*Cunt*

*Cunt*

*Cunt*.

He's looking at me pathetically. I loop my eyes into the air and let them fall into the opposite corner of the room as though I were actually physically shifting his sordid floppy-skinned puppy-dog-anima by its withered revolting neck.

'Would you please assume a foetal position in the corner?' I ask.

Cunts ad-infinitum, I undo the small wooden box from which I'd earlier removed the bird and take out a tiny trident. The Bishop of W., as instructed, cowers in a corner of the room, holding the trident to his bald, flaccid chest. He looks beseechingly upwards to the panelled ceiling.

The retinue creaks; by now as comforting and familiar a sound as the homely movement of familiar timber at sea to the crew of an ancient ship of the line.

Thus, God-Jesus–Christ-cunting forgive me, I harry the old man for days. Only ever deserting him to pace around the crucified figure of Jesus. To smoke and stare at his slanted wooden head.

To look into his sad,

wooden

eyes.


In "Jesus Is The One At The Top", the naked Bishop of Whatever stands in an imaginary landscape, a very obviously stuffed bird on the index-finger of his right hand. In the middle ground The Bishop of W., again, can be seen curled up at the entrance to a cave; clutching what appears to be a small piece of cutlery to his chest, he looks up and across towards a small hill from which rise three, tiny, crucified figures.

The foremost amongst them appears to be laughing up-roariously.

# THE ROAD TO DAMASCUS

I'm thinking I can see it clearly now: it's like a black and white WW2 German submarine.

This thing that I'm throwing all these obscenities at as I drive along. All the "Fucks" flying out of my mouth towards it.

It just bobs there in my head, regardless. Untouched.

I wonder quite what it is I'm so upset about. I can't remember anything specific but I keep laying down a blanket of obscenities towards the WW2 German submarine.

Nonetheless.

Just in case.

There's a woman pushing a buggy. I drive past her as I approach the last bend before the shops. The look she gives me breaks through my German analogy which sinks without a trace.

It breaks through most of the debris that's in my head like garbage in the gutter after a street party.

I smile back at her.

I take a deep breath.

I tell myself, well, nobody died.

I start laughing and can't stop.

Everything, being just a symptom to a major, underlying disorder.

This's all before I see the other "Her" in the messy little car park in front of the shops. The combination of three things acting on me like some comic-book poison.

I'm completely overwhelmed:

*by* her collar,

*because* she's a priest

and by the dog she's trailing that's a dead-ringer for one of my mother's-that-wasn't that didn't die of a stroke but lung cancer.

I witness the vomit leaving my mouth and hitting the tarmac in the same way I was witnessing the obscenities roll out over the steering wheel a matter of minutes before. Workless days like this, seemingly underpinned by blind panic and horribly sharp emotional transitions.

I think: 'Hold On.'

I think: 'Focus.'—Like this is only some horrendous kind of vertigo and if I just pick a spot and stare at it everything will be fine.

I feel like a bingo caller as I analyse random, popping elements that my head keeps throwing up out of nowhere.

That all seem bad.

I call out a few more.

I witness the Hieronymus Bosch painting in front of me right now. The one I've been walking out into for months. I want to go berserk and run around screaming and holding people hostage like Elijah. Everybody's seemingly exuding an horrendous psychic current. I try not to look at them. The air's thick with a residue given off by the badly conceived equation I believe most everybody to be.

Out of the corner of my eyes I see the priest and the dog enter the shop.

I follow.

I'm as aware of the priest's position inside this shop as I would be a lion's had I seen one going in before me and still felt the need to buy cigarettes and drink and a small piece of fish.

I can hear toenails clatter across the tiled floor. I jolt for a second but am pretty sure that the lion was just a part of some ongoing, alternative construct. I stand by a pile of cans, listening to the movement of those toenails.

Apart from the priest and the dog three other people are nearby: two young women and an old man. The young women are discussing the merits of potatoes they're holding between them in a plastic bag. They're talking in an Eastern European? language as they take turns feeling and nodding at the potatoes. The two young women, they look so miraculous in comparison to the old man. The boundaries of their bodies marking off everything about them that's well tended and serenely untouched by the effects of time or any other by-product of the basic laws of physics. I can't detect one scuff or smudge or stain or wrinkle between them. I think it fantastic how the chaos of everything else ends so completely at the beginnings of them. The old man, however, he looks like a repository for every lost scuff, smudge, stain, crease and aberration. The edge of him, his boundary, announcing the beginning of every kind of visual information that alludes to all that might go horribly wrong. I look from the two pairs of beautifully arched, dark, full, neatly tended, Japanese-zen-garden-eyebrows to the wrecked and worried face of the old man...

He looks like a deserted lot that's been overwhelmed by every neighbours' fly-tipping inclination. He's just one mass of off-loaded unwanted garbage.

He's such a well-advertised tip.

Somewhere, in the middle of thinking all this, I start to ap-proach the grey, nylon back of the priest. The closer I get to her the more *whatever-it-is* starts bearing down. My skin tingles. My hair stands on end. Every external molecule of me catching whatever's radiating from her in every direction. And radiating up, obviously, because the soles of my feet are yawning a big hello to the threat of something.

I think:'Just get beyond the heavy, leaden feeling in my lungs.'

I think: 'Just ignore the residual alcohol; the sense that I'm operating all this contraption-that's-me from some Heath Rob-inson apparatus on the dark side of the moon.'

I approach the shiny tight nylon of her back as she bends to pick out some vegetables from a big trough, in the knowledge that, to me, she's the epitome of what I don't want to be in close proximity to. Being:

The surface of the sun.

A virulent disease.

A hungry lion.

Just as I expected, her dog turns and squints an odd fucking look. I attempt to psychically bombard this dog with something as repugnant to it as the priest's whatever-it-is radiation is re-pugnant to me.

The air's thick with these repugnant ions.

I discharge everything with a whispered sentence as the priest's frightened head comes up from the vegetables. The eyes in it having just noticed the strange look on her dog's face.

'*I lick lovely oriental arse nightly*,' I calmly state, as she drops the vegetables back into the big trough. I finalise my relationship with this woman with another statement, as though it were a profound observation that she might actually find to be of great assistance:

'And they taste like sugar-fucking-candy.'

Somehow, now, I feel the universe to be a far more hospitable place.

I smile in a kindly manner at the lovely young Eastern European women who look at me from above their potatoes as though I'm some kind of threatening airborne blight.

I wink at the deserted lot, which sticks out its dry old tongue, widens its exhausted old eyes and winks straight back at me.

I really don't want to be seen as having any allegiance with the filthy deserted lot.

I give it a look I intend as some kind of psychic wrecking ball.

The Lot, Christ, it's still laughing horribly as I leave the shop with the tobacco and the drink and the little bit of fish.


Back at the flat I send a text to The Cloud:

HELP. AM SURROUNDED BY MONSTERS!

My body's rigid as I stare with a beer in one hand and a cigarette in the other at the TV and wait for whatever's about to appear from the blackness that's my TV warming up. I drink some beer, smoke the cigarette. Every question asked of me by the real world being answerable with that.

I remember The Bishop of Whatever.

I creep around the outside of why I hate the clergy.

Because of God.

I keep all of this in my peripheral vision because it's just too bad.

Because of God

Because of God

letting

my

dad

die.

The Cloud sends a text back: TELL ME ABOUT IT

# STANLEY'S DOG

'It's like we build a feast for the one-eyed fucking monster to come and devour,' says Vince. I watch his legs moving. Them being the only bit of him I can actually see beneath the scenery he's carrying to the truck.

'It's like a fucking horrendous myth,' he says.

Sweat's falling from my forehead. I watch it fall past the handle of the broom I'm pushing. I think of Number 5 and Nadia as I watch each drop plummet.

'And when the feast is fucking over, and the one-eyed filthy fucking monster's gone, we strike the set,' Vince says. 'We fill skips and load trucks. We wipe the filthy fucking monster's dirty arse.' He's got his hands out by his sides, palms up. His eyebrows are raised. He's been on about the warmer-cooler-higher-lower-piss-piss-people all morning. How they tweak the feast and faff with the seasoning and lay on the garnish. To make the monster happy. Everything we both say being heavily weighted in favour of construction—me and Vince—and damning of them, the warmer-cooler-higher-lower-piss-piss-people.

I look across at Vince. He's looking at something on the floor. Something I've yet to get to. He looks up and smiles.

I'm just slowly pushing a big broom across the width of the studio floor the same way you might mow a lawn.

One

stripe

at

a

time.

'Hey, Manny,' I can hear Vince say… 'Come and take a look at this.'

I drop the broom and walk towards him.

There's a piece of A4 paper stuck to the floor. On it's a before and after photograph of a Battersea Dogs' Home dog. The before dog has a bowed back, a skeletal body, a bouncy spine and protruding ribs. The after dog's fine. He's upstanding and muscled and healthy.

'Manny,' Vince says. 'Look, Manny.'

He's pointing at the dogs.

'*That* one,' he points at the skeletal dog, 'Manny, it's fucking *us*,' he says.

He points to the other dog.

'And *that* fucking one…it's fucking *them*.'

We take a break, sit on some steps outside and watch people walking up and down.

A rigger's on his mobile phone; he's pacing about, watching his feet, talking to his ex about money.

Men in white overalls and white hats unload meat across the way.

I light a cigarette and blow some smoke towards the rigger.

I've never seen a rigger that didn't look in control.

Vince and I sit quietly for a while.

'Stanley had a dog like that one,' says Vince. 'The Battersea Dogs' Home dog.' Vince's looking a long way off, remembering.

'…My friend, Stanley. Like the one in the photograph. The *well* one. He'd a dog just like that.

'…It used to chase sheep. It was a lovely dog, but it liked chasing sheep, and he was getting in more and more trouble with the farmers. He was worried that he was going to lose the dog.'

I watch the men moving carcasses about the loading bay opposite. Most of them laughing about something.

I've got this feeling, that everything that's said, everything I witness, is for a purpose. That there's something to be learned from everything.

Vince's saying that his friend with the dog was harried by farmers the same way the sheep were harried by his dog. That he left one rural district after another. That he kept on leaving until he found a Scottish island.

An island with no sheep.

I get this big sense that everything's OK.

That life is beautiful.

'There was one butcher's shop on that island,' says Vince.

'…The dog sitting outside it all day long.'

## GUMS

The girl momentarily fixed her eyes on the paint-covered man. He was always coming in for potassium pills and homeopathic prostate tinctures, stuff like that from the shelves and everything imaginable you'd think he might be ashamed of receiving from the pharmacy.

No such luck.

He was such a freak.

Why couldn't he behave like everybody else.

He said something to her by way of a prompt.

This was the worst-case scenario. Him wanting help. She looked blankly at some throat pills. Away from the man and all the other people waiting at the back of the shop who were too intimidated to come forward. The paint covered man, his eyes burning through her; staring at her face like that was the normal way to look at people.

He said something else. He said it like some TV scientist. Like he was an expert on the subject. He asked her something. He stared at some medicines while waiting for his next great idea. He was talking on and on but she couldn't hear a word. Nothing. She sent her eyes about the room like the room was a jungle path with certain hazards and pitfalls she didn't want to go near. She took big looping detours around the maniac; and the other shoppers; and the whole area around the pharmacist (who was pretending to be busy but still glancing at her occasionally). The maniac was holding several different packets, looking at them, glaring at the small print. She knew from all the pharmacist had said before that she couldn't be turning to him for help. He'd been embarrassed enough already.

The maniac brought his hands up and showed the girl an array of different packets. She watched him jabber at her. Whatever it was, the nonsense, she could tell by his intonation it included questions.

It was unbelievable.

How could anybody behave like that?

He had such a dreadful, sordid urgency about him.

'Well?' he asked.

She believed that saying yes was the only way out. Her only escape. She felt like she was trapped underwater, beneath a heavy sheet of ice.

"Yes" was a hole up there somewhere.

'Yes,' she said.

'Ok. Fine.' said the maniac.

/

All this with Doncaster and my near future coming like a weather front, that, according to every forecast, is unremarkable.

Doncaster, my next job.

Three weeks before I return and everything's different.

# ANTITALIBANAPOTHEOSISCITY

The city centre's a marked up extended arm offering for a pulse to be taken; about the pubs, clubs, bars and fast food outlets people are coshing themselves into submission with drink, drugs, fast food, casual sex and mindless violence. There's this constant shouted precursor; a demand in a screamed sentence; an emboldened Northern post-post-hippy expectation of the easy availability of free-love. Goose-pimpled, from behind boob-tubes, they're coming out like fucking mushrooms on just the right kind of autumn morning.

It's playtime and happy-hour in Sodom and Gomorra.

I'm whispering a 'Fuck' to every revelation of the ease of a Northern magic I think I like.

Big men in suits and overcoats outside bars, gargoyle-featured and dressed in black. Three girls crossing the street. I'm looking. I'm thinking it's spray on tan. Spray on tan/hair/nails/short-skirts and cleavage. Heels and bags. They get into a taxi, two of them yanking up their skirts to force their arses against the windows and scream. One of them's no knickers. I tilt my head in my mother's Mexican-hairless' stupid corkscrew fashion to better witness that. The other girl, she holds the hole of a fist to her mouth, sticks her tongue in her cheek and crosses her eyes.

London seems a long way off.

I picture the tide of gentrification that's swept across London, rolling everything over until it's gaudy side down. I figure that the big energy behind that wave must've dissipated way before Doncaster. I imagine the demarkation of that—a line of on-coming piled up Pret-A-Mangers and Starbucks somewhere south; a Hadrian's wall to a Southern kind of progress.

I pick up a girl in a bar.

She gives me this New hello that's a coy varnished finger slowly in and out of her glossed-up lips, to—one leg up on a tan plastic bench seat—be easily slid gleaming under her micro-mini, tight past her thong and up her cunt. All the while she's smiling and pouting and licking her glossed-up lips beneath eyes which won't break contact with mine.

Her mouth tastes of rum and coke and cigarettes and gum.

We fuck standing amongst garbage in an alleyway out back.

I buy her a kebab.

We walk down a street, eating, her with a look on her face like she knows the world's going to end in five minutes but doesn't care. I remember the sublime women in central London, how lost they looked.

She doesn't look lost.

She looks like she's enjoying fulfilling realistic expectations.

My little interlude with her, I'm thinking it's one of the most honest exchanges I've ever had with another human being.

She ruffles my hair, kisses my cheek and runs a hand down between us to squeeze my cock and balls.

By way of goodbye.

It's like for five minutes we've shared the same fucking fox-hole and heard no artillery.

I go to join the Germans at the Hotel bar.


The crew is entirely German. They immediately begin expressing serious concerns for the well-being of the people of Doncaster. I'm the only Englishman present.

The proxy-expert on Doncaster.

'What's happening here, Manny?'

'It's like the Wild West.'

'That's right. It is. Most unusually. It *is* like the Wild West.'

I smile.

'Girl. *Girls*, Manny everywhere. Young girls exposing themselves.'

A whole lot of Germans nod.

I look at them. I haven't been in close proximity to a German
in years. Somewhere in the distance, I can't help it, there's Adolf
Hitler and a whole lot of jews. There's German precision en-
gineering.

They expound rational theories as to the nature of the de-
cline and fall of Doncaster. They whittle down Doncaster and
find it wanting. Every theory they fabricate, they hold it up like
a thermometer they expect to be sucked by the infected-proxy-
host that's plainly me.

Maybe its all the black and white WW2 movies lying as
sediment in my psyche but I'm feeling really protective towards
the women of Doncaster. The glossy-lipped painted-nailed
micro-mini'd goose-pimpled-cunt-thrusting beautifully-titted
ebullient-explosive nature of Doncaster women.

I picture the girl with her kebab.

I attempt to imagine some structured, stolid German equivalent of Doncaster.

I can't.

I run my tongue around my lips to still better-taste the bar-girl. All this reverie, it's segueing a new long-lost finale to all those black and white WW2 films.

'Why?'

'What could be the reason, Manny…

'for Doncaster being like the Inferno of Dante?'

'It's because…' I say—way back this small boy with a fascination for tommy-guns is smiling—'It's because…' There's this pleasing yearning blankness to only blinking German eyes.

'The Prime Minister Has *Two Tits*,' I tell them.

I'm on this little wave of citalopram where the sun's always shining.

I smile at them.

'There's one for the middle class and there's one for the working class,' I say, gesturing about my own chest by way of explanation. I can see they're wondering where all this is going. These Germans.

'The one for the *middle class*,' I tell them, 'it contains nourishment.

'But the one for the *working class*…

'What might you think *that* contains?'

I look at the Germans. The Germans look at me. They don't advance an opinion.

'*Shit*,' I elucidate.

'The Prime Minister, he suckles two children. *One* he wants to prosper. The other he wants to fucking fall off and *die*.'

I feel like I'm behind glass in this room full of Germans.

The combative TV expert on Doncaster.

'You can see it, this tit, clear as fucking day,' I say. I tell them it's hanging withered and limp above the insanely lovely filthy fucking streets of Doncaster. I walk to a window and heave back the curtain material to gesture out theatrically into the Doncaster night.

This anti-Taliban apotheosis.

'Shit,' I conclude.

Hans, the German producer, he looks at me.

'Manny,' he says. There's this drawn out pause. 'You know Mr. Meshershmitt?' he finally says, like that's the way conversations like this are supposed to go. Mr Meshershmitt, apropos of nothing. I look at Hans.

'After the war…' he continues, he makes eye contact with some Germans, as if indicating that they should all rally and advance on me behind the banner of Mr. Meshershmitt.

'He, well…he wasn't allowed to make planes any more. But Mr. Meshershmitt, he vas a very clever man, Manny. He started to make these little cars. You know these cars, Manny?'

There's more eye movement amongst the Germans.

I can only assume this massive deviation is some common post-war German tactic for evading confrontation.

I nod at Hans.

'What was strange was that these little cars still had tiny *little wings*,' Hans says. He goes on and on about the whys-and-wherefores of these little wings as though they've proven mesmeric qualities for foul-mouthed Englishmen.

'Yes,' I say.

I believe it to be really important to halt them in their tracks, these mobilising Germans. The more I think on it the more liberated and wonderful the women of Doncaster seem. The more they need protecting.

'They would, wouldn't they?

'Have them. *Wings*. Have wings,' I say.

Hans looks at me.

All the Germans are right behind Mr. Meshershmitt.

'Why, Manny?' he asks.

'So zey could ztill come und *Bomb* vucking London,' I say. All flouncy and Faux-German.

I grin at them.

They're not grinning back.
They don't grin back.
Of course not.

# RETROSPECTIVELY KILLING RONATA

All this dormant backlog of karma I'm kicking down doors to get at, it's waiting for me three weeks later in London.

As retribution:

> *Dear Mr. Lipman,*
>
> *Sorry I haven't written for a while, but, what with one thing and another, I haven't found the time.*
>
> *The strangest things have been happening and, funnily enough, they have led me to feel much better about my own situation.*
>
> *Last year everything seemed such a burden, but thanks to a new prescription from the doctor and the blossoming of a friendship with a man I met at St Catherine's, things do seem to be very much on the up.*
>
> *Shortly after Elijah's Thorazine lobotomy I met Varley Thistlethwaite. We struck it off very*

well. Poor Varley's wife Ronata was down the corridor from Elijah in Lady Churchill Ward. She'd been seeming to make such good progress with her chemotherapy and, apparently, had every chance of making a good recovery, but, as you must have read in the papers, she was mercilessly shot by a cold-blooded madman. I know nobody seems to know the answer but why would anybody do such a thing to an old woman who'd already suffered so much? Mr. Lipman, it was all so very terrible. And you must think me awful, but what with Elijah's lobotomy and Varley's tragic loss, we (Varley and I) fell together as friends who were both suffering too much.

Elijah is also very much on the up.

We've even recently spent a very pleasant afternoon at the Rectory Rooms. And, for the first time in as long as I can remember, I managed to feel relaxed in Elijah's company in the knowledge that he was incapable of embarrassing me as he had so often done in the past. People seem to understand his present incapacity in a way they never could his behaviour of before. Really, Mr. Lipman, everybody has been so terribly attentive.

Anyway, the upshot of everything is that that poor, lovely man Varley, has moved into Becky's room as a lodger and he has proven such a godsend. The driveway and the windows are now not so much of a chore as, believe it or not, a pleasure. Even Elijah in his own way does more than before.

*Varley's religious beliefs have been a rock and Varley, Elijah and myself have become very much a part of life at the local Baptist church.*

*And to think of all the self-pity I had been wallowing in and all the dreadful things I have said about black people in the past.*

*Life is very strange.*

*The Lord moves in mysterious ways.*

*Love*

*Beatrice.*


*ps it's rather bad but here's a photograph of me and Elijah and Varley.*

*pps if you look very closely you can see one of the squirrels. It's to the right up a tree in the background.*


I see the floor coming towards me as my conscious self vanishes like the burnt out centre of a fine fuse.

I feel myself falling.

I'm in a garden with a shiny silver gun. The holster for it on a special belt with little flat silver horses studded around it. Those flat horses just the perfect emblem of my childhood happiness.

I'm smiling at my dad.

My dad's smiling straight back.

Then there's nothing.

This, some weird scrabbling for safety before I'm semi-conscious and dialing up what I feel I need; which, thanks to London, is only ever a phone call away. Before I'm swivelling naked in my chair, a big, slapped down, badly-glued collage of a nightmare in my head. The cold gun that killed Ronata Thistlethwaite in my lap. Every bit of me guilty and worthless. The gun next to my penis. I picture the girl from Doncaster.

The bullet after Ronata's; a little brass brother to the ones that killed her, it's waiting for me. I think as long as I'm thinking something, maybe I've got a chance. I hold the gun to my head and say, 'Bang'.

Just another big insult to the ease with which Ronata Thistlethwaite died.

Me, the cold-blooded madman killer.

I try and picture the bald figure in the hospital bed.

Nothing.

I try to imagine how I might have believed her to be Elijah.

Nothing.

Me, the cold-blooded madman killer.

The stuff enters my body the same furtive way I'd enter number 5.

I slowly turn and float and yield to an endless black meniscus. Covering God-alone-knows-what as far as my worth's concerned. A sense of wonder forming from this infinity of stretched out vacant nothing that's me. Slowly, a few disparate pieces in my head collide and stick and roll to form an idea. An idea way away from death. Like a little moon forming from the remnants of an impacted earth. My moon, made from the girls at number 5 and Jabba and The Cloud, Elijah and Beatrice and Ronata and Vince.

Everybody.

Even Franky hung over it as decoration—a little draped constellation of Bling.

My big bang of a revelation heralded by a tiny small twitch of a smile in this dark room.

The logic of an idea appearing to illuminate one last tunnel; a worm hole of a way out for Manny. One last project that seems worth doing well.

Also amongst the mail was confirmation of my exhibition in America. An exhibition of my blue paintings.

Two possibilities, out in front of me like two small islands I have the option to swim to.

I kneel, naked, in front of the gun, remove the magazine, remove the topmost bullet from that. I swallow it as though maybe ingesting it like that might count for something. I bend over and slip the next bullet up my anus because somwhere in my addled mind I think it's being requested of me.

I drink some wine and fall asleep on the floor.

I sense Jabba later. Him, seeing my recent history in the kitchen; I sense him at my door and at his games console, running it only tentatively tonight as he's listening out for me.

Me, floating on the floor of my bedroom, hearing Jabba driving a long way off.

Smiling to myself for the love I feel for Jabba then.

Even smiling for Svetlana.

## PORTRAIT NUMBER 9: MR. and MRS. RUSSIA

It was all too easy. Every portrait opened a door; slid easily into an invisible lock out there somewhere and opened it with an imperceptible click.

The portraiture door opened neatly every time.

I figured it was exactly because God knew how much I didn't like what was behind it, that's why the portraiture door kept flying open—God was having a laugh:

A businessman in Russia, he'd seen reproductions of my latest work in an international style magazine; he was determined to secure my services. He couldn't help himself.

Had I realised earlier what kind of business the Russian businessman was in I would've behaved differently. I wouldn't have gone through that door with such confident disdain. I wouldn't have fucked his daughter. I'd have been polite. I would have tempered my English-village-amateur-dramatic-society version of conflict.

It being a long way away from real guns and torture.

Mr. Russia, deftly managing to teach me something different; something I wouldn't ever be able to forget. Mr. Russia, this man, having been nourished since childhood in a real 100% hothouse of murder and mayhem. His bullish disregard to the suffering of others easily extruding money from all manner of misery. This man, employing an army of craftsmen to generate a magnificent dacha from a gigantic clearing in a mosquito infested forest that was the largest lot on a piece of real-estate prized by his peers. He wanted to live there amongst them. He intended to diminish them all with massive excess.

Containers of glass by Liberty and furniture by Chippendale were shipped out. As gilders burnished miles of gold leaf painstakingly applied to the most ostentatiously bold ornamental plasterwork, so was Manny/Emmanuel Marbas/Me—shipped out. The bold, brash portrait painter from England.

Svetlana was Mr. and Mrs. Russia's only daughter. She met me at the airport. The moment I saw her was the foundation to something coming; I knew that much: I felt as though I was beginning a shape in my head to which I was immediately making alterations and revisions, determined by what I was guessing at, what I was hoping for and, ultimately, what I'd find out later. All of this, hanging on an armature that was nameless then but which I'd soon call love.

Everything I found out about her, every alteration I made, just tied me to her the more.

For as long as she could remember, her parents had been busy finding new and more expansive ways to spend their money. She felt she'd lost them as a small girl. They'd left her in a gilded pram for a shopping spree from which she knew they'd never return.

That was the first confidence she made to me.

She was prone to whimsical analogies.

She'd made a life for herself in Moscow but a manifest hatred had caused her to be waiting for me at the airport. She hoped that by way of the solace she found in sex I might be able to help her disrespect her father.

She looked like she was on a mission; she had the open expression of a gymnast about to do a series of complicated tumbles. As soon as she could, she pulled the big car over.

I stared through trees and reckoned that had I sold everything I possessed, I wouldn't have enough money to buy the clothes it took two minutes to take off Svetlana. She, to me, already like a magnificent advent calendar. Everything I touched. Everything I opened, revealing something yet more beautiful.

The shape I was making in my head was begun with a few crude images. Having my cock sucked in a top of the range Mercedes her head something I'd just held dropped straight from heaven. Holding her cool hips on the edge of a Russian forest. Licking her cunt like every movement of my tongue was some invisible stitch to bind us.

A few crude images: big bold brushstrokes to the ruination of both our lives.

She introduced me to Mr. and Mrs. Russia in an entrance hall large enough to diminish everything except the look in Mr. Russia's eyes. The recently lavished pheromones, they bowled right in. They made a post-sex slight permeation of a big hello—Svetlana's small token-idea of an airborne homeopathy generated out of hate.

I thought it amusing as Mr. and Mrs. Russia contemplated that.

That's how fucking stupid you can be.

I thought it was funny.

I held my penis through my trousers, rearranged it slightly while smiling at them. That's how I decorated my first Hello. I embraced Mr. and Mrs. Russia, aware I was meeting two people I detested while completely oblivious to the authority held by one. Not for one moment noticing anything significant in the

180

gaze of Mr. Russia; oblivious to whatever might be sitting quietly beyond the retina of a man who at the age of eighteen had tortured three men to death; who still watched the video of that event with pleasure, despite one of those men having been his brother. The talent I had for recognising the smallest changes of colour and tone—for spotting the slightest deviation in a line determining something as delicately curving as the loop of an eyelid or the turn of a mouth—was plainly of no avail to me now, when it came to spotting the differences between an English Bishop and a leading member of the Russian mafia. I was crippled by a clumsy overriding fear of the nuances of everything; seeing danger in minutiae, while perceiving none in a man capable of having me permanently and painfully extinguished with a nod of his head.

I couldn't see the elephant for a blade of grass.

The sun for a mote of dust.

I was busy regarding the interior of Mr. Russia's dacha over Mr. Russia's shoulder—my fingers pulling tightly against the fine cloth of his jacket; my chin jutting into his scented neck: I was busy experiencing a wave of aesthetic distaste.

Svetlana watched me, her comic-book ragtag Icarus, flying too close to the sun. But she was full of duplicity then; she knew what her father was rumoured capable of, but she was still desperate to see him suffer.

It was the kind of interior you wouldn't want to give a blind man the fucking gift of sight in. That's what I was thinking.


Svetlana showed me to my room.

We popped another advent calendar window and wanted more.

It's like this in my head now: a three dimensional collage; a paper dolls-house dacha. Me and Svetlana, fucking. Mrs. Russia in the kitchen. Mr. Russia, moving on through other rooms. Purposefully. Hindsight building this paper nightmare. Me slowly fucking Svetlana. Fucking her up the arse. Both of us sublimely quietly anchored like that. Her and I against all our fears like that. Me, invading Mr. Russia's territory, happily, like that.

A fantastic disrespect to Mr. Russia making my cock grow harder.

Mr. Russia, finally seated in a dark room in front of a bank of monitors.

Because he liked to know what people were doing.

He liked to watch.

Paper me, in this dolls-house dacha, only ever able to position these characters correctly later, curled up as in a catacomb with Svetlana.

Mr. Russia, governing an intense hatred for me for the envy he felt at watching his daughter being fucked. Wanting to kill me the same way he'd killed Venson Arkonovitch, when he'd still done the killing himself.

But Mr. Russia liked to watch.

He liked to watch a lot.


This whole series of events, it's covered in a kind of scar-tissue from the damage done later. The memories distorted, reassembled and marrying up badly:

Her, a beautiful mathematical equation. The shapes her muscles made under her skin. Around her belly and hips. Looking at me from the edge of a mirror as she arches her back and her breasts rise and she pulls her hair behind her head. Svetlana, doing a faux clumsy dance.

All these years later I can still hold my hands out to the memory of her hips.

We were at the beginning of things.

The tenderness with her from the start; the big sex and the small tenderness. Kissing her like there was a sheet of rice paper between us; both tilting our heads like slow purposeful railway signals indicating a clear passage to love.

This paper figure, later, this Manny, standing over the place where we'd made love, trying to make it real; smoking a cigarette and saying her name for the first time ever:

'Svetlana.'

/

The next morning I met Dimitri, Mr. Russia's projects' manager. We stood in a giant room that was more a massive argument of inanimate things.

I was myself again: this fucking cunt from England.

'Manny, it's good to meet you. Very much at last. Did you sleep well?' asked Dimitri.

'No,' I said.

'Why not?' he asked.

'Well I had this dream,' I said. I looked about. 'I was on a hillside,' I confided in him. 'In the country, by an old ruin of a building. And there were lots of dead sheep lying around. And out of nowhere there was Mr. Russia. And Mr. Russia pushed me over and started dragging me backwards over these dead, bloated sheep.'

Dimitri stood there looking at me. There was this delay; it reminded me of feeding my hamster as a boy; Dimitri, digesting my dream the same way the hamster would sit there and chew on a seed I'd just given it.

'It is easy to see you have very much the sentiments of an artist,' said Dimitri.

He unrolled two large drawings and laid them onto a Louis Something table. They were drawings I'd sent ahead of me from England; my response to the detailed brief I'd been given. 'They will make very exceedingly lovely murals, Manny,' said Dimitri. He cleared his throat. He had a habit of clearing his throat in the middle of most sentences. I felt it must be his unconscious way of punctuating a lie.

We looked at the drawings.

On the East wall drawing, the centrepiece was a bare breast-ed, beautiful Mrs. Russia, rising like a large exotic pearl from a clamshell. In the foreground, the little spume-tipped waves that she rode broke onto a small beach, where a young Svetlana languished as a naked nymph. An Italianate landscape undulated into the background; it was populated by various members of Mr. Russia's household performing menial tasks with oxen and sheep. Two of Mrs. Russia's dead baby children flew incongru-ously about her head as angels in a cobalt-blue sky.

The first drawing I could just about cope with. I felt that the limitations imposed on me by Mr. Russia's conceit had some-how forced me into creating a strangely surreal and wonder-fully comic work. The second drawing—content wise—was far worse; being Mr. Russia's coup-de-grace, the one he'd had me hone and sharpen for his hapless neighbours. On the west wall drawing, Mr. Russia led a triumvirate of very Russian looking Wise Men. He was the only handsome, young and athletic Wise Man. With great poise he proffered a gift to the tiny figure of the no less than baby fucking Jesus. The setting being an open-topped manger. Mr. Russia's other company, a pair of soon overridden, long-dead business mentors holding gifts of frankincense and myrrh, they looked old and ugly, defeated and crestfallen, as they awaited the baby Jesus' obviously favourite

Russian son to finish. Bizarrely, the figure of Mr. Russia was presenting a miniature rear axle; Mr. Russia's first substantial legitimate financial killing having been made with a company that manufactured rear axles.

I looked at the drawing.

I looked at the small pencilled arrow that led to the rear axle.

I read the word *Gold*, at the base of the arrow.

'Beautifully, Manny. Most poignant and most marvellous,' said Dimitri.

He coughed.

I summoned up an image of Svetlana's anus.

Fixated on it like a mantra.

I looked up.

Years later I'd remember myself and Svetlana looking up a lot. Me to God, her to corners of different rooms.

Me blaming God for making me a portrait painter.

Svetlana, in my mind, blaming her father for being a rapist.

'We have prepared the walls for your magnificent renditions,' said Dimitri.

The walls had been swathed in plastic sheeting to protect all that was revolting below. Two fifteen foot by twenty-five foot naked, preoperative landscape rectangles were waiting for me to perform a final revolting act of self-exaltation.

I tried not to flinch.

I intended to make eighteen thousand pounds and run.

I felt as though I were holding my breath, walking across the seabed in an old fashioned diving suit.

The only air being Svetlana.


We fell into a routine.

Mr. and Mrs. Russia were mostly away on business or at the family home in the city.

I spent ten hours a day up a scaffold tower in the giant room. Often, with Svetlana. She squared up drawings, helped me grid up the walls. She posed as a Nymph in the evenings. I drew her every night. I began a small sketchbook dedicated entirely to her cunt and her arsehole. We'd draw like that and fuck, then draw some more. I had a carpenter make a three and a half foot by five-foot wooden panel with four three-inch-square doors beautifully cut away from its face. Behind each door was a pristine two-inch deep recess. The panel was boxed in at the sides and the back. I applied acrylic gesso to the face, the sides, the little doors and the recesses behind them. I sanded the whole thing down and repeated the process again and again until the boxed panel shone like a church candle. The shut doors, almost invisible.

Svetlana posed for the face of the big white box–advent-calendar.

She stood naked, with her left forearm across her breasts and her right hand concealing her cunt. The delicate way I had her shape her fingers, it made me want to cry. She had her head turned to the side and looked down across her left shoulder.

She looked vulnerable and sad.

It was only much later that I could do the maths and work it out.

As ever.

The information coming retrospectively, in bits. Only illuminating the later truth fitfully. The truth, the thing coming from the shadows being bad. Vague, low-watt bulbs then, flickering on, off and around it.

I was surrounded by a cacophony of excess. The riot of which only made Svetlana more an angel to me. The contrast was too much.

Something happened in the second week.

Lying together, every part of our bodies that could saying the occasional hello. It was something to do with a particular look we gave one another with all the filters down.

I was getting to a place I'd only been once or twice before with another human being. The furthest point out in my experience of human affection. I drew a line up her torso with my finger. I remember drawing a straight line up her torso and saying to her that this is where we'd been, the path of that line, and then my finger made a deviation to indicate a slight barrier and then it rode straight on through to God knows fucking where.

Years later, The Cloud, he'd tell me how I was forever building things up high so they'd have further to fall. In Russia, it must have been the same attribute manifesting itself then, with me building up high this love for Svetlana. The Cloud, he'd tell me I was like a monkey addicted to shaking trees laden with coconuts. So they might fall on my head the better for it.

The way things changed between us, was strange. It happened quietly with shared cigarettes and small glances. We exchanged the truth about ourselves like that. Little nothings, meaning more than anything else. That seemed to be one of the good things about painting people—being with somebody, in silence, as just yourself.

She wouldn't make love.

We spent a lot of time holding on to one another and kissing in silence and not knowing why.

I can't remember a single conversation we had now.

I can remember the overriding emotion, the newness and the wonder of that. But there are no words.

## TOO BUSY WITH MY COCK FOR SUICIDE

Since Beatrice's last letter I've had this problem that I don't see can be related. I've been urinating too much. My suicidal inclinations have vanished because of it; my entire psyche's so otherwise engaged with urination: I'm getting out of bed in the middle of the night to urinate; stopping my car with urgency to urinate wherever seems most appropriate. Sometimes, there's nowhere appropriate, only the side door of a regular suburban house in broad daylight or the nearest tombstone in a churchyard. I'm forever jumping fucking fences I never wanted into parks I never cared to visit.

*I'm far too busy with my cock for suicide.*

This cock that's betraying me.

The doctor across from me's female. She's about twenty-seven.

Really attractive:

'How are you doing doctor,' I ask, 'OK?'

'Yes, thank you.' She looks at her notes.

'Manny,' I say.

'Manny, yes, thank you. Manny. What seems to be the problem?'

'I can't stop urinating.

'It's been going on a while.'

We begin skirting around the subject of my cock like a couple of African hunters sizing up a lonely wildebeest.

'Does it hurt when you urinate, Manny?'

'No.'

'Do you attempt to urinate and not be able to, or have to wait to be able to?'

'No, it just comes straight out.'

'Do you urinate and feel as if you've emptied your bladder only to have to urinate again soon?'

'Exactly.'

I feel that this wildebeest is a fucking sad, fucking lonely wildebeest.

'It's unusual in men of your age, Manny. In a man of your age, Mr Marbas.

'It sounds like your prostate.'

There's this ongoing pause. Like she's giving me time to go through the formality of a hello with my prostate.

'I'm going to have to do a D.R.E,' she says, finally.

'A *D.R.E*?'

'A Digital Rectal Examination.'

'O…K.'

I notice this mixed expression on her face: she looks sympathetic—sorry for having seen my wildebeest for what it is, and, as she pulls on a latex glove, she's wearing this look of grave resolve and fear; as if she were going to put her hand down a hole in which any old angry animal with teeth might be hiding.

Apart from my t-shirt and socks, I'm naked on the doctor's couch, facing the wall, my knees drawn up.

'This may be somewhat uncomfortable,' she says.

She can't see me smile.

I like having her fingers up my arse: greased, slim and elegant. They feel really nice. I make out I'm finding it uncomfortable so that she might linger; intimate moments with strangers like this being so hard to come by. I get dressed. She's safely behind her table. 'Your prostate gland,' she says, 'it's fairly enlarged.' She's blinking much more than she was before. 'It's obviously causing the problems you're experiencing.' Apart from the blinking, she's her normal self. 'This prescription should cause the symptoms to subside,' she says. She completes a prescription.

The way those shot animals on TV slump to their knees, look confused and die; that's what my wildebeest is doing.

'Just a couple more questions for your record:

'Do you drink alcohol?'

'Yes.'

'How much... approximately?'

I look up at the ceiling and hallucinate a supermarket drinks section.

'Well...four or five pints and a bottle, maybe two, two and a half, of wine...maybe some cognac.'

'A week?'

'...No. A day.'

'A day?'

'Yes.'

She writes something down.

'And...have you had the same sexual partner for the last year?'

I believe that to be a strange kind of question. I'm feeling a couple of things: I'm thinking I don't want to tell her about all the prostitutes in case I've still got the slimmest of chances with a young beautiful doctor who obviously finds me odious, to say the least, and I'm kind of resenting the imbalance here between my unstated but definite desire to have sex with this woman and her obvious revulsion to me.

'No,' I tell her.

'I've only had *you*.'

## ST LOUIS

Fragile fat people, slathered in angst: the place is fucking full of them. The one with the bulging eyes immediately behind me, he's tutting his displeasure already; like he's a cicada or something and this is just the right time of day to be making fucking noises like that.

Fuck him.

OK: so these fat people, so they're all intent on not being an incendiary punctuation on a news item in a few hours time.

OK.

OK: so we're all trying to get to America just a few days after the latest aeroplane related terrorist outrage. OK. But christ. Fucking-*really*.

And the woman at the desk—Jesus: a hat, scarf, big smile and these heavily made-up eyes.

'Might that be possible? An *aisle* seat?' I'm pleading. I'm pleading already on account of my *condition*. On account of all the fear and abject humiliation attached to it. A condition like this.

The hat gives me this look and drops some heavy lidded/ painted eyes to a monitor.

I asses the condition of my bladder.


I hadn't been able to travel out to America for the exhibition opening. All the flights being cancelled. Not that I wanted to go anyway—I didn't. I was intent on pursuing the revelation that'd occurred to me shortly before deciding not to shoot myself— that being thankfully so distant now. Seeming, as it does, like a dream already—but the gallery in London, they'd suggested that the gallery in America might not be willing to give me another exhibition if I didn't appear to be at least a little enthusiastic. Whatever that meant. I was assured that collectors in America liked to meet artists, purportedly to get an insight into their work; that's what they said, but I wasn't convinced; I didn't believe it at all—I felt as though these collectors were holding the prospect of cash for me on the same basis, and with similar intent, as I, the prospect of cash for girls at number 5. The difference being that whereas I always felt duty bound to hand over my cash to any girl working at number 5; however appealing or not she might be, I appeared to be expected to flaunt myself for the wonderment of these Americans with absolutely no guarantee of any financial reward whatsoever. I resented their inability to echo my generosity to London prostitutes in their dealings with me. It appeared to be paramount, however, that I should mingle amongst these tight-fisted connoisseurs, no matter how much the gallery in London believed me to be a significant liability.

Caroline was thrown at me: Caroline, my conduit to the gallery owing to Austin's complete inability to relate to a living artist. She was so fucking prim it just made me want to hold her buttocks and stick my tongue up her arse. Her psyche gave me a hard-on every time:

194

'Manny, we really *do* think it's important that you should go.'

'Caroline.'

'Manny.'

'Caroline.'

'Manny, seriously… Austin is un-moveable on this.'

'How is Austin?'

'He's fine, Manny.'

'How're all the dead artists doing?'

'Fine, Manny… Manny, *Don't*. The business is doing very well. Thankyou.'

'Does that mean you're going to be feeling the need to give me another exhibition soon… *Caroline*?'

'Manny, don't be so paranoid. We love your work. We really do. We've sold a lot.

'…We're doing the best we can. And things aren't going to get better. The market's completely flat with all that's happened in America. It's just another reason why you should be willing to hold your end up and go. You did neglect to sign the pieces we sent…knowing that to be a proviso.'

'I never sign my work. It seems the ultimate conceit, *Caroline*.'

'I know… but you did know that the American gallery were expecting it and you neglected to do it all the same.'

'Why don't I just sign fifteen little bits of paper.

'We can post them. They can stick them on with fucking glue.'

All this time, I'm in the bath, on my mobile, making suds for Caroline. Her buttocks and shining anus shifting explicitly amongst polystyrene ceiling tiles.

'Manny.'

'Caroline.'

'Manny.'

'Mmm.

'You're like the snake in The Jungle Book.'

195

'Pardon?'

'You know the sssnake. Sssexy sssnake.

'Very sssexxxy.

'Mmm.

'The sssnake in The Jungle Book.

'You're Austin'ss sssecret weapon. Your big eyessss keep going round 'n round and your sssilky voice goeszzzon 'nd on—and I fall backwards off the fucking branch and wake up in fucking America.'


The pleasant separation I've been feeling ever since ingesting the bullets is good; it's as though they've successfully inoculated me against the seriousness of my own life. Somehow. I'm thinking it's the bullets; the bullets plus the Seratonin-re-uptake-inhibitors, plus the alcohol.

And the Tamazipam.

And, all the other shit I had with Cloud last night.

If it weren't for my fucking prostate I'd be fine.

The very fat cicada's reaching some kind of crescendo. Being a hideous litmus to the anxiety in this airport terminal: chipping and fucking clicking and whirring as it languishes behind me in its fucking hideous shirt.

'Do you *Fucking* mind?' I ask its huge shirt.

'Pardon, sir?'

'Sir?' I echo. 'Hahh. Jesus-Fuck. You. You are a complete fucking aberration.'

I focus in on the fat cicada.

'A fucking fat-mountain,' I gesture to the shirt, 'adorned with this elephantine-prayer-flag shit,' I announce.

The largest of its chins, it's crept a short way down its chest to accommodate its mouth being open. I keep on with the shirt: 'Your shirt,' I tell it, 'is as repugnant as your inability to keep a respectful silence while waiting in a fucking queue.' I'm model-ling the dialogue on Ignatius Reilly, for sure.

I fix it with what I hope's a most insane and manic stare. 'Jesus-Fuck-Hahh,' I say. 'Whoaa,' I add for luck.

The fat cicada gazes back at me. It stupidly pulls at its shirt and raises its eyebrows.

'Fuck off,' I instruct it.

It falls silent.

The hat's eyes stonewall amongst its scarf, smile and make-up; I feel I'm standing by some deep and dangerous water with the hat's eyes building me huge concrete boots. I feel completely fucking powerless.

'An aisle seat. *Please. Fuck*-Shit 'n Christ. How difficult must it be?'

'Chip-chip-chip-chip-chip,' the shirt begins again, tenta-tively.

'Sir, we do not *condone* profanity,' says the hat. *So* calmly. Really, really calmly. Just to let me know how completely she has the measure of me.

'May I ask—why, sir? *Why* you want an aisle seat?'

chip-chip-chip-chip-chip

'*Sir?*' the hat says firmly.

I lean forward, slowly.

The hat looks suspicious but cranes itself towards me.

'I've got a *prostate* gland the size of a fucking ping-pong ball,' I begin. 'Up my arse it is. This *elephantine* clitoris, so to speak. It's holding on to my urethra. *Hijacking* me. I need to piss all the fucking time.'

The word 'Hijacking', it works like some kind of vile fast-acting yeast.

It rises:

There's fear amongst the fat Americans; a kind of latent hys-teria…and there's anger under the hat.

'I'd *really* like an aisle seat,' I insist. 'You know, in close proximity to an *aisle.* So as to easily be walking down it to the toilet. To facilitate speed and not inconvenience my fellow passengers with the contents of my fucking *bladder.*' (It's looking at its fingernails and scowling at a cuticle. I sense I've walked in to some kind of airport check-in endgame.) 'Over which I myself have such unfortunately demonstrable lack of fucking cunting-control; being as I am *so easily* about to illustrate against your pristine fucking-cunting counter.' I'm sweating. The effort of talking and not pissing at the same time's way too much.

The hat multiplies.

It takes forty-five minutes and a Doctor's letter to convince the millinery that only my bladder's likely to discharge at any minute. The other passengers, however, above the Atlantic, they're not so sure. They're convinced I'm building a bomb in the toilet—it's palpable. This man, up and down the aisle to the toilet. *Constantly.* Every fucking fifteen minutes. This man that's me building a bomb in the toilet.

*Definitely.*

Only the cunting drunk are not convinced.

At thirty thousand feet I lose an on-going battle between my will to live and my desire to not be humiliated by randomly urinating in public. Sitting, squeezing my eyes shut and picturing myself pissing in my trousers, I begin praying for a bomb to go off: the Iron Clad Fist Of Fate's so completely convincing grip on my urethra's made the prospect of free-falling and pissing-at-will for the last few minutes of my life seem so totally fucking sublime.

I'm met at the airport by a stretch limousine.

It's just a question of urinating twice in the cocktail shaker on the way to the gallery.

# DUDLEY SAYS IT'S SAFE

The gallery's all lit up.

Well-dressed people are standing around my paintings. As the limousine slows, I put the cocktail shaker full of urine into my hand luggage; I feel that as far as the driver's concerned—spending his whole day being subservient—what he doesn't need to find is someone else's piss in his cocktail shaker.

Heads start to turn in the gallery. People smile.

'Manny, it's *so* good to meet you at last,' says Hilary, the gallery owner, emerging onto the pavement. She looks deeply into my eyes. She instructs the driver to drop my luggage off at the hotel ahead of me.

The limousine drives off.

I discover where the toilet is.

I mingle.

Relax.

Start drinking champagne.

Hilary introduces me to the biggest collectors of modern art in the midwest. I feel like a benign 1950s alien coming down the ramp of a spaceship. That's the way they're looking at me.

The bad messages coming from my bladder and penis, they've mercifully stopped. The runaway vehicle my body had recently become, this piss-machine, it's miraculously been overhauled; there's no longer a ravine coming with my brakes shot and engine ablaze—I'm motoring easily along somewhere picturesque. It's got to be the pills.

I'm thinking how much I like it. This picturesque place.

I feel reprieved.

Reborn. Miraculously so.

Sublime.

I look around the gallery to see if I can spot one of Jabba's sci-fi, temporal warps, some kind of portal I must have just fallen through amongst all these Americans.

That's how weird I'm feeling.

Hilary introduces me to Mr. and Mrs. Big Collector. The biggest of the big collectors in the mid-west.

Mr. Big Collector's plainly very impressed by the look of me, Manny.

This Manny possessing about him a strangely peaceful beatific angstless charm; the like of which Mr. Big Collector's sure he hasn't witnessed before.

I know that's what he's thinking.

I can sense it.

I'm fucking radiating love and wisdom.

I can sense it.

I'm feeling such a pleasantly transient residence in my own mind that life's suddenly become the most beautifully impersonal and unthreatening experience. I feel as though I could walk through the middle of a hideous battle and calmly wonder at the beauty of blood and the intriguing sound of men screaming.

The release from the way I'd been feeling earlier, it's

that extreme.

I smile at Mr. and Mrs. Big Collector.

Mr. Big Collector, he looks at Mrs. Big Collector. 'I told you, darling,' he drawls, 'anybody capable of painting such dignified, contemplative images as these…' but he fails to finish his sentence, he's so completely fucking entranced by the vision that's me.

The serenity of it.

The Collectors come in close like an imposing ship looking to dock at an oddly captivating jetty; an oddly captivating jetty maybe projecting from a beautiful faraway island. That's how it seems.

'Manny, we do *so* love your work,' says Mrs. Big Collector.

I turn the wrist of a hand over until the hand's cupped with its fingers gently apart. The Collectors, they're noticing the most divine barely perceptible smile. They're noticing a look of complete and shocking inner calm as I contemplate the remembered beauty of oriental Angel's heavenly arse.

How I'd been amongst it only days before.

'Mmm,' I moan. I can't help but let my tongue through my lips and wiggle it about the same way a dog might start flapping its feet if held above a body of water. I moan some more.

To me the moaning, it's sexual prurience, to them it's a heavenly mantra.

I know it.

I'm *so* wonderfully sliding far out there somewhere through circumstance, alcohol and countless self-medications.

Looking above The Collectors and picturing Angel's arched back and shining oiled buttocks, I exude a sigh.

'Such a demeanour,' Mr. Big Collector whispers to Mrs. Big Collector.

I notice something on the floor between Mr. and Mrs. Big Collector. I smile at it. I'm not sure what it is but I think it might be the only one I've ever seen that I actually like. The thing on the floor's looking at me; it's got these lovely little eyes: *twinkly*.

So deep and kind and brown.

It's got this dainty bit of tartan.

God, it's adorable.

I hand Mrs. Big Collector my empty champagne flute.

I touch her wrinkled wrist with a stroking free finger.

I crouch down in front of *the thing*.

Mrs. Big Collector, she's remembering a painting that belonged to her mother, a painting in which the figure of Christ was *so* reminiscent of me and my bearing now.

I embrace the thing.

The thing,

It

L

i

c

k

s

Me.

God. It's *so* nice. Its little hot tongue on my skin.

'*Mmm*,' I moan.

'Good Lord, *Dudley* just *adores* Manny,' says Mrs. Big Collector.

*Dudley*. Obviously *This* is Dudley. '*D u d l e y*' I say. Dudley—Mr. and Mrs. Big Collectors' dog. He's renowned for loving no one. I can sense it.

The American patrons are regarding the artist from England and Dudley-the-dog.

Dudley and I, we're the living-cunting-embodiment of a Fra Angelico; a Giotto, we're that serene.

Dudley jumps up on to my lap. He tilts his head and makes a

very timid apparently un–Dudley-like loving sound. Everybody present's caught in this moment of awe; knowing, as they do, this foul dog's temper; its bad reputation; its history of violence.

We're witnesses to something most profound and extraordinary.

We all know that.

The room's absolutely completely still for a moment.

Dudley alone perceives a slight compression meeting the exterior glazing of the gallery; his head tilting to an almost imperceptible sound, as seven blocks away the cocktail shaker full of urine is detonated in a controlled explosion.

/

The limousine driver's talking to a reporter in the street as I'm led from the gallery in handcuffs; some camera flashes lighting up my beatific face. Manny, me, I'm like an Indian sadu unashamedly regarding a self-atrophied limb:

I'm feeling no shame.

Nothing.

Nothing can touch me.

'Yeah, that's the man,' says the limousine driver 'That's the *god-damn-fuckin'-Osama-Bin-maniac* from England.'

Hilary watches me go.

She watches the old money go. The new money. Only Mr. and Mrs. Big Collector remain.

And Dudley the dog.

*Lovely* Dudley.

He's *so* gorgeous.

He's whimpering at the sight of my face as I look out from the back of the police car.

His face is so beautifully confused, pathetic and sad.

A big, gum-chewing face is opposite.

I smile.

'Who the fuck's Mona Hatoum?' it asks.

'She's an artist,' I say.

'An artist?' says the gum-chewing face.

I smile.

This is how we're laying down one another's foundation

'According to Scotland Yard, you destroyed her work?'

'Yes,' I say. I watch the big jaw compress. I wonder at the many bulges of muscle surfacing in the face that's looking at me as though gum-chewing faces like that know, with complete certainty, that they have a monopoly of wisdom of every kind.

'What was in the metal tube, Manny?'

'Fascinating,' I say, in reference to the jaw muscles.

'Huh?

'You what?'

'Urine,' I say.

The face stops chewing.

'The cocktail shaker,' I say.

'Huh?'

I just smile.

The face busies itself with some papers. It runs a big flat hand across the bristles on the back of its head. 'Let me get this straight,' it says, 'you had a cocktail shaker full of urine in your hand luggage?'


I'm questioned for two days. On the third day the forensic results return from Chicago. These results, along with the limousine driver's only just discovered taped rendition of the defilement of his cocktail shaker are enough to curtail the face's constant assurances as to how I'm soon likely to be suffering every manner of humiliation and discomfort. Thankfully, the limousine driver, he'd installed a camera in his vehicle, so that he might later backtrack to all manner of daily defilement of his carpeting, upholstery, entertainment systems and mini-bar. He'd only this very morning witnessed me slipping my penis into his cocktail shaker, three days after the event on tape.

The metal tube picked up by the Hotel security X-ray machine is only now believed to be the limousine driver's missing cocktail shaker.

The St Louis Police Department, they've apparently agreed to overlook the limousine driver's intrusion into my and whoever else's privacy on account of the value of this particular concrete evidence to them. They've even expressed an interest in his sordid back-catalogue of defilement.

The videotape the limousine driver's provided so surprises the face.

It'd been so desperate for me to be a terrorist of some standing.

The face is completely crestfallen as it repeatedly watches me urinating into the cocktail shaker.

There's this immediate and complete loss of interest in St Louis' nearest thing to America's Most Wanted. Three different Agencies, they'd been crawling all over me as flies over putrefaction.

They're absent now.

I can't help but fucking miss them. Never, plainly, having received enough attention from my mother that wasn't.

Me, the physical embodiment of their own unbelievable stupidity and fiscal recklessness.

My downfall does however cement my relationship with Mr. and Mrs. Big Collector; in their eyes the public humiliation I've received only serves to beatify me the more convincingly.

Mr. Big Collector, he comes to liberate The Urinator From England in a big gold Lexus.

Dudley's in the back.

'Manny,' he says, 'me and Mrs. Collector,'—he's staring straight ahead, looking close to tears—'Well, we feel you've been very badly done by.'

He tells me how he and Mrs. Collector would like to apologise to me on behalf of the people of America.

I look out the window, distractedly, at a long, drawn out, passing strip of St Louis.

I feel fantastic: calm, concrete and devoid of anxiety. I smoke a cigarette as we roll along. It so perfectly punctuates this moment.

Mr. Big Collector's watching Mr. and Mrs. Big Collector's litmus in the mirror. Mr. Big Collector, who'd been moved as a child by the story of Androcles and The Lion: he's remembering Androcles and The Lion as he watches Dudley slowly ingratiate himself onto my lap, turn himself upside-down and look longingly into my eyes while appearing to raise whatever passes for eyebrows on Dudley.

Mr. Big Collector watches Dudley look up at me. Dudley's eyes two small brown beautiful pools of love from my diving-board of a head.

Mr. Big Collector's never seen Dudley look at anybody like this before.

He remembers Androcles and the lion. He bites his bottom lip. His eyes fill with tears. There's this big, beautiful, cathartic moment in the Collectors' Lexus. I lean across and squeeze Mr. Big Collector's big, soft, age-speckled hand. We're like that for some time; my hand and Mr Big Collector's hand moving the steering wheel together. Big switches are being thrown in Mr. Big Collector. Gateways to huge surges of love and compassion.

Mr. Big Collector, he's riding a big sublime wave of love.

The constant information that had been this long strip of St Louis, it's degraded to the occasional big American house / big American porch and big American flag, then a space, then another repeat of the same.

The spaces stretch on out, the houses become less frequent, until, finally, the biggest furthest-away house appears.

We stop outside it.

It's Mr. and Mrs. Big Collectors' house.


Mrs. Big Collector's old; there's this riotous overabundance of information coming from her face as far as lines and creases and wrinkles are concerned.

You can't help but try to settle on some simplification.

The way you might attempt to hear the melody amongst the sound of an orchestra.

That's what I'm doing.

Mrs. Big Collector, however, she's still a young woman when compared to Mr. Big Collector, who's ancient; his orchestra though, it's less intrusive, having collapsed amongst its chairs with its instruments scattered about.

Mrs. Big Collector's Mr. Big Collector's third wife.

Whatever children they've had together or apart are long since gone.

She meets me on the porch and guides me into the house with a smile that's the whole orchestral shabam.

Dudley and I, we walk on by: Dudley following me like he needs air and my leg's a nebulisor.

Incessantly building my credit with the Collectors.

They show me their house.

I collate the art like a cat burglar:

Elsworth Kelly,

Jasper Johns,

Andy Warhol,

Jeff Koons…

it goes on and on.

'The two we have of yours, Manny, they're at Martha's Vineyard,' says Mrs. Collector. 'They do *so* suit the lightness of the house there.'

This statement leads me to speculate as to why I have no money.

I picture the London gallery's web site—my surname surreptitiously sandwiched about those of Matisse, Modigliani, Morandi and Moore.

I stare at a Warhol tin of soup.

I attempt to find consolation in my new, significant alter-ego. Me:

The Piss Bomber of St Louis.

I hold on to this small notoriety as though it were the only flotsam in an endless and hostile sea.

The Collectors show me to their pool house, where I'm to be staying.

I sleep with Dudley for two hours on a bed that's a beautiful patchwork quilt amongst acres of white painted wood and huge potted plants.

Mrs. Collector wakes me with a cup of tea and the wood-wind section playing something romantic.

She's got plans.

# THE BLIND DATE

The four of us leave in the gold Lexus for the oldest roadhouse in St Louis.

We pick up a woman on the way.

Mine.

A blind-date.

She must be fifty-five.

She has the shoulders of a miniature quarterback, but I'm still pleasantly in an unfamiliar zone: I'm in love with everyone.

My seratonin levels. Christ. Everything I can get my hands on's a tactile wonderland. Everyone I witness, a thing of wonder.

The blind-date's got an odd little house by the side of the road. Mr. Big Collector's swung the nose of the Lexus in next to it but he's having trouble getting the car back out again. Mrs. Big Collector, the blind-date and Dudley are in the back. 'Come on, darling,' says Mrs. Big Collector, 'It's safe,' she states. She looks at Dudley. 'It's safe isn't it Dudley darling?' she asks Dudley.

'Yes,' she says, looking at Dudley. '*Dudley says it's safe.*'

Mr Big Collector makes the car complain but gets it back onto the road.

I tell the Collectors and the blind-date that "Dudley Says It's Safe", it should be America's new catch-phrase.

I can see it all.

'How's that, Manny darling?' asks Mrs. Big Collector.

I enlarge upon a notion in which Mrs. Big Collector and Dudley appear twice daily on Mrs. Big Collector's huge porch for CNN. 'Just You, Dudley and the anchorman. And he, the anchorman, he'll ask "Is It Safe?" and you'll say "America," and look at Dudley, and hang on this big pause and then say:

"America... Dudley says it's safe."'

The Collectors just adore the notion of Dudley's fictitious stardom. The blind-date wriggles her miniscule plastic skirt into the leather upholstery.

I stare out the window but am otherwise completely engaged with a stream of foul presumptions relating to liberties I might later be taking with the blind-date—I feel I've accrued enough interest with The Collectors to maybe be already blatantly anally raping the small quarterback; to be revoltingly enmeshed amongst her ancient arse and underwear as we drive along, and for The Collectors to somehow still reason that that's morally acceptable behaviour. Dignified even. I turn around in my seat and look at her. My blind date. She's wearing make up, a tight leopard-skin-print silk top, a short, yellow pseudo-snakeskin skirt and a flirtatious smile.

I ogle her dark brown cleavage.

I look up at her and smile.

I look back down at her cleavage, lick my lips, raise my chin and smear this big sex-glaze across my eyes.

The Collectors coo.

The Lexus hums.

I adjust my crotch.

The roadhouse is full. We participate in a little ritual with the Maitre-D: some jungle-clearing-moment. The Collectors being the oldest of old money they don't have to dance for long. We're ushered in to an inaudible fanfare of grace.

The place is wooden-panelled and plush.

I stroke the linen tablecloth, touch the fancy tableware and beam. I adjust my crotch; the aerial antennae to however many milligrams of Ciallis and Viagra I'm still harbouring. I can't leave my crotch alone.

Grey haired white old money sitting at nearby tables acknowledge us with white eyebrows 'n tiny nods.

A big fat woman sings to a piano player at the end of the room.

All the waiters are black.

The money shows no obvious signs of recognising the much recently reported, heavily-televised, infamous Piss Bomber Of St Louis.

'The steak is sublime, darling Manny,' assures Mrs. Collector.

I smile and engage the blind date's nearest leg under the table.

The blind date reciprocates with polite vigour.

'Henry,' says Mrs. Big Collector to the nearest waiter, 'could we have one of your delicious porterhouses for Emmanuel Marbas from England?'

Henry's a sounding board to everything that's absent around him. I'm thinking he must have found a convincing repository for all the outrage he's so effectively banished from his face, which betrays nothing as he notices my unshod foot slide up the inner thigh of the ancient blind date and penetrate the confines of her tasteless skirt. He just stands there like this dominant, carefully carved, black chess-piece amongst the heavily ornamented, age-albinoed, moneyed legion of diners.

He's this taut black flag flying amongst a white doldrum

of plenty.

He takes new insults and our dinner orders to the kitchen.


You can sense a special entrance to the room.

It's the sort of place where people's sensibilities part ever so slightly to accommodate truly-moneyed celebrity. It's just a nuance but it's as obvious as the parting of the Red Sea for Moses as The Budweisers glide on in.

Two of them.

Mrs./Ms. Budweiser cross the carpet.

Vintage DNA.

One regressed on the other with surgery.

The Budweisers stop at The Big Collectors' table.

They're big about the shoulders too. These cross-dressing linebacker twins.

There's another Jungle Clearing moment.

'Why, daarrlings,' says Mrs. Budweiser, 'This must be your famous young artist from England.' The tiniest movement of one bonsai'd eyebrow amongst this heavily conserved face might, or might not, reveal some judgement on my recent, sordid past.

The two-part Budweisers are wearing heavily ornate brail-couture-bolero-jacket-type combos. I stand up and kiss all the hands of the two-part Budweisers.

I'm magnificently priapic.

You have to be able to read these ancient inbred facial nu-ances like a coprologist a stool sample.

There's the slightest blip—an ever so quiet, dull Thud of impropriety.

I eat my steak.

I carefully cut off choice slivers and neatly place them on my side-plate. The small sacrificial offering, an unlikely ticket to

214

soon be copulating with my blind-date.

We dance.

Her and me.

Her stomach accepts my erection like badly behaved white corpuscles engulfing a foreign body.

I make our plans.

The subversive nature of dancing with my ornate herald of this white Midwest dining fraternity, while so plainly manhandling areas of her body that every right-thinking person would know to be not caressable in public, it's fucking divine.

I reclaim my penis from her compliantly soft stomach.

We sit back down with the Collectors.

Pick at the pudding.

'Why don't we let's go and give *poor* little Dudley his dinner,' I say to the big, wide-open, shining eyes that have overrun the face of my blind-date.

I remove my hand from her underwear and pick up the side plate.

'Poor old Dudleykins. Stuck in the big bad old car on his *lone*some,' I say.

'Oh yes, *Daarlings*. Do,' says Mrs. Big Collector. 'Go on—off with you both to *poor* starving-hungry-darling-Dudley's aid.'

She's punching my ticket past the blind-date's gusset.

I can't fucking wait.


Dudley never gets his dinner.

Fuck Dudley.

I slide it into a bush.

Me and the blind date, we find the Lexus in the dark.

Dudley's awoken from some doggy-dream to fast be staring transfixed at the blind date's gyrating naked breasts as she's spread-eagled, prostrate and moaning across the boot of the car.

He looks so fucking astonished.

His big brown eyes staring at the big jumping wide ones that're staring straight back at him.

Fuck.

Her breasts semaphore Dudley something unbearable in canine.

Dudley. He's going berserk.

His crazed barking, it's a

*Yap Yap*

metronome

*Yap Yap*

to our

*Yap Yap*

fuck.

I get a purchase on the underside of the blind-date's breasts. I make them pert for Dudley. He looks down at them, critically. *Fuck*. It's fucking cunting sublime. I ride the yellow faux-snakeskin skirt up as high as it'll go. I better pull down this combination of corset, tights and panty-pad. I leave the mess of that about her knees. The flat of my palms separate her cold, cold buttocks. *Fuck*. I'm in amongst the beautiful, adorable heat of this musty herald of the midwest. Into defilement big-time:

America,

up the arse,

against the back of a Lexus.


Mrs. Big Collector and Dudley sit up front on the way back.

I'm remembering my mother that-never-was while whispering *Coochy-koo Coochy-koo*, repeatedly, on-and-on-'n-on through the big hoop earring that's miraculously still attached to my blind date's ear. Her eyes are all glazed over, her lipstick smudged into a shape that's exaggerating the small, steady smile below it.

She looks like she's had a fucking stroke.


Two days later I phone the Collectors' number from the airport:

'*Darling*, Manny.'

'I just wanted to ask Dudley something,' I say. 'I've a quick question for Dudley.'

I think that this little silence on the phone now, it's beautiful.

'It's all right Manny,' says Mrs. Big Collector. '*G*et-on-the-plane…you naughty-*Naughty* boy,' she says.

'*Dudley Says It's Safe.*'

# THE FUCKING ENIGMA OF THE LANDSCAPE DOG-FLAP

Ten hours after arriving back from America, I'm at Vince's Arch in Battersea. Vince is opposite me. The Human Abacus, Vince's business brain, he's pacing between us. We're in the tea-room, which, like the rest of Vince's Arch is a testament to The Human Abacus' obsession; his ever-compelling, pulsating magnetic-north of a fixation: thrift.

His perpetual abhorrence of waste has long since turned the tea-room into a surreal cinema: two rows of six cinema seats are secured to the floor, their mottled old velvet the colour of dried blood. Other flotsam from previous jobs has been salvaged and screwed down: a large coffee table, emblazoned with the painted screaming head of a long since forgotten OD'd singer, awaits its destiny as a valuable piece of pop memorabilia; a carved African figure hangs crucified by coach bolts next to a health and safety poster, curiously printed on what looks to be papyrus, illustrating Egyptian stick men lifting loads or slumped to the floor after sustaining electric shock.

The fabric of the place in itself is another witness to The Human Abacus' thrift: the walls are quietly erupting, overrun by untreated damp. New and extraordinary growths blossom daily like calcified deposits upon the luckless skeleton of Joseph Merrick. It's as satisfactory a place of work as a small chalet on top of a friable and fast diminishing cliff might be a holiday destination. It's as though all the airtight, new, dry, minimalistic condominium towers that have surfaced South of the river have channelled Battersea's residual damp towards Vince's ancient and decrepit arch.

Vince's testament to The Human Abacus' clinical obsession.

Ostentatious proscenium arches sulk against damp, curving walls, hopelessly awaiting a minimalistic modern designer to bafflingly request a scenic throwback to seventies glam-rock chic; they allow passage now to only damp spores and MDF dust and endless vistas of rotting stock scenery. Ancient, un-serviced, imperial circular saws sit fat, stately and archaic in the workshop, lethally awaiting the next big job. The Abacus' obsession, evident throughout. Every tool's as conspicuous as a musket loading rifle in the hands of a 20th century soldier. Museum-piece nail-guns correctly propel one nail in twenty into cut-price timber and dissipate the flagging capacity of the always overheating and foul smelling compressors. Suspicious carpenters on day-work shepherd vicious chop-saws and hostile routers with the intent and focused concentration of those knowing only too well the heinous reputation of the Rott-weiler while resentfully attempting to control one they'd never hoped to have the custody of.

Collections of bent and dull salvaged nails 'n screws wait like bowls of free sweets in a cancer hospice.

Stacks of off-cuts wait.

Paint, long since crystalline or repugnantly loose and putrid waits in tight-shut, hammered down ancient tins.

All this, decades of traversing coloured balls on taut wires running constant economies and punctuating endless quiet victories for The Human Abacus.

The big doorway to the loading bay as always marked by a gargoyle of a truck driver, eaten up with hatred for The Abacus—the drivers' heads forever awash with endless requests that always, somehow, leave them longer in their cabs for less money. They *will* The Abacus to trip and be crushed as he dances urgently down the workshop with yet more weight of cumbersome, rotting, mould-blown scenery to be loaded.

The Human Abacus, urgent, as always, and with great purpose.

"Time is Money" to Little Abacus, from his father, sticking tight as a bug's wings to flypaper.

The miserly Human Abacus. Loading trucks and calling out a roll call of biblical restraint:

'*Two* paint kettles—

'*one* roller tray—

'*one* bucket—

'*one* rag—

'*five* litres of white.'

His roll call often initiating urgent phonecalls from London studios:

'Hello, London Construction.'

'What am I?—Jesus-fucking-Cunting-Christ?'

'Look, Manny…what do you mean?'

'I *mean*. I *mean* the sardine and the two fucking buns. And me with the fucking multitude of cunting *Piss-Piss-People* gagging to be fed.'

In front of Vince, in the tearoom, this remembered, hauled up hologram that's me, clutching a torn out, degraded piece of recycled trouser and shaking it at an empty stage.

'And what's with the fucking-cunting rag?'

'Manny, look. It's cheaper than the white rag.'

'It's the fucking arse-flap of a pair of cunting corduroys. Abacus. Fuck. We just can't do this fucking loaves and bastard fishes thing every-single-fucking-time. Abacus. Christ. Fuck.'

The Human Abacus, he's pacing back and forth, back and forth, because he can't abide the alternative. The alternative being a posture that's the physical admission of a willingness to interrupt the constant throng of economy that wages in the marketplace of his head. The Human Abacus, as likely to sit as a hovercraft to deflate its skirts while out at sea. The Human Abacus disliking any notion of time frittered away in himself, despising it in others. The look he's giving me a mixture of complete disdain and absolute incomprehension. People all too willing to sit and haemorrhage their hourly rate to the detriment of the company at any time of day being an anathema to him. He's running everything pertaining to Emmanuel Marbas that's detrimental to the company through his head. This is our set pattern of behaviour. He opens his mouth to form the beginning of a sentence that's meant to chastise. He shuts it again. He so obviously doesn't know where to start. There being so much profligacy and waste attached to every passing thought of me. He paces the tea-room some more, fashioning his complaint with the same zeal that led him as a child to be able to stand for three hours stock-still with his right Clarks' Wayfarer firmly planted on a fellow pedestrian's mislaid five pound note. He's leaning his whole psyche against his nightmare scenario of profligacy in general, and wastrels, like me, in particular.

I talk about America.

Tell the Abacus and Vince about the exploits of the Piss-Bomber of St Louis.

The Urinator From England.

I watch The Abacus not be drawn. He won't collude in the comic irrelevancies of exploding piss-filled cocktail shakers. It's like expecting the time of day, a look of affection, from a dog attached to a fetid bone.

The Abacus focuses amongst the air somewhere close by.

He's fixating on a wasted three-foot length of timber.

You can shut your eyes and hear the Scottish drone of his long-dead father intoning the virtues of thrift.

You can feel his mother, rigorously about him, at any sign of Little Abacus' betrayal of his hammered-down, rigid DNA.

'Fuck. Jesus mother-fucking Christ Almighty,' I say.

'What?' asks The Abacus.

'*You*. You won't be pulled away from it, will you?'

'What?'

'All this Abacus shit. Everything coming back to money.'

The Abacus looks down at me as a disciplined general, who's just observed from the safety of a hilltop the eccentric meanderings of a small, disgusting rabble army.

I look at Vince: 'He's like a huge fucking expanse of water with this one big underlying foul strong fucking current.'

The Abacus cranes his head back, as though the rabble army, well, as though it might be even more uncontrolled and repellently meandering than he'd at first thought.

'Wherever you drop a conversation it skids along the surface towards his fucking Niagara of an obsession.'

'Manny, that length of flooring; the three foot piece; the one for doing the test piece on; the sample—where is it?'

'See?'

'See what?'

'See what I fucking mean. *You*...

'You *know* where it fucking is. I saw you staring at it. It's in the fucking bin.'

'*So*?' requests The Abacus.

'So what?'

'So, why?'

'I didn't need it,' I tell him.

The Human Abacus, just looking at him I can see the boundaries of his dilemma. He's feeling that whatever weapon he approaches with, however appropriate it might seem, it just morphs into something else—like a good sharp reliable blade into a fucking banana or something.

That's how all at sea he's looking at the moment.

'I *despise* profligacy,' he states.

'Oh, fuck off. *Profligacy*.

'Thank fuck you weren't a carpenter at the fucking crucifixion. You'd have economised on everything, cut back on timber / made a *tiny* cross / hammered Jesus up with *itsy-too-small* thrice-used-fucking-rusted nails; Fucked him like that. He'd have died doubled up as if he were taking a shit.' I get off my seat and squat down with my tongue sticking out.

I make myself a big puppet to persecute The Abacus.

I look up at him.

'You could have started a firm specialising in economical crucifixions,' I tell him, with malice:—"The Human Abacus Let's Crucify Cunts Cheap Company". Except it would have made a hopeless fucking spectacle—no one would have been able to see a cunting thing.'

'Fuck off, Manny,' says The Human Abacus.

The Human Abacus:

The millionaire.

Who owns several properties.

A barn full of vintage cars.

Who sends his children to private schools and comes to work like a voluntary patient to an insane asylum solely to lubricate his compulsion to keep his father's diabolical dreams of thrift alive.

I stare at The Abacus.

Vince stares at The Abacus.

'You see the way we're looking at you?' I ask The Abacus.

The rabble army to The Abacus now, its weird manoeuvres bearing no relation at all to anything you could adequately combat with normal textbook military strategies. The Abacus, staring down his nose. His nostrils, those two holes, his only available and too often used calibre of artillery.

'It's called fucking disdain.'

The Abacus turns to Vince. He's craving a soft, paternal, downy embrace of a familiar fiscal blanket to enfold him. The Human Abacus and Vince are preparing scenery for a commercial being shot the following week. They discuss their budget before approaching the often surreal finer points of the job at hand:

'We've got to find two dog-flaps for the door I'm working on,' says The Human Abacus.

'Right,' says Vince.

'And we've got to make a breakaway section around one of the dog-flaps. The gag is the dog runs through the door and takes the flap and some of the door with it.'

'Right,' says Vince.

'The problem is finding two *landscape* dog-flaps.'

'What do you mean, *landscape* dog-flaps?'

'The director, he wants the dog-flaps to be wider than they're high—*landscape*—something to do with the shot.'

'Who's ever seen a *landscape* fucking dog-flap?'

The Abacus, who's no interest in creative technicalities, stares back at Vince.

'You mean like a big fucking letter box?' asks Vince.

'Exactly.'

As with all the three arches, and all the particular areas within them, that make up Vince's *Arch,* the tea room's covered in a layer of MDF dust: a molecular ghost of past scenery stretching back over thirty years; the settled remnants of days spent making real the surreal dreams of designers, copywriters and creatives.

Vince, The Human Abacus and I set about the most recent—*the fucking enigma of the landscape dog flap.*

I stir some paint, match a colour, take a mohair roller from my bag. I find an image of the blind-date's recently frequented arse in the back of my head; I stand staring at it for some time, taking part in some sexo-cerebral battlefield re-enactment. My tongue skirts my lips lazily. Eyes gone completely as far as focus is concerned. The long-handled stirring-brush's hanging from my hand. My mouth's open. Amongst the mould spores and the MDF dust I've got a pretty convincing image of the blind-date's gusset about her ankles. It's delicately cradling a panty-pad. Gravity's slowly adding a thread of dull colour to the MDF dust that's always slowly falling.

The Human Abacus, he's looking on disapprovingly from behind a workbench.

I don't even need my fucking peripheral vision to tell me that.

## THE BIG DAY


I don't want it to come—The big day.
    Facing up to all those fucking consequences.
    Digging up all those fucking memories I've so badly buried.
    I'm too busy doing Harry Houdini shit in this straightjacket
the exoskeleton I'm making.
    Down at the bottom of this icy fucking river.
    Solitary.
    Down here.
    Still putting shit on instead of taking it off.


It was Russia that threw me in.

# MR. RUSSIA'S BIG SURPRISE

I sensed that the forty-watt bulb thing was drawing to a close; the fizzing and buzzing in the circuitry of it was becoming angry, like it was heralding something big. I knew that much. The stop-motion terror of it, I could feel it coming... though a whole decade's what it'd take to lift me up and carry me off to look with accuracy back and properly scream. Then, I was too busy looking elsewhere; too distracted—completely engrossed with Svetlana.

Forever watching her.

Wondering at the way she'd recently become so demure. Wondering why. It seemed such an anomaly. She'd surprised me earlier by parading her naked body; by arching her back, craning her neck, cranking a hip to get fucked with abandon and ease.

By flaunting herself.

Her body, this poultice to me.

An empty hold in my head fast filling with images of Svetlana: naked on the painted walls downstairs, naked on my big advent calendar homage; the panel with the little doors—each door hiding her observed cunt or arsehole. She'd shown no inhibitions when she'd posed for me. It hadn't seemed a problem. She'd wanked in front of me. Put fingers up her arsehole. I'd painted that. Those images were behind the little doors. But all the rooms in which she'd been so brazen were the rooms in which she seemed so reserved now. Now, she was only naked in the darkness of the house, or outside, off paths through the forest, as if she had no qualms about being naked at all.

I considered it like some lazy conundrum.

I thought about the portraiture door; the portraiture door that had turned into the sex door that had turned into another door altogether. I'd walked through the last door into a place that had only existed for me before as a vague, unbelievable notion. I'd have thought it more likely I might have walked into a world inhabited by my favourite childhood animated characters with my dead Dad somewhere amongst them. Maybe a real, 100% loving mother too.

With Svetlana, information, as ever, it paired up and walked hand in hand with strange revelations: Mrs. Russia not being Svetlana's biological mother at all; Svetlana's biological mother dead and gone, only a handful of stories now; her strict frugality seemingly determining them all; Svetlana mining that vein for me—the reused English advent calendar each christmas for Svetlana and her brother. Them, apparently, excited by the familiarity of it every year. It becoming somehow precious. Parcity stamping a closeness and a strange appreciation. The mother's regime of snacks and treats not freely given but bought for cash. One bag or item at a time between the two children being their limit; that limit forcing an elegant compromise in which one sibling would divide two equal portions, leaving the other to choose the portion thought preferable. Some kind of magic out of meanness being made by their mother, a poetic frugality: the treat of a boiled egg in a packed-lunch, a story written small in pen, wound about its shell in tiny words. Svetlana weekly unravelling miniature episodes to her friends, all of them standing, watching the egg turn.

Her mother's home-made paper-wrapped pie, a pencilled list of ingredients on that:

Worms 'n bones

Frogs 'n hair

This small girl, for me, seperating crisps—one portion of curled / one portion of regular. Keeping the curled pile smaller because she liked them the best.

Svetlana lying there,

looking at the ceiling,

remembering curled crisps.

Details as footholds for me...to climb further in love with Svetlana.

I felt like a blank piece of paper then, that could have been anything had she wanted it.


Out of nowhere, she asked me to go to Moscow with her and just leave the walls incomplete.

For a while.

For us just to go.

That, maybe being the exit for me and her to make a life. But I thought of the money I'd lose and I stayed and she stayed with me. And I stitched us both to that nightmare house and our subsequent futures. This being two weeks before the fucking monster finally walked into the light and ate everything up:

There being no Mrs. Russia. Only Mr. Russia and three men that even I could tell had nothing to do with any kind of regular business at all. There's this line from them now, through the future, to loop around big men standing like black gargoyles

229

outside clubs in Doncaster.

Years after the big lights coming on all at once.

Mr. Russia, he didn't look at the painted walls. He didn't care to look at the walls at all. He stood off to one side. He watched the three men leave the room. The expression on his face was fluctuating, going through some kind of transformation.

Svetlana came in with one of the big men.

The other two came in carrying the crate in which I'd packed my advent calendar homage to Svetlana.

I was playing catch up with my senses as they began breaking it open. As the perfect white box of naked Svetlanas was removed. As Mr. Russia walked up to it, and, watching Svetlana, put his hand to one of the little doors. I thought he seemed really familiar with something he should have known nothing about. He opened the little door he had his hand on. He stared at a beautiful four-square-inch rendition of his daughter's cunt.

There was this strange look between Svetlana and Mr. Russia.

All the ghosts in the family came screaming out like banshees.

Everything turned to shit.

They dragged me upstairs. There was this comical figure in my head pulling on a circuit breaker. An invisible cloak flew off Mr. Russia. I was slapping down these glued fragments. Mr. Russia said nothing to the two men with me. They just naturally seemed to recognise the second the open season on Emmanuel Marbas started. That's what I was thinking as I witnessed myself being tortured—I was thinking how they knew exactly what they were doing as I cut my losses again and again and began expecting less and less of life until the very idea of just being allowed to live seemed good enough for me. That's what I was thinking before they pulled me into a small room full of monitors and dumped me into a chair. My thumbs tied together behind my back.

My face was fine.

I sat there thinking that they hadn't done anything to my face. All this, just a remembered thread of events, like recalling the bald facts of a nightmare without caring to get too specific about the overwhelming undercurrent of terror that was the tune being played—the music. The remembered thread being just the notes on the page.

My face was fine.

I held onto that observation without actually thinking that it meant they were likely to let me live.

That would be a challenge to God, after all.

Mr. Russia said something to the two men. They left. I was like this skinned animal. Just billions of naked receptors.

Any spare space in the room was covered with outrageous images of Svetlana.

Whittled down like that. In two hours. From wanting Svetlana and money to just only hoping to maybe, possibly, hopefully live. Mr. Russia introducing me to someone I'd never met before—a coward that hated pain and would do anything asked of him. A compliant victim of rape. A compliant victim of rape who'd say 'I'm sorry / I'm *so* sorry / I'm *so* sorry,' over and over and over again to the man fucking him. Every thrust promoting a sorry. Mr. Russia'd taught me a lot already.

He was intent on teaching me more.

He selected a DVD from a shelf and put it into a machine. The screen lit up the room. I watched myself fucking Svetlana. Mr. Russia changed the video. He wanted to teach me a thing or two about a different kind of parental love. I started walking back through these doors in my head.

I knew where I was going.

I kept on back until I found the last door, the one that was truly mine…went in, bolted it behind me, piled furniture against it…went back to the same corner of the same place I'd been for all my remembered life before Svetlana.

Whatever they gave me it successfully obliterated from my memory the conclusion of my business in Russia.

The money was wired to me in England.

I burnt it down the bottom of the garden with Charlie. Charlie, not saying a word.

I stopped painting people.

Left the country, moved to London

and

took

to

drink.

## JOHNNY ROTTEN'S UNKNOWN SISTER'S SCREAMING

Austin deposits me with a small pristine man and his large pristine wife. The pristine man wipes his hand on the side of his trousers after shaking mine. I've come straight from work; he can't get over the look of my clothes. The pristine wife can't stop grinning.

'Austin,' begins the pristine man, 'he says you do contemplative, restrained, blue paintings. He's holding his head way back, as if there's some weird gland he needs to be using at the tip of his chin. 'What are you working on at the moment?' he asks, his eyebrows pulled up casually.

'A dog-food commercial,' I tell him.

'Ohh,' says the pristine wife.

The eyebrows stay where they are.

'Yes,' I say, 'it's very interesting…there's this *very* picky dog…' I get up and running about the dog, that's ok, but the part of me that swallowed 50 milligrams of sildenafil before leaving the car's not, it's completely captivated by numerous different longitudes and latitudes in this room; every elegantly swathed crotch, breast and arse, palpitating a signal directly to my penis. 'The dog won't eat anything apart from this particular brand,' I continue. 'And the dog, it's always surrounded by these *bitches*. And the *bitches* just *love* this dog.' I'm picking up signals from the pristine wife. The eyebrows carefully watch me elaborate about dogs and bitches to the eyebrows' wife's cleavage and crotch. 'So, the idea is, the dog's owner, he wants to economise, and because he wants to economise, in an effort to do that, he starts feeding the dog different dog-food—inexpensive dog-food—Bang, all the *bitches* disappear.' My eyes feel like they're being pushed out of my skull by whatever's in this drug that increases the pounds-per-square-inch-pressure of my lazy smoked-out arteries.

There's a vein's emerged on my neck like a big fat worm after heavy rainfall.

I can feel it.

Pulsating.

My eyes, they're burning holes in the obvious bulge that's the pristine wife's skirt as it gently circumvents her stomach. I stare beyond the pattern of her skirt to where I suspect her Mound of Venus's hiding. I can distantly hear myself groan. I feel like a small burrow-dwelling animal, dreaming up the pleasant confines of its childhood home. My cock's a rigormorticed corpse pinned down under a scanty tarpaulin. The pristine couple, they're staring transfixed at this haphazard mess of bad animal information that's me.

I tell them about the end shot:

'The end shot's this fucking stupid dog looking out of the window at night; really fucking crestfallen with words coming up on the screen:

KEEP EVERYBODY HAPPY—GIVE YOUR DOG BESTBITS.'

There's a protracted silence.

'I don't understand,' says the pristine wife. 'I thought you were an artist.

'...What exactly *do* you do?'

'Well, for the latter part of the day,' I elaborate, 'I was kind of standby dog-flap-holder-opener. But I did paint a bit of a wall this morning. And I painted a white mark on one of the *bitches'* noses; hardly anything to do with contemplative anything, really.' I take another glass of champagne from Caroline who's passing. I make a point of letting the pristine man and his pristine wife see me stroke Caroline's arse. Caroline shoots me a look that's frighteningly for once the real her. She walks away.

I pull at the corpse and smile at the pristine wife.

I whisper to her tiny neat ear. The fragrance from her neck nearly making me pass-out for the beauty of women in general.

I smile at the pristine man.

With the absolute authority of my eyes I drag the pristine man's across the room and adhere them to Caroline's arse.

I wink at him.

The whole disgusting confection that's me, this cocktail-party anarchist, ended, topped-out, pink-frosted and glazed with a protracted moan:

'Mmmmm.'

We take a taxi back to Caroline's.

She wants me to keep my work clothes on.

Her liking painters.

She starts with the noises. In this unexpected collusion, I begin unwittingly conducting an increasingly raucous downward-sliding audio-dynamic of class distinction: from Hunting Pink to shell suits 'n Burberry in sex-sound. Her sexual scenario. The starting point—the zenith: politely retarded posh exclamations like a subdued hubub at a garden-party—A giggle / A squawk / A chortle. I start to home in on her, as one might a foreign musical instrument. Experimentally. Getting her knees up to her shoulders seems to effect a change. That's obviously the kind of instrument she is. Without so much as a nod of an introduction, I unceremoniously feed my sedanafil'd cock into her like it's some endless wide rope attached to a solidly berthed boat. I'm overwhelmed by this force-fed goosenecked rigid virility.

It's fucking *divine*. Being right there. Amongst bovine moaning. I shut my eyes to better envisage this coup: I picture Jesus ejecting moneylenders from the temple. I watch the length of this monster goose-neck-cock as it does a slow, wet jack-in-the-box easy slide with Caroline's cunt. The way a little wave of her cunt's holding my cock like the ripple of the sea across ribbed sand on a beach.

I fuck her all the way down to a subbasement level of class-distinction.

I extricate the monster. I pull a bolster down her back and settle her arse upon it. I put my hands behind her knees and push them way up to better say a repeat, big, intimate hello to her shoulders. Her buttocks, this taut, shining, wide rimmed solitary drinking vessel in the whole, entire Mohave fucking-desert to me. I put my mouth to her arsehole, my nose to her cunt and suck and lap and drink and glut at that like this latched-on engorged temple-pounding parasite that's my re-volting drug-induced self.

There's this riotous East-End hen night screaming every cunt-fucking profanity to that.

Whatever I'm intent on ingesting from her, in my mind it's deep-seated, well-anchored and calling for all the right songs to be sung: I've got to magic its release like some tight-fitting barnacle from a reluctant fucking rock. I clumsily introduce the special internet device onto my tongue. I set it for its enamel-chipping urgent journey. My silver bullet vibrator; the one I've bought specially and strapped to my tongue with an inadequate pink plastic band. I switch it on. The whole room's filled with Doppler-waved orgasmic barks and yelps.

The barnacle's being liberated.

Johnny Rotten's unknown sister's screaming. Running rampant, completely fucking unhinged amongst this cunt-party. Cunt-ramming-crazed. Running-amok. Screaming about our cheap boob-tubed fuck-summit of a mountain. Flying off the ejaculating cunting-top with this plummeting, magnificent cockney-fucking-Howl:

'Aaaaooooowwooooowwooooowwwwooooooo.'


Half an hour later her phone rings.

'Hello.'

'Oh, Austin,' she says. *Ohh-so-fucking-innocent.*

'*Yes,*' she says.

'No, Austin, that's all right,' she says. 'I know It's late,' bla-di-bla-di-bla. 'It's OK. Absolutely. Yes. I was just reading actually.'

'Phone who, Austin?'

'Mr. Van Stratten in America…yes.'

'Yes.'

'Yes.'

'About the cash sale next month—yes?'

'And what's the figure on that, Austin?'

'Two hundred and fifty thousand.'

'That's dollars?'

'OK, Oh, pounds? OK. Yes. I'll do that right away. Yes. Yes. Yes. OK, Austin. Goodnight—No that's fine. Goodnight.'

I listen to Caroline talking to Mr. Van Stratten in America.

I hear her mention the day.

My cock, it's jerking to a slow pulse.

I hear the time.

# RONNIE AND MARGARET GO FUCKING BALLISTIC

'Hello. Could I speak to Caroline please?'

'This is Caroline. Who's that?'

'I'm terribly sorry. I don't know how it happened.'

'Pardon me? What? Who is this please?'

'I'm *so terribly* sorry. It's Tarquin—Tarquin Ottershaw.'

'Hello, Mr. Ottershaw.

'…How can I help you?'

'It's your cat. It's just. I was just. I was coming back from my swim. Same as usual. Christ. And. And / *God-fucking* / Pardon / Pardon me / I'm *so* sorry. I ran over your fucking cat. Pardon me. But, and—and a neighbour told me where you worked. Fuck, I'm *so, so* sorry.'

'My cat…oh God—Oh shit and fuck.'

'Exactly. But the poor darling's not dead. I'm ah—I'm here with him, umm her?…is it a her?

'What?'

'Sorry. Never mind. Completely irrelevant. I'm here with *it*. With it. Now actually. At the animal hospital. In Bleak Street.

*Oh, Christ.* Sorry. It's just seeing the poor thing looking so mangled and hopeless. God. Fuck. Number 43. The vet says it's touch 'n go. I'm so, terribly, terribly sorry.'

'Oh shit fucking Christ. Where?'

'Bleak Street. Number 43.'

'B-L-E-A-K? Is that right?'

'Yes.'

'I'll be right there.'

The Cloud hangs up. He's got a small twitch going on around his mouth that's nearly always announcing that whatever he's been doing, he's been doing far too much of it.

'What?' he asks.

'Nothing,' I say. 'You were brilliant,' I tell him.

'We're doing this aren't we?' he says. 'Now,' he says. 'We're actually doing it.'

'Yeah, we are.'

'Have we got everything?'

'Yeah. We have. I think so.'

He does a bit of his limbo thing as we embrace but I think maybe not as much as usual.

I tell him I love him.

'What was the pill, Manny?'

'Viagra.'

'Viagra?'

'Yeah.'

'Why?'

'It's all we've got left.'

We put our helmets on, get on our bikes and drive up Piccadilly.


Austin's sitting upstairs.

He watches the pair of us walk past the window.

He watches us come into the gallery. Two men / dressed in leather: Black leather, black helmets, black visors. One with a gun.

*Both* with erections.

'Get downstairs cock-sucker.'

'Oh my God. What the fuck is this?'

'It's going to be male-fucking-rape if you don't get your cock-sucking arse down those fucking stairs.

'Arse-wipe.

'Shit-head.'

I'd told The Cloud he'd have to do all the proper talking. I'd been very insistent on the particular type of language. I'd bought a DAT recorder. Used a voice synthesiser programme (the same one as Stephen Hawking)…the aim being to confuse: I've got all these choice fucking profanities on a loop. I press a button. The voice of Stephen Hawking says:

'*You-fucking-cunting-shit.*'

We take Austin downstairs, both pulling huge masks over our helmets.

Austin turns around at the bottom of the stairs.

Two men with erections—one with the gun and a huge Margaret Thatcher head, the other, a wrecked and distended Ronald Regan. Two passé western leaders with neurofibromatosis adjusting their cocks. Margaret Thatcher's cock appears enormous.

'Fucking please, oh fucking mercy. No.'

'*Cunt-face-shit-head.*'

'Shut your fucking filthy mouth. We've got the fucking gun
—'

'*You - Cunt.*'

'—and the gun buys automatic fucking respect—'

'*You - Shit - Rag.*'

'—and it means we get the monopoly on fucking everything

—even the cunting foul fucking language.

'OK, cock-sucker?'

'OK. Yes,

'Yes, *Sir*. Sorry.'

'*F u c k e r - F u c k e r - F u c k e r - F u c k e r.*'

I give the gun to the Cloud, dump Austin into a swivel chair, pull the chair into the middle of the room, walk out of the room and down a corridor to the racking system where the paintings are stored.

'*M o t h e r - F u c k e r.*'

I feel good in that "out of body kind of way" you can get at number 5.

I pull out the big Bonnard and go back to Austin and The Cloud.

'Oh, Jesus,' says Austin.

'OK cock-sucker, where's the money?'

'What money?'

'The money *in* the safe arse-wipe.'

'*T h e - Q u e e n - o f - E n g l a n d…sucks-filthy-fucking-cocks.*'

The Cloud looks at me.

I shrug.

'The money fucking Van Stratten gave you fucking half a cunting hour ago.

'Don't fuck with Ronnie and Margaret.'

Austin watches the man with the Ronald Regan head, the gun with the silencer and the erect penis swing around and shoot the Bonnard:

one

two

three times.

'The money in the safe is *in* the safe—it's in the fucking safe. Sorry. *Safe*. There—*there*.' Austin points to a big safe in the corner of the room.

'*F u c k—T h e—shitcunt—P r e s i d e n t.*'

'You have 10 seconds to get the money...

'Time starts now:

'one...'

Austin leaps up and runs to the safe. I follow him.

'*F u c k—T h e—Q u e e n 's—s t i n k c u n t i n g—saggy— a r s e.*'

The Cloud shoots the painting:

1

2

3

4

5

6

7 more times.

I turn my big head towards him to indicate why didn't he wait the full 10 seconds.

He just shrugs.

I'm amazed at the money in the safe. Like I'd been amazed at finding girls at number 5 who'd let me fuck them. The same way. The same feeling. Like this alternative life's always been just an arm's distance or one door away.

'*C u n t i n g—J e s u s—C u n t i n g—C h r i s t.*'

The money, it enters my soul as a balmy breeze an airless room. There're no mountain ranges to be traversing. There never have been. I experience a moment of complete serene liberation.

I look through the visor and the holes in Margaret Thatcher's head. I stare at the money. The sound of my breathing's trapped and magnified inside the helmet.

I look at Austin.

He's shaking.

I fill mine and The Cloud's shoulder bags.

We tie Austin up, pull off our masks and leave…

I'm expecting a hostile army waiting in the streets. There isn't one; only a multitude of well-dressed people armed with Starbucks.

I'm expecting the bikes to be gone. They're not. They're right there where we left them.

The Cloud and I set off in different directions.



I'd been to a Sports' Physiotherapist before going to America. She did a few tests; got me to walk about a bit, stand on one leg, bend this way and that. Do a few things with my eyes shut.

After that, I'd sat on the edge of her couch in my underwear. We got into conversation:

'How do you feel in the morning, Manny?'

'Well, I feel as if about three hours before I wake up, a group of men've been in my room beating me with sticks.'

'Every morning?'

'Most every morning.'

I fell asleep on her couch as she worked on my back. I dreamily pictured Nadia, prostrate and complaining.

The Sport's Physiotherapist sat at her desk and wrote up my notes.

'Manny, your proprioception it's really poor—about as bad as I've ever seen.'

'My what?'

'Proprioception.'

'What's that? Proprioception?'

'Its your brain's sense of what your body's doing in space.'

'My brain…it doesn't know what my body's doing in space?'

'You've become too reliant on your eyes, Manny. For balance. That's why you have trouble on escalators—the visual signals become confused, your balance goes.

'Your brain's communication with your body is very poor.'

She'd raised an eyebrow, as an Emperor might a thumb in the Coliseum.

She watched me struggle with my trousers.


I ride across Battersea Bridge at peace with my new, novel understanding—my alpine deceit. I come around Queen's Circus and turn sharp right under the railway line. I accelerate up the service road towards Vince's arch.

The Cloud's bike's there.

I see it before I see The Abacus' large corduroy-clad arse—this real, one-hundred-per-cent-kosher cotton-covered mountain.

I go for the brake.

Miss.

Lunge forward, crank my wrist and accelerate (...as Austin liberates himself in his basement; unfettered Austin thinking Austin thoughts; getting up, taking a blade from a drawer in his desk, hesitating, then calmly cutting his big Bonnard from its stretchers.) The Abacus, meanwhile, he's happily engaged in a final numerical mantra—counting sheets of ply:

'Sixty-six,

sixty-seven.'

As the bike and I, we slide.

To The Abacus.

Sending him, a sheath of money and the figure 'Sixty-Eight' leaping into the air. The Abacus, a comic, unlikely, computer-generated-super-hero rising; he looks suprisingly graceful, right up until the bad 'clack' noise, like a row of balls on an abacus coming together.

The airborne money comes down slowly.

I notice The Abacus's expression:

*Little* Abacus on Christmas morning—early. He's peeking through the flickering curtains of his eyes, witnessing the most beautiful kind of snow. A charming little smile's at the top of his twisted body.

I know that buying his silence would be impossible.

The Abacus, he stores up information on people. It's part of his Abacus thing—running accounts to the detriment of everybody. Bad information stacked up, screwed down and waiting. Fucking Abacus, counting ply when he shouldn't even be here.

I drag him into the last arch.

The Cloud's face, it changes in an instant.

I need to think.

'm o t h e r - f u c k i n g - c u n t i n g - s h i t - h e a d.'

I've got this big taut penis in my trousers. I walk to the toilet at the end of the arch, collate my head, pull out an image of Miki's arse, pull out my penis, stand slowly masturbating amongst the mould spores.

I can hear The Cloud miles away:

'Manny, I think

he's

fucking dead.'

# DILDO EXPRESS

The police show Austin photographs of the dead dispatch rider and a Ronald Regan face-mask. Two policeman.

One offering photographs, the other talking.

Austin sucks his psyche like a retracting gastropod deep into his cranium.

'Sir, is there anything about this man that might lead you to believe he was one of the assailants?' asks the First Policeman.

Austin looks at the photograph: A large man. Limbs very badly arranged. Plainly dead. Dressed entirely in black leather. Black helmet/black visor. Austin looks at the man's crotch—there's a grossly distended bulge. Austin wonders who this dead, obese man in ill-fitting black leather is. He's confused. He fixates on the man's stomach—corduroy and white belly erupting from  excruciatingly tight black leather trousers.

'Both him and the bike found by a dog-walker, yesterday morning. Sir.'

Austin stares at the man.

'Anything about this man, sir?'

Austin's gastropod psyche, it turns in its confinement. 'Everything,' says Austin. 'That,' he says, pointing, 'in particular.'

'I know sir, it's very strange. The rider. Very odd. He was wearing a black strap-on.'

'A what?'

'A black strap-on, sir.'

'Jesus.'

'Do you recognise the graphics on his clothes sir?'

'Yes, definitely,' Austin says.

'Would you care to take a closer look?'

The second policeman hands Austin a detailed photograph of a leather jacket, and, another photograph, specifically of the dispatch company logo: on a printed, white background there's what appears to be a black penis with wings above the dispatch company name: DI. LDO EXPRESS.

'Were they Fucking Welsh?' asks Austin.

'No, sir, that is to say...that hasn't been ascertained. Welshness. I don't think this particular gentleman was Welsh, sir. He seems to be very much an English gentleman. Decidedly upper-class. Ignore the punctuation, sir.'

Austin looks again.

'God.'

'Was this the pervert that did all the talking, sir?'

Austin puts down the photographs, twists a wrist, gently turns a gold, monogrammed cufflink in his shirt cuff and lifts his head: 'Yes it was.'

Austin resigns himself to make no mention of Stephen Hawking.

He believes he must be frugal with what he knows, to avoid confusion.

For some reason the old oil painter's logic of "start lean" seems to be being communicated to him. 'The Ronald Regan one—the one that did all the talking. All the talking and the lacerating removal of my Bonnard.'

'I suppose, sir, he'd have had to do that, what ever kind of deviant he was, sir.'

'Pardon?' says Austin.

'What with him being on a bike, sir. To cut it out to steal it. Being as large as it was.'

'Oh, yes. Definitely. Of course.'

'A most unusual case. On paper this deviant's a very wealthy man, while his job description is *Carpenter*.'

Austin's looking at the floor, thinking—Dead, Dead is good. Dead can't deny.

'I think you might have had a lucky escape, sir. We've been into the man's hard drive: a complete forest of filth.'

'Really?' says Austin.

'And we suspect terrorist links on account of the post-it-note.'

'Post-it note?'

'Yes sir, attached to the—' the second policeman produces another photograph, it shows a yellow post-it-note attached to the end of an enormous, shining, heavily veined black dildo.

'Jesus Christ. This just gets worse. What did it say?'

The first policeman looks at the second policeman then back at Austin. He inhales. His nostrils flare:

'"*FUCK THE ARSE-CUNTING-PRESIDENT. THE DIRTY-LITTLE-SHIT*", sir.'

/

The Dildo-Express-Heist captivates the tabloids for two days. On the third day two bombs explode in London. I'm picturing The Metropolitan Police turning their cumbersome weight like a huge, slow-moving vessel out at sea. Way out at sea myself. The maths being simple: cash+drink compulsion+chemical compulsion+sexual compulsion = Me, out of sight of land, in a surreal shipping lane, barely afloat, witnessing: A titan of a vessel with a huge *helmet shaped bough* slowly turn and head off towards International Terrorism and away from the dead Abacus. Me, the only witness to its monstrous reality saying, 'Fuck Off.' to its enormous blue stern, turning to Nadia and surveying her beautiful cunt and thinking of Stephen Hawking's mystical answer to everything.

I finger her cunt.

The wonderful, elaborate, external geometry of it, so familiar.

'Are you in there?' I ask her cunt.

'Fuck off, Manny,' she says.

'Is what in where?' asks The Cloud.

'Stephen Hawking.'

'In her cunt?'

'Maybe.'

'He's dead, Manny.'

'So?'

The Cloud's looking at me. He's gone way beyond the stage of his mouth being able to twitch.

We smile.

The radio's on, a familiar voice states that a government computer knows if we have or haven't paid our tax.

Nadia's looking beautiful.

The three of us wrap ourselves about one another like figures from Gericault's The Raft of The Medusa.

I can feel Nadia's pulse at one part of my body.

The Cloud's at another.

Nadia's looking at me.

She does something she's never done before: she smiles at me without a prompt of any kind.

## AUSTIN FINGERS THE HUMAN ABACUS

The First Policeman has a second and final interview with Austin.

The First Policeman plays Austin a DVD. A middle-aged man is with his children in a garden. Austin thinks the man looks quite reasonable.

'I would like you to concentrate on the man's voice,' says the First Policeman.

'Daddy, daddy.'

'He had two young children,' says The First Policeman. 'Blonde. Both very lovely.'

'No darling don't,' the man begins. 'Put down the cauliflower. *Sweetie.* That's better darling. Where's Toots gone? Can you see him Pop? Pop, darling don't.'

Austin surveys the room from the confines of his skull; as though it were a concrete emplacement sitting amongst a small war.

He shudders.

'Are you all right, sir?' asks the First Policeman.

Austin puts his hand to his head. 'Would you mind? Would you mind, officer? Sorry. Sorry.'

'Oh, of course, sir,' says the First Policeman, ejecting the DVD from the machine. 'This must be very upsetting.' The First Policeman watches Austin. He's pampered a lot of delicate, moneyed middle-class victims.

He gives Austin some time.

# THE ABACUS GOES DOWN

In the short time it was newsworthy, the convoluted story of the The Abacus' demise attracted a lot of attention.

He became something of a martyr to a mixed community of sexual minorities: his state of attire was well documented; the contents of his hard drive hinted at; the cause of his death debated—the police stated that his injuries were consistent with their theory that he had lost control of his high-powered bike, but the purported massive bruising to his buttocks only fuelled the ferocity of the growing enigma that was The Abacus; The Millionaire Carpenter; the black leather clad, dildo wearing, fanatical art thief.

The Abacus, crucified by the press, dead…soon to be buried.

At the beginning of autumn, everything and The Abacus passing into stasis. All kinds of minuses everywhere as God turns down the brightness, the colour and the contrast, trips up England with an outstretched foot and sends it sliding into a mean configuration of frugal, washed out and depleted tones.

His idea of autumn.

Some ancient, low-budget, black-and-white afternoon-TV-movie of a season.

I smile by a gash in the ground near where the Abacus had been a child. In this, his village. The country's turned opaque.

But things are different now.

Opaque's good.

Even the radio's fucking fine.

The TV's great.

Everything's OK.

The Abacus' family haven't deigned to come to his funeral; likely not appreciating the notoriety. It's easy to picture them trawling back over The Abacus' past, conveniently finding previously innocent memories to be full of portent. Posthumously recreating The Abacus so they might find him a monster.

For simplicity's sake.

Representatives of the Film Construction Industry fail to recognise one another in suits. Rough people in city clothes around a grave, haloed, at a distance, by a scattering of leather clad deviants, who, with small floral tributes and personalised newspaper cuttings, move amongst crucifixes and statuary, intent on saying good-bye to their black-dildo-wearing luck-less-martyr of an Abacus.

Everything opaque in the damp of an English autumn.

A Zombie Film of a funeral.

Different gazes around this sodden cut in the ground. I smile at The Cloud. He's looking down. Vince 's smiling at me. I smile back. Traffic's Appalling, he's obliviously running a big rough hand over his braille message of a face, while glaring at the funeral hymn-sheet as though it were just another menu holding a different riddle to be solved. The Priest's coughing for attention. He begins to usher his face and whatever appropriate's left of The Abacus closer to God.

Poor, vilified, disowned and crucified innocent Abacus.

I smile a pleasant, easy, drug-induced detachment.

The Cloud has tears in his eyes. I know that his big proxy heart'll have to do for the both of us.

Mine being dead and buried with Svetlana.

# VERNON PRENDERGAST

Vernon Prendergast was a sadistic vegetarian who liked to be in control. His control extended past his pale living-room carpet's network of plastic carpet-protector-strips, past his many pairs of identical shoes; polished and boxed and pristine. It extended past his kitchen hygiene—his two wall-mounted tin-openers (one for Vernon, one for Vernon's cat), and way out into the limited spheres of Vernon's existence.

Vernon had a whole bag of compulsions, at home they were easier to control, at work it was more difficult. Method was the thing. Vernon hid behind method. It was his mask and his body suit. His way of stopping the world from seeing him a monster. His need to be invisible had spawned a gift—the ability to recognise anomalies in others; like the man at the hospital with the loose walk and the expression that was good; good, but not perfect.

Vernon was a technician. He'd been employed for many years but had always lacked a vocation. He found his vocation the afternoon he saw Manny.

One of Vernon's obvious traits was his punctuality. His punctuality ruled many of his compulsions. A natural by-product of two of his compulsions was his presence in the restroom at the end of Chamberlain ward, at 12:30pm, three times a week. The first compulsion being to evacuate his bowels at 12:30 on the dot. The second, to witness Nurse Cunningham in the corridor outside, or thereabouts, at approximately 12:42. Three times a week Vernon would attempt to re-create their first meeting. The wonder of that. The frequency that he witnessed Nurse Cunningham in the corridor outside the restroom, in Vernon's mind, correlated not to chance at all but directly to the degree of affection in which Nurse Cunningham held him:

If she loved him, she'd be there.

Vernon was completely delusional.

Nurse Cunningham was in love with a urologist. The only thing that occasioned her to notice Vernon at all was his terrifying expression. He looked like a monster and it made her flinch. Vernon, in turn, read this reaction as a fetching, coy shyness badly disguising her obvious desire to make love to him. On the day he'd witnessed Manny, he'd firstly acknowledged the lack of Nurse Cunningham.

*There was no Nurse Cunningham.*

There was only Manny.

Where Vernon had trouble with reading natural facial expressions, he had no trouble at all in divining artifice.

He saw it in Manny immediately.

He followed Manny down the corridor.

It changed his life.

There was a big black wall that stood between Vernon and his relations to the rest of the world: his narcolepsy. Vernon's type of narcolepsy was especially cruel. It was initiated by excitement. It proved a bad old fuse-box to Vernon's progress. It often caused the world to cease to exist for him when he longed for it most. Vernon had fallen asleep on or around seven women in his life. Each time he had reached a point which his fantasies only had allowed him to pass, his narcolepsy had betrayed him. An erection for Vernon became a heart-stopping, momentary glimpse of an enemy flag being terrifyingly flown over his capital city, shortly before the enemy would mercilessly, cruelly dispatch him.

Seven times he'd woken to find himself vanquished.

Three times at home.

Twice in his car.

Once in a field.

Once in a storeroom.

Twice he had woken up in his car with a no longer erect penis for all to see. He'd woken to an audience of strangers seemingly all too happy to witness something of no use to anybody.

It wasn't good to wake up to the sound of people laughing.

It just made things worse.

In the field he'd woken to two pensioners on a tandem, looking at his penis as if it were a compass bearing.

The storeroom was worse.

The storeroom was at work.

He didn't want to think about it.

Once in his car he'd woken to find his penis carefully put away. This remained the solitary act of kindness of a girlfriend that never was.

In an effort to trick the switch that controlled his narcolepsy, Vernon went into training. He started buying mail-order porn. He wanted to systematically assess and slowly increase the level of stimulation he could endure. He intended, like an artist, to start off lean—to start off dilute and harmless and cautiously proceed to full-bodied hardcore.

He spent a cathartic weekend blacking out.

After three months Vernon reached the top of his first mountain. He could repeatedly watch "Granny Vixens" and remain conscious. It was a strange mountain to climb. Vernon didn't find old women in the least bit attractive, but that wasn't the point—this was his first summit; he planted his first flag and moved on. He moved on to bestiality. He thought that if being repulsed proved to be a safe technique, he might as well just hold on to being repulsed.

It was a kind of personal homeopathy from hell.

It left its mark on Vernon.

After half a year he'd developed a particularly sordid technique. While climbing his personal Matterhorn, he looked beyond it and thought of his mother. He was repeatedly watching "Heaven Bentley's Ass Worship", looking through and beyond the TV and thinking about Gladys Prendergast. It was disgusting, but it worked.

Heaven Bentley, the beautiful American soap-actress enigma. Vernon wished he had some of Heaven Bentley's good fortune. She'd set all manner of precedent. Not only had she weathered the storm of her pornographic-industry *Teenage Revelations,* but she'd gone on to be the first prime-time soap-Queen to have a successfully expanding back-catalogue of classic pornographic re-releases and remain in employment. All this by way of her much publicised *special relationships* with the Judge presiding at at her unfair dismissal case and the handsome young star-attourney making himself a hero by successfully commanding the highest dollar-sum ever paid in out-of-court settlement for personal damages.

Heaven Bentley had brought an entire Hollywood studio to its knees. She had taken its money—she had, by public demand, been given a cast-iron contract with another studio.

Heaven, Vernon's favourite, by far.

Heaven, sexually and socially a heroine to millions.

Vernon wondered at the good fortune of lives like that, like Heaven's, as he attempted to focus slightly beyond the TV. Focusing slightly beyond the TV obliterated detail, it took the sharp edge off full-frame-labia and allowed him to proceed. Plus the constant mantra of his mother's name. The constant mantra of his mother's name somehow kept the images moving without catastrophic failure but it built up bad silt in the psyche of Vernon. He began to feel a growing resentment to her presence in his newly found playground of sex. Gladys was still holding him on the swing and catching him at the bottom of the slide as his resentment went through guilt, slipped about through anger and fell into malignant pathological hatred.

Vernon refined his technique.

The effort of staring through the TV to someplace not too short of infinity was causing him to suffer migraines. He stole a pair of thick prescription glasses from a patient at the hospital. He wore them instead. They allowed him to gaze out, with a correct point of focus, but still have the detail of vaginas and anuses pleasantly smudged. His spectacles were a successful volume control to the screaming sex-flesh of the TV. At weekends, after long bouts of training, Vernon only suffered mild cranial discomfort. The glasses were a godsend. He kept them in a neat aluminium case on top of his DVD player. He felt good just looking at them. But he intended to betray them later. That was his goal: He wanted to stare Nurse Cunningham straight in the labia with nothing but his 20/20 vision.

For the first time in Vernon's life he felt a certain prowess. He could cautiously masturbate without blacking out. The strange thing about Vernon's new-found prowess, was how it appeared to be unlocking other passions, the potentiality of them; particularly the one that had lain dormant since witnessing Manny:

M u r d e r

Vernon loved just thinking the word *M u r d e r* .

Murder being Vernon's vocation-in-waiting.

The pot of gold at the end of his rainbow.

*M u r d e r.*

In the past months his subconscious had been quietly making plans for a different kind of coup. His subconscious couldn't wait to make a start, being desperate to use the same tools of distraction but for a different end. Sex had a finger on the invisible switch that blacked Vernon out. As did any manifestation of anger. His temper had extinguished him on many occasion. He sensed, however, that in making careful preparations for one magnificent culmination he'd made a wonderful template for another.

His personal potential for sex and violence loomed in front of him.

The summit of Vernon's destiny had initially appeared singular but a big cloud shifted easily to reveal a second summit and cause him to smile.

The Twin Peaks of Vernon's destiny rose up before him.

It was an Alpine kind of a revelation.

Gladys would be the first.

There'd be sense in that.

Vernon's weekends were always spoken for. He limited his sexual training to Saturday. On Sunday he took to haunting local beauty spots and mercilessly killing small wild animals. His methods were limited by his thick prescription spectacles and by his cowardly vegetarianism—his abhorrence of the sight of blood. His traits and his very much diminished perception of the visual world ruled out the use of firearms, knives and all but the very bluntest of implements.

Vernon fell into strangulation by default.

Strangulation presented its own problems:

1. *Strangulation is one thing*, wrote Vernon.

2. *Finding something willing to be strangled is quite another.*

Vernon was into lists.

The exertions involved in creating the possibility of the first notation by hotly pursuing any potential member of the second caused him to be discovered twice after periods of unwanted sleep. On both occasions he was discovered holding small dead animals instead of his penis. Vernon found this to be a far more acceptable form of humiliation. It even engendered in him a strange sense of pride. Disparate synapses fused in Vernon's brain. With each blackout came a profoundly morbid mental realignment in the already addled thought processes of Vernon.

With each awakening a slightly more monstrous bastard child was born.

Vernon began enticing neighbour's pets into his garden with the aid of food bought for the only safe animal in the area— Vernon's cat. Local pedestrians were soon confronted by an odd kind of paper spring as notices erupted on trees and lampposts beseechingly requesting information as to the whereabouts of missing cats and dogs. Snapshots of pets were taken from drawers and fed into scanners as Vernon's cull continued. The consensus being that a modern day Burke and Hare were active in the area; maybe supplying some heinous laboratory. Local residents fell badly asleep at night. They slipped into fitful dreams where much loved pets were tortured in the small hours by cruel men in white coats. The sale of litter-trays and para-phernalia for keeping pets indoors rocketed in the local pet-shop, which itself was festooned with A4 litanies of personal grief. It couldn't last forever. After three months the supply that had been so bountiful, became fitful and Vernon, at the zenith of his powers and awash with a new-found virility, stridently moved on to badgers. He overcame two with chloroform and remained conscious during the struggles, which were noisy and protracted.

He buried them alive.

Such was the measure of Vernon.

He was ready for Gladys.

He'd reached the end of his second volume of neatly self-prescribed expectations. He ruled a tidy line through objective number 84. Objective number 84 stood out most beautifully on the page. Vernon's calligraphy was impeccable. The embellishments and flourishes that announced objective 84 were particularly fine. He was cautious enough to encrypt his listings:

84. 1st culmination: $5+1$ = Vernon had watched five hours of blissfully uninterrupted hard-core. He'd ridden the biggest, most sublimely sensual wave of his life and not been wiped out by narcolepsy.

Vernon, at the age of thirty-two had finally achieved ejaculation while conscious.

He fetched a glass from a cupboard in the kitchen. He stood looking at a bottle in the fridge for a long time before removing it. The bottle was a gift to himself he'd thought to buy in anticipation of this moment seven months before.

Vernon stood looking out into the darkness of the small pet-cemetery that was his back garden and toasted himself with Spumante.

It was a Saturday he'd never forget.

He looked forward to the future with a new-found, wonderfully benign optimism.

He was ready for Gladys.

He was ready for Nurse Cunningham.

He was going to throw down a gauntlet to his narcolepsy with some serious sex and violence.

# GLADYS PRENDERGAST

Gladys didn't expect much from Wednesdays.

Not since Vernon's father's mid-week business trips had stopped. The ones that kept him away Wednesday, Wednesday night and most of Thursday and let her get her pin money.

She stood in her kitchen, regressing through Wednesdays; drawing up men from the silt of her memories—a big old grab handle of a function bringing up random faces, torsos, penises, grimaces and smells; smells of lavender scented air freshener and sperm and lube and condoms. And Montel Danson. Montel Danson, whose years of treating her like an angel had imprinted the smell of him onto her memory as profoundly as the internal organs she'd seen on a TV medical programme had accommodated the shape of their neighbours.

With that kind of permanence.

Like that.

Shapes pertaining to maybe a liver and some such else drifted in front of her.

All the colour torn out of Wednesdays by Vernon's father

resigning himself to hanging about every day of the week until he finally did the decent thing and left to meet Jehovah. *Finally*. When even a body as beautiful as hers had been wasn't beautiful any longer.

She let a hand range over the obvious contours of her body. She tried to remember the taught little nuances that had been there before.

The logic of Wednesday gone.

A big vacuum behind it.

A big guilt slowly grown there about her first-born who'd gone for good with the man most likely to believe him his son.

Way before Vernon coming out of her like a booby-prize.

She pictured Wednesday.

Sitting there in the middle of her week.

'A little island of nothingness,' she said to her kitchen.

Wednesday, that had hidden behind a gaudy curtain as everything that was exciting and nice but had come out as a midweek declaration of all that had gone amiss for Gladys.

A radio was on in the kitchen.

The TV was on in her living room.

The radio alarm clock broadcasted a radio play to her silent, empty bedroom.

She was lonely.

Most of all on a Wednesday.

She'd missed her boat.

She was in the winter of her life.

God only knows where her boat might have taken her. Sailing off for good the day Vernon was born. It could have been anywhere by now.

Somewhere sunny perhaps.

Gladys, standing on the quayside of her kitchen, wondering where her boat might be.

'My boat,' she said blankly.

She stared at the fridge magnets. The colours of them against the white door of her fridge. The most prominent amongst them in her mind being a plastic boy on a skateboard. A gift from Vernon. (He'd some notion that as a child he'd borne a resemblance to this handsome little plastic boy—whatever the truth of it, in the absence of Vernon, the plastic boy took precedence: the plastic boy *was* Vernon.)

Gladys took a great deal of pride from her grasp of English, her second language:

'You're a fuckin' *anathema*,' she said to the plastic boy. 'You always fuckin'-*were* and you always fuckin'-*will* be.'

She remembered little Vernon stunning his extended family with his vocabulary, as highfaluting words with solely negative connotations backed up in his little brain and were liberated by his mouth. Their wonder, soon superseded by concern and fast followed by embarrassment as Anathema turned to Enigma by way of Abomination.

Vernon's pronunciation of Abomination was superb.

Soon, everyone knew to begin talking loudly whenever he showed the slightest inclination to open his mouth.

At the age of four, Vernon was witnessed by his uncle Cylus talking to his reflection in the bathroom mirror. Vernon's uncle Cylus had a dramatic sensibility which coloured the delivery of any event he tried to describe:

'*Crestfallen,* he was, with his *sad* little face, his *weighed-down* little shoulders, and all the while saying: "Gorms, Gorms. *You've* got no Gorms.

'*You're* camp*letely* Gormless".'

The story, often repeated, soon became a warn out banknote of old denomination in the already unwanted currency of Vernon.

By the time Vernon began attending school, he'd learnt to only betray a normally bad understanding of the English language. He was worldly-wise because of an overbearing sadness. Marginalized because he was different. He had one perfect, profound understanding: his mother had missed her boat and it was all *his* fault.

He seldom had cause for excitement. The first time he did, he wished he hadn't. He said a big hello to narcolepsy.

Gladys was in the habit of twisting the little plastic boy anti-clockwise on the fridge. Twisting him into a *fallen-over* position.

Vernon never failed to notice it when she had.

She gave the plastic boy a little tweak. She left the radio on in the kitchen and took her sandwich into the living room.

Another nothing of a Wednesday nearly done.

Only the one treasure still tagged to the end of every Thursday.

Only that left now.

# TWO VERNONS AND THE THING ON THE FLOOR

7:50pm.

That's what he kept thinking: 7:50pm. All day long, that time.
As though it were a target in his head.

7:50pm.

Vernon was planning on being punctual.

His birthday.

The time of his birth.

7:50pm.

He was going
to murder her
on
the
dot.

The glasses were just a fail-safe. They felt awkward and cumbersome. In front of the TV it was one thing but out and about it was another. He couldn't help it, though. They weren't indispensable but he felt them necessary.

It was just a matter of trying to pretend they were an essential part of his mission.

Like they were night-vision or something.

He was aware of himself, as if from a distance, creeping around the familiar back garden that was his mother's.

He was dressed in black. Being sharp and confident; running a sharp, confident mantra of death through his imagination. Along with Preordained. The word. He kept thinking that word. His feet, even the steps they were taking. Preordained. Falling into exactly the right spot for Vernon's feet to be falling into. Each step, every time, falling correctly, as Vernon prepared to wreak revenge on Gladys.

He pictured the basement of the hospital. Where there was no CCTV and he wouldn't be missed. He'd made one appearance for the front desk CCTV earlier. He'd finish throwing this gauntlet down to Gladys, get cleaned up and make one more appearance for the front desk later.

He thought of his hourly wage.

Tonight, for killing his mother.

He felt immune to pretty much every kind of possible danger or outcome. Even if he left behind a trail of incontestable evidence, what could they do, after all? The narcolepsy he had a history of since childhood, the evidence of that made him inviolate. The family doctor had known for well over a decade that Vernon couldn't even masturbate without passing out.

He couldn't help but smile under his mask.

What possible harm could he be to anybody?

Inviolate.

In the darkness of his mother's garden he pictured his fine calligraphy pertaining to this day, the most special day of the year for him and his mother.

He was going to celebrate it with her in a way that even she wouldn't be able to ignore.

She'd be doubtless fixing herself a drink soon. He looked at his watch. In three minutes time. Or thereabouts. To get back to her chair for the beginning of the penultimate episode of a programme she'd never miss.

The one she wouldn't ever see the final episode to the following week.

She would never let him visit on a Thursday for the sacrosanct nature of this programme. The Thursday night series: Reality Family. This series of programmes, some black family out of poverty with more money than they knew what to do with. Them being the latest Reality Family. Vernon thought it odd that whoever the family had been, over the years, whatever demographic type, she'd been besotted nonetheless.

Every Thursday for years.

Their ridiculous stereotypically told story would be finishing seven days after she'd been blotted out.

He could see her shadow fall onto the kitchen floor.

Like a stain, thought Vernon.

A stain soon to be expunged in a sanitary fashion.

Vernon had come prepared.

He pictured the implements and packaging and plastic sheeting he'd brought to keep all this tidy.

Vernon caught sight of his mother stopping in front of the fridge. She said something to the fridge-magnet plastic boy and hoiked his little skateboard to leave him yet more upside-down than ever.

Her, being like that, in her kitchen, insulting him for the very last time ever.

He thought she looked a bit overdressed.

She had "The Stockings" on.

"The Stockings", her way of referring to which ever pair were her favourite at the time.

Vernon lifted the thick prescription spectacles, adjusted his mask, acknowledged "The stockings" and replaced the spectacles.

She was wearing heels also.

He noticed, with surprise, that she was partially undressed. That's how it seemed. He thought he even saw the dark shape of one of her nipples lifted out above the neckline of her dress. He couldn't be sure, though. What with the slatted blinds on the kitchen window and her having disappeared back into the living room by the time he'd removed his spectacles to get a better look.

Whatever the noises were coming from the living room now, they seemed to include her laughing.

He held his narcolepsy at bay.

He looked at his watch.

It was just after seven thirty-nine.

He refused to feel himself on a narcoleptic tightrope and liable to fall anywhere as he waited and gave his mother ten minutes and thirty-seconds-counting to live.

Throughout Vernon's rigourous training he'd had a growing sense of a doppelganger-self; the emergence of a doppelganger self. He was close at hand now. The doppelgangar-self. The other Vernon. This clone borne out of hate. Forged from anger. Conceived for company on nights such as this. Vernon couldn't exactly look at the other Vernon full on. It wasn't as easy as that. His existence was far more ephemeral. But, he implicitly believed him to be there. Vernon looked about as best he could. He found what he thought to be a likely spot, nodded to it and gave it the thumbs up.

He'd been talking quietly to the other Vernon for months.

The two Vernons agreed on everything implicitly.

It was comforting.

They finally agreed on opening the back door by way of smashing it down with a big fence-post-sinking-tool from their mother's garden shed, this, an implement they'd not thought to bring because of Gladys' door being invariably on the latch.

The Vernons determined to make nothing much out of an anomaly such as that. They both felt *very much* as though they had carte blanche for extremely clinical brutal murder as they burst through their mother's back door in perfect unison and rushed through her kitchen. Charging into her living room like a small medieval army with foul intent, believing that they alone had the monopoly on surprise—to be confronted by naked black and coffee limbs amongst discarded clothes and witness their old mother's face about the genital area of a fat black man which neither of them knew from Adam. Their old mother raising her eyebrows to them like a greedy child caught with the lollipop of the fat black man's penis still rooted in her mouth. A drop of sweat fell from the fat black man onto their mother's forehead. Her, blinking and reversing her mouth down and off Montel's penis which was still very much erect.

Montel, because with her mouth liberated that's what she was repeatedly saying.

Montel's face a picture of astonishment and growing concern.

Montel, naked apart from a big pink brassiere the Vernons recognised as belonging to their mother.

Him, wearing only that.

The fat black man Montel farted. His only declaration. As Vernon and his doppelganger-Vernon-self in turn experienced a shock-wave that separated them momentarily and caused a big black neon sign to slowly pulsate and buzz the word NAR-COLEPSY/NARCOLEPSY/NARCOLEPSY above them, as though advertising an American TV motel straight from hell.

The Vernons fought to stay conscious and together. To slaughter two instead of one. Not with leisurely intended strangulation; the strangulation of the Vernons' mother that was in preperation always almost calm, but with the reckless wielding swing of a heavy garden instrument and the subsequently disgusting colossal loss of blood by the nakedly conjoined thing on the floor.

Half of it more naked than it had been on the day these Vernons were born.

And all of this without any provision being made for bodily-fluids by way of plastic sheeting...forgotten in the rush with so much else. Such as method and preparation.

'And, you. You *eradicate* him! And, I. I'll *expunge* her!' Gladys witnessed Vernon screaming to himself. Not recognising him at all. At first. Animated. Dressed in black. With a black balaclava. And ridiculously thick glasses which he would keep flipping up to get a better look at her to only be dropping them right back quickly down again and start swinging a big tube of something thick.

Something of enormous weight.

Something made of iron.

She'd gone from feeling so terrified to feeling so relieved when she'd put together enough bits of this person for it to become Vernon. Then she'd held there at the top of this dreadful arc, only to be swinging on back to being terrified and straight through that to this place she never knew existed before as far as fear was concerned.

All she heard herself saying repeatedly being: 'But Vernon, you don't wear glasses.'

Gladys, holding onto the hope that Vernon's endeavours with Montel would cause him to black out at any moment as Vernon in turn repeated:

'I—will—make—love—to—Nurse—Cunningham—*yet*.'

With every word a blow to Montel's head.

The blow with every '*yet*' by far the heaviest.

273

CRACKS

It's in the plane coming back, looking out the window—little phantoms of Heaven Bentley floating about my head like tiny upward burning pages of the Kama Sutra—coming back from painting Heaven Bentley, that, out of nowhere, memories of an old car I was driving years ago come into my head. I remember not being able to stop fixating on the windscreen in this car. The state of it. That, and the driver's side window which was broken too. It'd be shut, but off to one side, off its seating behind the door panel, a gap at the top of it and a triangular gap at the side by my shoulder.

The electrics were bad as well.

The crack in the windscreen stopped a few inches short from where it'd really get in the way of your field of vision.

I was sure it was getting bigger.

Longer.

Hardly able to drive for looking at it and wondering that.

This bubble of a memory of me and her, by then a complete caracature of what had been odd enough to me at ten, in this

274

car, driving along.

Me, and the mother that never was. About the only time that she'd ever left the house.

A few miles back I'd pulled over and marked the end of the crack with a chinograph pencil.

I kept checking that mark.

Driving thinking about it and then checking the mark and looking past my shoulder at the triangular gap.

She'd asked me what I was doing? What was wrong?

I didn't say anything.

Some Arabic music was playing on the CD.

The CD player was on the way out too.

Jumping.

The whole car was fucked.

I remember feeling like everything was a little test. An assault course of some kind. Or as if everything-maybe in the real world was only a reflection of the imbalanced state of me. Thinking that and checking the mark on the windscreen. Plus, she kept saying things that didn't make any sense.

'I bought him an Ohm,' she said.

'What do you mean, you bought him an Ohm?'

'You know. That word you say when you're doing yoga.'

I didn't know specifically who the "He" was and I didn't know what she was talking about in general.

'I don't,' I'd told her. 'I don't do yoga.'

'What?'

'Do yoga.'

'No, but he does.'

I just kept checking the mark on the windscreen and driving along. 'How do you buy someone a word?' I asked her.

'You know, on a thing for round his neck. I thought it'd be nice. You know, that word you say, "Ohm".'

The CD jumped. That was from the time when in changing

275

to the radio you invariably got the man with throat cancer or the girl warning they knew you didn't have a tax disc, or they knew you were signing on and working. Any number of things like that.

She had her window open. Her window worked. She held a clear plastic bag on her lap, it was full of smashed up bits of fried bread. She'd been throwing handfuls of fried bread out of her window as we drove along and saying, 'The birds will like it. They really will. Darlings.'

I remember looking across at her, solid and static, with the landscape flying by outside. She was wearing the kind of frock she always did; something big and colourful. Like a set of curtains. Like the one she'd worn a lot the first year I knew her; the one she'd said was her first "suicide dress". And out of everything I remember about this woman, this last revelation comes as a complete surprise. That she had a dress she referred to as her first "suicide dress", and that I'd forgotten everything about that until right now.

It's night outside.

I can see myself smiling in the plane window.

I'm thinking it must be the pills.

This wonderful sense of a calm stretch of distance between me and important events in my own life. Like suddenly realising after all this time that she'd contemplated suicide before I came along all those years ago. It makes me feel better that she had. Not that they were sure it'd been suicide anyway. What with her being found dead in that house after having lain there for so many weeks.

I can picture that.

All the familiar furniture.

The state of the place.

Another dead dog and a half-eaten bag of liquorice toffee doubtless somewhere.

I'm staring through the aeroplane window. It's dark. Speckled with stars. Amongst them the reflection of my smiling face.

## HEAVEN BENTLEY

Heaven Bentley's gone from being so familiar and real to something I have to cobble together in a meandering photo-fit collage.

Just like that.

In no time at all.

I can't even remember the colour of her eyes.

I can remember the taste of her mouth, though. How she'd latch it onto mine. Me shutting my eyes and trying to put together the pieces with her mouth on me. Painting her portrait. Her sitting there so sure of herself for a day and a half. The famous American sitcom actress. Her first film. Sitting there in period costume; her drop-dead breasts, gorgeous in that costume. And I'm telling her what to do. Where to look. Getting her to move minutely. There's all that, then she's suddenly on me like I'm beautiful myself. It turning out that's to do with the fight I got into with one of the carpenters, the state my face was left in and me being gruff. The gruffness and the state of my face reminding her of some resolute old dog she had when she was a girl. A dog called Bunga. Bunga, who'd always be getting into fights. She couldn't keep her hands off me after she'd decided how much like this old dog of hers I was. Not caring what people knew, thought, heard, anything. Three days in and I've got a necklace come dog-collar engraved with *Bunga*. I'm sitting painting her in-situ on the set, in this 17th century interior. Carpenters mooching around. It's OK until the dog noises. I don't know if it's to do with my collar or what. By then, already, her and I, we've taken so much of what someone as famous as her can easily be getting hold of it's a wonder I can stretch my arm out with a brush. It's the first time I've bitten anybody all the way to stitches and a tetanus. There's no more barking, though. Somehow, the painting's looking as good as any painting I've ever done. Maybe better. That's the only thing the producers are pleased about. The painting. Everything else is worrying them. The fighting, the bites, the sex, the press being outside the studio and the hotel. Heaven's been on the slide for two years already back home but the public, at the moment, they love her for it. They want more.

They're getting it.

They're getting *Cocaine Fuelled Canine Love Romps*. Thanks to a telephoto lens they're getting *Bunga in Heaven*.

I'd never seen a photo of my arse before either.

With her mouth on me and my eyes shut, it didn't make any more fucking sense than with them open.

Any of it.

I loved her cunt, though. I can remember that. The taste of it. The look of it. Smell of it. I've never been so captivated by a cunt. I loved just looking at it. There was a lot going on with it externally. It had some kind of narrative; not all tucked away, shy…it was theatrical like her. As theatrical as her standing there with a strap-on and a lead to my collar with my howls racing about the corridors and down the lift shafts. Her lean and taut body with a glaze on it. Me, finding a way of getting her clit under my tongue while sucking it into my mouth that fed her soprano up through the 5 star hotel like smoke through a beehive.

The hotel register oscillating to that.

Maybe I shouldn't have let her wear it on the balcony. The strap-on.

It was so nice, though.

Anal.

It was really, really nice.

But the evidence of it, it kind of opened a door to what they'd soon be concluding about me and Jabba.

I keep picturing the transition a firework makes. From a big explosion of colour to a wet, bedraggled, carbonised stick in a backyard somewhere.

Being back to Jabba.

This place. The trashed kitchen. The bathroom. Him, chemically dormant in his wrecked lair of a front room.

Stupefied.

OK, so I'm helped in realising the full horror of this English nightmare by the squalid photographs in a gossip magazine I'd never heard of before last week. God knows where they got those pictures from. I've no memory of anybody taking a photograph of him and me in the front room like that. Heaven looks beautiful in her photographs; maybe just a bit depraved, then there's me looking crazed and pictured living here amongst so much filth with Jabba who's without doubt my fat oily boyfriend.

The kind of thing someone like me's longing to be sharing a bed with immediately after Heaven Bentley.

Obviously.

Jesus.

Now, nobody's happy: Jabba, the neighbours, the landlord. Seems to take nothing at all to get things fast unravelling. Plus, the photographs of me outside number 5. If there was anything left between me and Heaven there probably isn't now. I've been ringing her phone the same way an ancient Roman might have delved into animals' entrails to answer an urgent conundrum. To work out an overbearing problem. The answer to my conundrum, it's just this automatic pit on her phone.

The sound of her voice and I'm slid right into it.

The lights shining in my direction are already picking out some zombie characters. The old Irishman for instance. The ruckus over that.

I couldn't care less.

Truthfully, I couldn't.

Fuck 'em.

It's all like some badly scripted TV drama anyway.

One I tune into every now and then.

On sufferance.

My life.

Maybe the guy lurking about with the camera, maybe I sensed him and that's why I pressed the wrong button. Made a mistake like that. Anyway, where finding number 5 had taken a bit of determination, a conscious effort, finding number 23 took no more than a lack of concentration.

It's all good though.

Apart from the images of this orphaned TV monkey coming from way back out of nowhere. The laboratory one that was lured into loving a tube of cardboard in a bit of fur. The one I thought poignant as a child even though I didn't know why. Watching it cling to any old rubbish for the sake of being convinced it had a mother.

Out of nowhere like that.

I looked at the number 23 just as I pressed the button and thought, Fuck. I'll just have to say *Sorry. It was a mistake. I got the wrong button.* What I got though was a different voice. A different voice saying the same thing:

'*Yeah, darling. Hello. Come on up, darling.*'

Indian. She sounded Indian.

I remember thinking maybe the whole block's being run as some kind of sex co-operative.

Fifteen minutes later and I'm behind this beautiful girl from the Indian subcontinent, trying to forget Heaven Bentley and wondering who might be next door. That's what money can do for you.

Get you squandering pleasures for contemplating the easy availability of the next. And the next. And the next. Me, like that already. That's what I was thinking as I watched the figure that I knew to be me in the full-length mirror on the wall opposite, in a bored, distracted way.

My own bored face watching my own bored face.

Bored. Watching the beautiful Indian prostitute's arse ripple to my oscillations.

There was traffic going by outside.

Somebody laughing.

The Indian prostitute making these noises; a prostitute's equivalent of herding some stupid, dumb animal towards its final destination.

I was looking above her and trying to not comply.

Thinking *L i f e   i s   R i d i c u l o u s .*

Contemplating the difficulty in aligning what's actually happening to my perception of it, the perception of it always being slightly adrift like some old dinghy being dragged along in the wake of a ship.

On a long, long rope.

The transition always too quick with prostitutes, from being outside behaving normally to inside behaving like a timid rapist...what you get as result, this weird separation, this lag between what you're witnessing and where you are in relation to that event.

Invariably way away.

A big fuzz in my head and all the lazy cash in my wallet, the rope to the dinghy being about ten miles long.

Maybe I wasn't even in the fucking dinghy.

The only evidence hinted at in the corridor was that the neighbouring practice might be German. I was thinking that German girls are to be had at number 24 on account of the Germanic ceramic plaque on the front door which recreates a Heidi-like figure, holding a staff, next to some gargantuan German dairy cow emblazoned with the number 24. Anything seeming possible and likely, probable even, to a man who gets off with an American porn 'n TV star. A man who gets away with murder. A man who can be with somebody as beautiful as the Indian girl at the drop of a hat.

She had a really beautiful slim back and her arse was fucking unbelievable.

The missing thing, OK, there's no frisson of whether they will or they won't...but what can you do about that?

Me and the Indian girl both easily going through the motions of what's expected of us. Her, a petite-moaning shepherd. Me, this dumb-moaning sheep.

Mainly thinking about Germans.

My one concession to humanity, a finger gently tracing the tattoos on her back.

# I LUF ANAL-ZEGS

Three nights later I consciously press the button for number 24.

I can't help myself. My life's not my own for wanting to bury Heaven with sex.

I've got what I'm going to say all worked out: *Hello*. Once. That'll be it. Everything else will take care of itself.

All this, half an hour away from putting on my shoes to leave the flat.

Thirty five minutes away from 50 milligrams of Viagra and a big glass of water.

'Hello.'

'Hello.'

'Hello.'

'Hello.'

'He-*llo*.'

'*Hello*.'

No *Come-on-up-darling* or its German equivalent. Whatever that might be. I'm phased but only slightly. I imagine this to be typically evasive German behaviour. How like a German to stonewall over an intercom.

I picture the TV monkey with its cardboard tube and tatty bit of fur.

'Hello. Are you German? Du bist Deutch, ya?'

'What?'

'Du bist Deutch, ya?'

'What?

'Christ. I do believe you're *German*?' I say, patiently, to this buffoon.

The buffoon breathes and thinks.

'Eine frauline, bitter?' I nudge him from a concealed box. The buffoon knowing nothing of his lines.

'What?'

'Are you fucking German?' I shout.

'Am I what?'

'German.'

'Do I sound cunting German?' he shouts back.

I think about it.

'No, but that doesn't mean you haven't got a nice German girl up there. Eine *Deutche* frauline.'

There's this long, long pause. In it I try to fabricate the man I'm talking to.

'You *what*?' he says.

There's lederhosen and braces, no matter how trifling the evidence. It doesn't seem to matter that it's a man I'm talking to, either. That, in all my experience of prostitutes the only time you get to talk to a man is when you call up to order a visiting prostitute; then there's a man, maybe; and he's only meant to intimidate you into behaving at a distance. Then maybe a man with a voice like this gets to talk to you.

Not otherwise.

Whatever the signs, I'm desperate to believe this cockney's actually a gargantuan male madam for German prostitutes.

285

He remains, in my mind, the custodian of the bovine ceramic on his front door.

I can't get beyond the physical evidence of the bovine ceramic.

He's the most unusual madam in London—it's just a question of believing it.

I plainly need far less information than even the TV fucking-monkey with its cardboard fucking-tube and tatty bit of fur.

The good thing, though, with the SRIs, things that in the past might have seemed an indictment against my character, now, they're just vaguely interesting.

I like it that I'm more easily convinced than the fucking TV monkey.

'Well?' I demand of him. 'Are you going to ask me up? Icht meuchters ein bumsen, bitter. I'm gagging fur e fuck. Vot do you hef up there?

'I'm prepared for anything.

'Anything will do.'

'...The only reason I'd ask you up, you cunt, would be to throw you out of the fucking window. You *f u c k i n g  Nazi*,' he bellows.

I visualise the demented greyhound in the stalls, the me under Viagra.

It's shaking in anticipation.

It's got this three foot sticky-stamen hot-house-monster type penis.

I reckon I've nothing to lose in delineating the anything I'm prepared for in my best German accent. A vaguely desperate thought process being that if incredibly poor people *really* can win the lottery, and actually *truly* do become millionaires, there's still an outside chance this obese German lunatic's only pretending to be cockney.

'I em villing to zpend a lot ef munny on anal-zegs.

'I luf annal-zegs. Much, murch, munny fur de anal-zegs.' I tell him. The old greyhound, shaking its attachment like some kind of foul jousting accoutrement. '*Feel gelt*,' I persist. 'Bitter. Bitter... A *vife*. A dorghter? Bitter, bitter, pleeze. I hev much money.

'*F e e l   G e l t*'

You can just tell by the way the intercom goes dead that the mammoth's coming down the stairs.


He's big, fat and panting but he can't see me crouching in the bush.

Crouching in this bush and smiling.

Humming slightly.

The big fat cockney/German? stands there for some time. Opening and closing his big hands,

looking about and breathing hard.

Breathing hard and looking about.

He can hear the vague persistent melody of the German national anthem in a distant, irritating, nasal hum:

Mm.mm.mm.mm. Mm.mm.m,m,m...

/

There's an odd little rationale going through my head that re-
volves around the pills making me happy and me not being the
same man at all because of it.

The same man who did all those dreadful things.

Previously.

And it's a really liberating feeling, because, somehow, it means
that all the guilt I should be harbouring, I'm not.

Nightly, I send a caretaker around every dark old curious
room that together comprise the ramshackle building-of-me.

He repeatedly fails to find one incriminating thing.

Each time he goes away
he comes back to me
with nothing.

# TOXIC DIALOGUE

'No she didn't. She had no idea.'

'I don't get it.'

'Well, he found a secret way up there, didn't he? He made a little door she's never known about. Did this tricky bit of carpentry amongst the tongue-'n-groove on the upstairs landing. He's been there eighteen years now. Now he has. *Eighteen* years. He's a sitting-tenant. Anyway, he completely redid the attic and made it really-really-nice.

'Because it was nothing before.

'The other tenants, they *know* he's up there, but they don't *care*—what's it to them? *Nothing*.

'And now he's got this nice little secret gaff and he's making his film.'

'He's making a film?'

'Yeah. He's got it all set up. On the cheap, though. 35mm camera. From Russia…it arrived *beautifully* packaged. Covered in all these *lovely-Russian-stamps*.

'*35mm*.

'And he's up there in his attic gaff making the beginnings of this film with a little diorama and a tiny model biplane on a *wire*. He's always been the same. With his *projects*. No money coming in but always some project on the go.'

Xav and I, we're sitting amongst our gear beyond the turf lawn that the palm Brokers laid yesterday. There's a small dog passing the big picture-window on a sit-on lawnmower with its paws on the steering wheel.

That's the gag.

It's on the story-board.

A lawn-mowing dog.

People around the camera whistling, banging anything that comes to hand as the small dog passes, to get its attention, because it's supposed to be looking through the window, the big picture window; *casually*, like that's something it's used to— mowing lawns and gazing about. The dog-handler's screaming at the dog to *Stay*. Somebody's banging on a short scaffold tube with a hammer that's the dominant noise amongst a whole chaotic orchestra coming from that kitchen as the dog sweeps past over the green, green grass on its red, red lawn mower.

Looking petrified.

Looking as though it knows everything there is to know about anxiety. Every inch of its attitude's hackled to the proximity of the grey wiry hair and the red crack of a mouth that's the ancient dog-handler.

The whole dog-fucking vision propelled by means of a long wire and a pulley.

The clients are sitting nearby watching the playback monitor as hilltop Generals any past disaster. On their periphery, everything they might want by way of fruit. Their conversation, it drifts across when the noise from the kitchen allows.

We watch the small white dog being dragged backwards on the red, red lawn mower across the green green grass.

The clients are watching too.

'What do you think?'

'Yes. I agree,' courtesy of the kitchen, comes their conversation.

The dog, slowly reversing by way of the pulley and wire.

'—I think a larger spot on its side. Maybe joined to the one that comes over its shoulder.'

'Brown?'

'Absolutely.'

'It'll make it look… What's its name?'

'Gorby.'

'Gorby? That's the name of the dog?'

'Yeah.'

'OK. *Gorby*. It'll make *Gorby* look a bit more compelling. Don't you think? A bit more eye-catching.'

'Absolutely.'

I look at Gorby. Gorby, going backwards and trembling. His ears telling you everything you need to know about his state of mind.

'Or maybe black?'

'Maybe black. OK. *Yeah*. I like it. Black.'

'Black.'

'Absolutely.'

The Absolutely-man catches me looking at him. I smile. Give it all I've got as far as teeth're concerned. My mouth a mess of recent bad dentistry. My gums rough, abraded—slashed purple.

'Black then?'

The Absolutely-man's staring back at me.

'Black? Black then?'

'Yes…absolutely,' he says.

I think of children dying of malnutrition. All the cliched bag of wars, iniquities. Of The Hadron collider. I think of how well all of that sits against the significance of a lawn-mowing dog.

For some reason, every time I move my right shoulder a jolt of pain hits a back tooth. Fuck, it hurts.

…I feel I'm a wiring diagram that makes no sense. I see: shoulder / big arrow / tooth. I see it like a 1950's educational film. That kind of style.

'You see the fence panels at the back?'

'Yes,' the Absolutely-man says.

The group he's in, there's about ten of them altogether— clients / copywriters / producers, whatever. With the same attitude as always. Visiting a maternity ward to bitch about their baby.

Every little fucking freckle and blemish.

'Well, I'm convinced. I think maybe *that* panel… Don't you? I think its a bit too o r a n g e. Don't you?'

'Yes it is.'

'It's *very* orange.'

'*Really* orange.'

'Absolutely.'

'I don't know how I didn't notice it before.'

'How didn't we notice it before?'

'I don't know.'

'It's unbelievably, incredibly orange.'

'Too orange?'

'Well, *yes*. Don't you think?'

'Yeah, definitely. It's a real distraction.'

I'm thinking, I'm not sure, but I'm thinking in all these years I've never seen any of these people actually eat any fruit.

'How did it ever get as orange as that?'

'It's *far* too orange.'

'*Absolutely*.'

'Yes. It is.'

'It's *incredibly* orange.'

'What's wrong with these people? Who are they again?

Who's responsible for the fence?'

'Construction. They're the ones that put it all together.'

'Yeah. Them. How could they let it happen?'

'I've got no idea. I really don't.'

'You've got all these brown fences,' one of them begins; she actually starts picking them out with a polished nail on the end of a clean finger: 'One. Two. Three,' she goes. '…7, 8, 9, and then you've got this orange one,' she says, tutting. 'Ten. Yes, number Ten. You've got this orange one. After the ninth, you've got the tenth, the orange one.' Her little shining nail beginning a line to the fence. She tuts again and folds away the polished nail. The clean finger. The art-director walks across to suggest how he thinks I can best alter the fence and to explain about Gorby—who's off his lawn mower—to explain what he, Gorby, might need by way of alteration. He faffs a hand about his own shoulder as indication. He, the art-director conduit between me and Mount Olympus, between me and the privileged huddle with the fruit ten feet away, goes on and on about the fence and Gorby. I set off towards the orange section of fence with a bucket of dirty wash and a big brush. On the way I pass the old dog-handler. She's shaking what I suppose to be a small can of spray-paint-dog-dye. She's going to paint him herself, she says. She appears to be equipped for any eventuality, having doubtless seen it all before. She collapses to the floor with the can and an exclamation which sounds like 'Fuck', but I don't think can be.

She begins on Gorby.

Gorby, The Lawn-Mowing dog, his eyes are wide open.

The old dog-handler, she gives me a really weird look as I walk on by.

I show her my teeth.

She's not phased in the slightest.

I set myself up in front of the orange fence. Take a good

look back at the clients and whoever else. I think about the TV woman in the Sumatran jungle, the one I saw again last night, the one who's been on before; the scientist studying the court-ship dance of a small Sumatran bird. I remember the way she so beautifully mimicked that dance in a small clearing on the jungle floor. I wonder if she's there, in the jungle, right now... as I'm painting this fence. I think about her and the other woman on TV the night before. The other woman only still a girl. A sixteen year old girl with a baby boy...her, really thin, dying of cancer, talking to camera in her bedroom...only sixteen. Her sister crying to another camera downstairs while watching a video of her sick sister when she'd been beautiful. When she hadn't been sick. When she'd been well. I think of this girl dying in her bed. Her, just a normal girl, and I think of Jesus, who wasn't normal at all, dying on his cross. I picture his image being in perpetuum, everywhere, and hers only briefly on TV. I picture the beauty of a world in which people might wear stick thin dying normal girls in little silver beds around their necks instead of a Jesus on the cross.

'...Absolutely,' comes the ghost of an agreement from the Absolutely-man.

The old dog-handler's watching me as she walks up and down to dry Gorby the Lawn-Mowing dog. I can see by the way she keeps cranking her head in concert that she's picking up on the foul things I'm saying about Jesus. Every few steps, the Lawn-Mowing dog looks from the old dog-handler to me and back again. Like it's lip-reading. I keep muttering. The old dog-handler keeps cranking her head for my words every time; this old fish, taking my words like flies from the surface of the water. This old fish and me.

This man.

The abomination with the blasphemy, the laughter, the tears and the brush.

'Do you want the fish?'

'No,' I tell him.

'Would you like the pork?'

'No.'

'How about the pasta?'

'No. I don't want that either,' I tell him.

I move my shoulder and grimace while I'm looking at the thin black chef in the draughtboard suit. He's staring back at me with his spatula like a conductor might a recalcitrant first-violinist…asking 'Well, *what* then?' with his face.

I point at the mashed potatoes and stare at his perfect teeth.

'You want the mash?' he asks.

I nod.

'Only the mash?'

I nod.

I grimace him a portion of split gum.

He reciprocates with mash.

I sit at a table, delicately ply my mouth with mashed potato and reminisce on my enormously expensive dental procedures and my gum-line like it's all been a recent holiday destination. I remember the South African's look of surprise as I shook my head about violently at what was a critical stage in his drilling procedure.

I chaperone the mash with my tongue.

To enable him to slice up my gums with his drill and me to have good reason to pay him nothing at all.

The vicious old dog-handler, she must have off-loaded her animals to her assistant. She's across the room with a piece of pork.

Staring at me.

I suck on some mash.

I'd browsed the internet after the fiasco at the dentists. I remember out of curiosity finally typing in *Prostate Symptoms* and pressing enter to the enormous binary nightmare devoted to the prostate gland; the one I could either go on throwing pills at or have reduced through surgery. The surgery didn't seem attractive. Seemed a gamble. Three golden bells and you'd be fine, any messy grouping of fruit and you'd be fucked. I remember reading two words really fast: *incontinence* and *impotence*. I drifted down some pixelated backwater and found a doctor recommending pro-active self help in the form of pelvic-floor exercise.

I suck on a small slab of mash and tighten the muscles between my anus and the base of my penis.

My pelvic floor.

I attempt to hold my pelvic floor muscles tensed for five seconds:

1

2

3

4

5

It does something strange to my face.

Makes my eyes lose focus.

I'm vaguely aware of the vicious old dog-handler across the room. She's scratching her wiry grey hair and staring at me.

Her red slit of a mouth with a ripple in it.

She's concentrating on my face as though she's collating it. That's how it seems. As if she believes she knows me from somewhere but can't quite home in on the where that might be. Her being stuck amongst canine data. Lost amongst ruffled brindle patterns, the beauty of them, to her, like ridges in wet sand on a beach. Her head stuffed full of dog-camouflage. Her, never forgetting a coat. Trawling back through a big mixed archive of nose, length of leg and length of tail.

Looking for me.

'I don't like them.'

'Why not?'

Why he has to ask with the thing being right in front of us, I don't know.

The Afghan.

The new dog for the next set. The kitchen set. I look at the vicious old dog-handler's assistant. She's blond and has this arse honed by many miles of forceful dog walking. Everything about her betrays her earnest, diligent nature. She's bent over the Afghan. Rubbing it all over. The Afghan's wagging its tail and the dog-handler her magnificent arse in unison. 'Ohh, beautiful boy,' she's saying. '*Beau*tiful boy. *Beautiful* boy. Who's a be*au*tiful boy? Yes. *Yes*. *You* are. *You*. *Yes*. *You are*.

'Yes.'

The semicircle of clients and producers are watching the dog-handler and the dog too.

Xav looks at me.

I stare at the Afghan.

There's no way round the feeling I get about dogs. That, plus, there's revolting, bacon-flavoured air coming from the vicinity of the food-technology woman. She's sitting at a table full of dog-treats with a tiny brush and some colour, painting out miniscule faults left by some huge dog-treat machine. She's surrounded by curled, elegant, bacon-flavoured dog-treats. She's got one in her hand and is highlighting strips of pseudo-fat with a cream coloured paint.

I clench my pelvic floor:

1

2

3

4

5

She goes all blurry.

To the other side of her's a phalanx of huge, dark red, barley-sugar-shaped chopped sections of something formed from a sweating rubbery compound.

The vicious old dog-handler hoves into view.

Bent over as if walking in a hurricane to the dog-treat table.

She picks up a giant sweating rubbery treat. She takes it to the First AD, holding it away from her body.

The First AD looks terrified.

'Are *these* next?' she shouts at him.

The clients/producers with a grandstand view.

'Yes,' says the First AD. 'They are.' (You can see he's already thinking in terms of this being some long awaited moment of complete humiliation. That it's always only ever been a matter of time as far as him and this moment's concerned and that the time's most likely now.) The vicious old dog-handler's position's in everyone's psyches as forcefully as a well advertised incoming missile. Every personal radar's blinking a doppelganger to the laser guided old bitch holding up the leaden barley-sugar pseudo-meat-treat. Dangling it at arm's length, between her thumb and forefinger. A big denouement coming, a Bring Me The Head of Alfredo Garcia moment; this Treat—the culmination of months of market research, of endless meetings; a canine fancy that's intended to storm the market and engage the public's unquenchable desire to pamper their pets as never before... come to this.

Hanging there, in all its ugliness.

All these eyes watching.

'*This*?' she says.

'Yes,' ventures the first AD.

The vicious old dog-handler, she looks toward the Afghan. 'My *God*,' she says. Everybody assuming the position emotionally akin to some ancient French gentry with its head on a block. 'You can Fucking *Offer* it to him, *O-nly*,' she says. 'I Fucking am *not* fucking having *that* dog eating fucking*shit-like-this*.'

Her sentence pulls after it a weird enclosed silence.

A strange vacuum.

Her head slowly bobs a glance at the clients. Bobs back to the First AD. Lolling in an arbitrary way like a gnarled old buoy in a fast swell. She stares on out. The clients look back at her like famous neurological case-studies. The culmination of their meat-treat efforts, the dream of every morning frappuccino for months, hangs wasted; a twisted, blood-coloured stinking composite of fuck-knows what.

I tighten my pelvic floor:

1

2

3...

It has an odd effect. Somehow, it *really* intensifies the foul incoming airborne bacon-flavour information.

I gulp a mouthful of vomit.

The mouthful of vomit's a bitter-arriving bile trigger to the rest of the black checkerboard chef's immediately flying pap.

I watch a fully-packed rush-hour-train of undigested mash fly from under my nose.

The famous neurological cunts gape.

The vicious old dog-handler, her withered arm's still up in the air offering the giant pseudo-meat treat. She crinkles up her ancient eyes and stares into the splattering gloom that's me. Her head tilted horribly round. She smiles this baked mud cracking over a red-rimmed yellowed-keyboard type smile.

She starts laughing.

'Bingo!' she shouts.

She's banished the fur.

Skinned it to be amongst the bald-faced human archive. The old card index kind. The cross-referencing had been the problem. Leaving the industry cards and delving into the ones from up North. From when she'd been a young S&M madam come star-attraction in a bright green painted brothel in Barnsley. A magnificent pea-green channel to her passion for restraint. All those young, lovely tarts. She can see them in a roll-call to hairless hips, tits, faces, cunts and arses.

They're all right there.

She can see Gladys, the filthiest black whore... with always photographs of this little puking shit amongst them. Photographs that came every two years. From down south somewhere. The ones Gladys was forever always eager to show off as if the gormless little wanker were a Tribal fucking Chief or a cunting Sultan.

There's my puke like some kind of endless, foul ejaculate, this ongoing cum-shot with a stop-frame animation of the crazed
old-dog-handler's
laughing head
through my blinking eyes.


'You OK?' asks Xav.

'I'm fine.

'Yeah. I am. I'm fine. Honest.'

There's a different, huge dog now. A different set. A different dog. Its tongue hanging out. It's confronting a ladder that's leaning up against a wall. The wall, a tenuous memory of a brick paint-effect some time in the last four days. Behind the set there's another ladder, a very tall, platform ladder. The hapless dog handler's assistant's up it. The front of her hanging over the wall. Her mouth emitting a series of words meant to attract the huge dog's attention. The huge dog, apparently, it's called Harold. On the storyboard there's a badly drawn huge dog helping with DIY, keenly, by gaily climbing a ladder. Harold's supposed to be mounting the first few rungs of the ladder in an

300

enthusiastic fashion to become that dog.

Harold has the beginnings of an erection.

I tighten my pelvic floor.

Whatever the well-honed arse is doing, it's not working.

My mouth tastes of soap having been sucking on a bar in the toilet, there being no toothpaste. 'Harold. Harold. *Up*. Harold. *Har*old. Oo-uee. Up. Up. Up. *Harold*,' the well-honed arse pleads, changing her inflection as though Harold might notice.

He doesn't even look up.

He just lingers on the paving slabs in a private, Harold world.

There's him and his erection, then there's the catatonic producers/clients and then the First AD, who's wearing the expression of a Naturist just beamed to the Arctic.

The huge dog Harold's erection is getting bigger; it's registering the emotional temperature of this studio with the same steady increments of a large mercury thermometer. Everybody's surreptitiously sliding looks to Harold's penis for a reading as around the base of the set the wiry-haired warhead sweeps in an angry arc. The livid ratchet-mouth on it open. 'Oh, for fuck-sake,' it bellows.

Another weird door shuts in space.

The First AD feels the biting full-on cold of an Arctic winter. He covers his manhood with a clipboard.

'Jesus 'n *fuck*-sake,' detonates the head, swooping to the base of the platform ladder and completing an odd kind of pornographic triangulation between it, the well-honed arse and Harold's cock.

'Come down at *once*,' it explodes.

It instructs an odd exchange-docking-procedure with the ladder's platform and the hapless assistant. The old dog-handler, she's intent on forcefully engaging Harold from over the brick-work with one screamed command.

Harold doesn't stand a chance.

He mounts the ladder with an East-London, primeval gusto.
He can't help himself.


'God,' the First AD thinks to himself.

Every time he sees the old dog-handler, an evil finger runs
down his spine...he thinks the word *God*. He looks at the old
dog-handler. She's at the end of the hallway set. They've just
moved to the hallway set. She's at the end of the hall.

He smiles at her, weakly.

'*You* might want to be here all night, *my fucking dogs don't*,'
she says.

'Yes,' he says.

He thinks: '*God*.'

He tries to sound convincingly like an AD, but, *really*, what
was "Yes" supposed to mean? Him just saying "yes" like that. *Yes*.
He didn't like the pathetic intonation in his voice. He thought
that whatever it was, the *it* that was so important to everybody,
it was all in the intonation. 'Yes,' he repeats.

'*Yes*.'

He holds on to an image of his daughter.

He desperately wants to not be seen as ineffectual.

He thinks that forceful is good. Forceful is desirable. Purposeful is good too. He thinks that the old dog-handler seems
to have a monopoly on forceful and purposeful. He feels that
by having so much of both she painfully eclipses the little he
has of either. He concentrates on an image of his daughter. On
thoughts of income. Of expenditure. He stacks up reasons to
persist like small fuel for winter.

He watches the old dog-handler spin unsteadily and disappear down the hall with the new dog.

He tries to control his breathing by consciously exhaling
slowly.

She cranks her head back towards him.

'*God,*' he thinks.

The vicious old dog-handler makes a show of inspecting the rig that construction has built into the hall wall (a painter's roller-pole on a sliding bar), made to accommodate the new dog and the intended shot of it rollering paint onto the wall.

This day being full of DIY dogs who'd do anything for the product.

It being *that* good.

The First AD knows he can't afford to let the futile nature of his work become too apparent. He knows that if he does, then everything will be lost. It will all crumble. He watches the old dog-handler slide the rig back and forth and raise her eyebrows to the dog and shake her head in disapproval and say something to that dog that includes the word Fuck.

He feels negativity coursing through him as surely as if it were post-operatively hanging over him in a plastic bag.

As if he were watching its passage down a transparent tube and straight into his arm.

'Five more minutes, only,' he shouts as she wobbles off.

'*Five More Minutes Only.*'

Hopeless.


I'm hoiking at my crotch with one hand and rolling a paint roller in a tray of paint with the other as she comes around the back of the set.

'Hello, *Manny,*' she says.

I look at her. At the exploding grey-halo of her hair; the way it decorates the wrinkled epicentre of her face.

Smiling in an odd way.

She's looking up at me.

The dog's looking up at me too.

I look from the red gash of the old dog-handler's mouth to the dog's hairy face. I don't like the combination.

Her face/The dog's hairy face.

Both, looking up at me.

I think it strange she knows my name.

The wrinkled face keeps on smiling.

She looks down at the new dog. 'Just like his fucking mother,' she says. Then she really begins with your enlightenment by way of all she says she knows for sure about your past. The big bucket of communal vitriol out there, she's setting about it for the amount she feels necessary to throw at you as far as her idea of your lineage is concerned. Telling you like any other madman might that your mother was and always will be a black whore.

A black whore called Gladys.

That you've a brother also—a brother that your slack jaw and blank eyes are telling her you know nothing about either and that this brother is madder than even a wanker like you seems he might be.

Maybe it's your tooth or the extreme nature of what she's saying but you're not taking any of this seriously. It's not even vaguely presenting itself as a regular piece of a puzzle that's you to complete might. It's just the random abuse about people's mother's being black whores and their lineage being doubtful and their brothers being mad and all about as regular a form of it as you're likely to find anywhere.

As you always have found everywhere.

Balsworth, she's saying, looking off towards the back of the set and setting her mind to remembering a point that seems important to the lunatic that's her. Balsworth or Mendicment. Or Hendergast. Gladys Hendergast, she says with glee. The rampant black nymphomaniac whore that was and maybe still is your fucking mother. Though she's more than likely been fucked to death by now. She says.

Her being frighteningly opinionated and brazen about everything.

And Vincent, your brother. The mad disabled wanker that he was and most probably still is also. Mad disabled wankers like that being in her opinion impervious to most anything.

Or maybe Vivian.

Some fucking V anyway, she says.

Then she smiles some more.

Then she and the new dog leave.

I look through the air where she's just been.

One hand static on my crotch.

The other frozen on the handle of my roller.

For there was a Gladys from the lips of my father amongst the memories that's my childhood.

His face drunk and maudlin and sad and her name coming from it.

And there was a V too.

And the memory of them breaks the surface of me for a moment like a mammoth sea creature might a cold sea.

The bow of its back.

The big sliding shape wet up one incline and down the other forgotten.

# BIG KARMA SANDCASTLES

It comes as a text message in the middle of the night:
    YOUR MNTHER'S DED MANNY...YOU SHMULD HAVE
SEEN IT
    It means nothing to me.

# VERNON'S HYDRA

Vernon thought that culls like that were supposed to clear the air. To be liberating. But five minutes of peace is all there had been. Five minutes only. And then that. Like the room was magic. Like you killed one relative only to make manifest another.

Da–Da.

And there you were:

Another.

Both Vernons had noticed it amongst the steaming debris of that room. Protruding from his mother's left breast; partially freed from its small, specially stitched pocket in the left Double-D cup of his mother's brassiere. In all the excitement. In all the mayhem.

You couldn't help but notice.

Just like that.

Da–Da.

This little head squeezing itself reborn from the bloody pulped hydra of his mother's left breast.

What were the chances, though? It was too much to contemplate. He'd held the small bloody photograph and looked at
the face of a man he'd always silently suspected was out there
somewhere.

Gladys, his mother, the part-time prostitute, her dumb other
spawn.

Her favourite.

Gone for years and years and her nursing him still.

The left Double-D cup wasn't lost on Vernon. It being close
to her heart.

What were the chances?

What were the chances of anything? Being born Narcoleptic? This face being liberated from your mother's breast? What
were the chances? With a name on the back. His name. And
a beyond the not-even-dug-yet-grave message from Gladys in
her foul looping hand:

*My Beautiful Manny. My real and proper son.*

And three wispy kisses.

Vernon had to hold onto the sodden carpet with his feet as
though he were climbing a hellish mountain with his heels.

He looked around the room, ignoring the fresh, organic
debris and inspecting the soft furnishings for more unknown
relatives. Which had actually seemed likely. Them popping from
the velour. Skipping from the scatter cushions.

Vernon stared at the photograph.

This man.

What were the chances?

This man. For months now only the enigmatic murderer of
Ronata Thistlethwaite. Vernon's apotheosis. Vernon's murdering
master. The chances? *This man*, with the gormless, dreamy look
being Vernon's brother.

This familiar unfamiliar other boy.

Manny, his name.

His brother, Manny.

His brother, Manny.

Manny.

He looked up. There were no more relatives blossoming from the back of the couch or easing themselves from the shag-pile smiling.

No more ghostly Lazaruses.

Just the in-side-outs on the floor and this photograph of Manny.

Manny.

'Manny,' Vernon said to the room like a blessing.

Vernon looked about for the other Vernon.

The other Vernon gone.

Betrayal everywhere.

The moment stolen by Manny.

Manny, an unsheathed demon-head, strolling horribly through the echoing corridors of Vernon's narcolepsy as Vernon

fell backwards

onto the bulk

of his mother.

/

He got home with the black boiler-suit and the slip on shoes and the mask all being hospital-bagged and properly gone and him scrubbed pink but that's where the similarity ended between the actual aftermath of killing Gladys and what was intended.

Her and Montel *Whoever*.

Montel, the now dead until yesterday unknown lover of his late mother. Not that what he, the fat black man, was doing to her could have classified him as that. Montel Dan*Something*. That, the name on the fat black man's blotting-paper driver's licence.

Vernon definitely hadn't accounted for all the eventualities.

The ramifications.

The very idea that his mother might still be sexually active at her age. The very idea of that being the wire that ran along the ground and brought the horses down. Like in old Westerns. That's why he'd spent three days in bed trying to outwit his narcolepsy and its revulsion to the foul coppery smell of blood that emanated from everything.

Three days minus interruptions.

Only then had he been able to properly celebrate by drinking spumante; drinking spumante and opening his treat—the rolled up, tight, newly delivered celebrity newsmagazine that was so often running stories about the svelte oriental diver with the beautiful hips; by drinking spumante and carefully slitting the paper slip with his address on it that confined his favourite magazine; by letting the magazine fall open and inhaling the nice smell of the new shiny paper and looking down at the random page and seeing the expose or celebration or whatever it was exactly that was the revelation of Heaven Bentley's lightning affair with a portrait painting drug-crazed prostitute-visiting film industry painter with a fat oily boyfriend.

The glasses not being on Vernon's face for that for Vernon feeling secure and expecting only hips to please him.

Amongst the big bump of his heart, the smudge of an optimistic notion that the magazine would have his hated brother's number, then, only the horrible view of the fast backwards flashing texture coated ceiling and a peripheral knowledge of the spumante arcing out way beyond the carpet-protector strip.

He looked at himself in the bathroom mirror as he dried his body.

He'd rationalised events while lying on the floor as meticulously as he'd dealt with the spilt spumante later.

He'd slid all manner of irritating negativity into the white hot small furnace in his head.

He said '*Mother*,' in a horribly mocking tone and flounced into the living room in his kimono, his head full of long words from his childhood.

He wrote a short encoded list in a specially purchased ruled and margined book:

1 Find Manny
2 Kill Manny
3 Culminate with Nurse Cunningham

He crossed out culminate and wrote *Fuck* in his own personal gibberish.

He felt a cold narcoleptic ghost travel through all the molecules that were Vernon as he wrote those four letters and intoned them to his room:

'F - U - C - K. *Fuck*,' he said.

He took his glass, refilled it with spumante, walked to his garden-side first-floor window, opened it and gazed out with some small reassurance from that. Considering each stinking sentinel to the bodies in his childhood home quartered, hospital-bagged and gone to grace a landfill. With all the garden animals gone from here weeks before them.

The entire documentary evidence of his training gone.

The inside-outs gone.

Good.

He pictured the fat man attempting to defile the entrance to his only one-time peaceful home.

He was proud of the base of his feet as they kept faith with the ground.

He crossed the carpet-protector-strip and rearranged his list of objectives:

1 Locate Manny

2 F U C K Nurse Cunningham

3 Kill Manny

He considered the night with the blood and every manner of other unsanitary matter. Montel DanSomething's stinking filthy faeces for instance.

He considered the possible ramifications to all that mayhem that wasn't strangulation.

Never mind.

Vernon gazed out through the open window and into the night.

Things would be all right.

He'd destroyed the Vernons' clothes; the masks, the gloves. The shoes. All care of the hospital. That was the really important thing. The thing that mattered. He pictured the police from two days before, felling him with the discovery of his butchered mother. He thought he'd got the weight of all that about right. Blacking out the amount of times he had. However clumsy he'd been with everything else, it didn't really matter. He'd got that right. Strange though, the way things had worked out. The way you could try less and be better at things because of it. The police had hinted at suspicions of sexual rivalry.

Because, apparently, *Gladys* had kept a diary.

Because, apparently, *Gladys*, had kept some *clients*.

There'd been plenty enough by way of damning unsavoury information about Gladys to stop Vernon having to magnify his symptoms. He just let his narcolepsy be as domineering as it always had in the past.

For once, his medical history pleased him.

Vernon Prenderghast, the registered narcoleptic. Vernon Prenderghast, so trounced by his disorder that he could barely achieve erection without the universe turning its back on him.

It was all in the paperwork.

He smiled to himself, lit a celebratory menthol cigarette, blew a long funnel of smoke into the night and took a sip of spumante.

# NURSE CUNNINGHAM'S STRANGE EPIPHANY

Nurse Cunningham took the box of Laguna brown-umber and the box of black and put them on her dressing table. She stared at her reflection in the dressing table mirror. She was manipulating a familiar big abstract in her head. It seemed enormous to her, like a big block of something hard. She felt she couldn't see the edges of it. She thought that maybe, if she could, she'd be able to get an angle on unravelling it; of making some sense of it: of understanding herself.

It was too big, though. If it were just sitting, small within her field of view, she could manipulate it. Look at it from all sides and feel in control. As it was, with no edges, just the big solid flatness, what chance did she have? You suspected it just carried on up and down and left and right for ever and ever and ever.

She turned her face about as she watched herself in the mirror.

She thought that maybe it was like a big indecipherable letter. Like the letter "Y", maybe. She pictured the letter Y. She pictured the famous big "HOLLYWOOD" sign in America and imagined being really microscopically tiny on that sign. Just seeing a lot of whiteness on a small area of a particular letter.

The Y.

She thought that was what it was like, trying to understand yourself.

Impossible.

She imagined turning round this microscopic element of her and watching people down there in the Hollywood valley. Watching their occasional reaction to whatever all that whiteness was that you didn't understand but definitely spelt out the significance of something.

Of you.

She smiled at herself in the mirror because she liked profound things.

And that seemed profound.

She pushed her lips out and blew smoke and said 'Profound,' to her reflection.

She felt that when you were defeated by yourself, that's all you had to give you some purchase—other people's reactions.

Gauging other people's reactions.

She thought of all the messages he'd sent her. All the little things. His reaction to her. All the words and the indications of love that had made her feel special. Made her seem significant enough to comprehend. Now all of that had gone and she was back to the enormous hard shape with no edges and her being infinitesimally small and he was reacting to someone else.

Reading those messages, now, and looking at those things, the things he'd bought her, and remembering all the words just made everything worse.

Bigger and blanker.

She felt angry at herself for being able to remember so much. All the little intonations. The tenderness. She didn't want to believe that it all meant nothing. She wanted to keep hold of something from it that made her feel OK.

Made her feel that she could cope.

She thought of the microscopic her on that big, white letter.

She opened her dressing gown and stared at herself in the mirror. She smiled. She thought she had nice breasts. She blew some smoke at her reflection.

She felt her left breast with her right hand until her thumb and forefinger met either side of her nipple.

She mixed the powders together in a green plastic bowl.

It was only then she noticed some mashed up information in the corner of the mirror that she hadn't noticed before.

Some information that didn't equate to anything.

She squinted and looked at it as it started to move.

# BIFOCALS

She stared at him over the top of her bifocals.

She didn't like the way there was always someone like him on a bus.

As if the big dilemma of them, buses, maybe being the end of you, violently, weren't bad enough. Buses themselves. It was all *too* much. Just when you'd forgotten the previous outrage. Just when a bus was back to what it should always be—an A to B thing *only*. Just when it *was* that, they'd blow up some more and you'd be back to square one.

And then there was the constant threat of people like him.

'It's just a question of keeping in synch. Like before,' said the man to nobody at all. 'It's a question of remaining focused. Of discipline. We will *prevail* if we stay in synch.'

The woman pulled her shopping towards her on her lap. She didn't want to risk moving seats, what with there being only this man and her on the bus. She didn't want to draw attention to herself.

She put her book on top of her shopping and pretended to

be reading, casually.

'We need one another,' the man was saying. 'We *do*. We need one another. But, remember, you can only watch this time, all right? I *mean* it. *Only watch*. OK? It's imperative. I mean necessary. It's what we'll do. *That's* what we'll do. You'll only watch. All right?'

She didn't like the look of him at all.

She hadn't when he'd got on, and for the five minutes he'd sat there quietly, looking around. Looking *really* weird. Those eyes, she'd thought, before all of this with the words. The eyes looked like they held all kinds of nastiness. Horrible, *horrible* eyes.

'Leitmotif—a theme or image etc.,' said the man. Apropos of nothing. He looked as though saying the word was painful. He looked across to whoever it was he thought he was sitting next to. 'Don't look at me like that,' he said, 'I'm jettisoning these old words, that's all. I say one, think it, exterminate it. Kill it off. I'm doing it for both of us. We've got to leave our past fallow in order that our futures might thrive.'

The woman thought of all the things in her life that she didn't want to lose.

She held onto an image of Fanshaw. Fanshaw, her toy-poodle.

'Impecunious,' said the man; '—having little or no money. Poor. Penniless.' He spat out the words. She thought he was so, so horrible. Possibly the most horrible man she'd ever seen.

She was thinking she'd maybe be all right as long as he didn't turn and look at her again. If he did that she felt she'd be lost. She knew that whatever expression the emotion inside her was generating, it would not be one that that man would care to see. He was involved in some weird, private thing. She knew she shouldn't break the spell of whatever weird, private thing it was. She feared that her face would let her down.

She'd always known herself to be transparent.

She sat behind her book, desperately trying to assemble an expression that might look normal, as though everything were fine.

Hopeless. it was absolutely, absolutely hopeless.

'Panegyric—a speech or piece of writing in praise of someone or something, especially an elaborate one; a eulogy,' he said.

She thought it a bad sign that the more she pictured Fanshaw, the smudgier and less distinct he became. More than anything she wanted him to be crisp and clear in her mind. She sat very still behind the small barricade of her book and her shopping and replayed special moments with ghostly Fanshaw in her head.

She'd forgotten what his face looked like.

'He's brown,' she thought. 'He's got a little grey bit at the end of his tail. And a bib. A kind of white bib.'

'You just watch,' the man was repeating, 'All right? Just watch. This one tonight,' he said, 'She's *mine*.'

The woman didn't like being put in the position of imagining quite what this man might be talking about. What this person, the man believed he was talking to, should only be watching. It didn't sound healthy, or normal, or in the least bit pleasant. She knew that much. She stared at the band that went around the back of the man's head. She noticed how it held on his ridiculously thick glasses. He was unzipping a black bag that was the other side of him to whoever he thought was on his right. There was a crinkling sound that sounded like the noise a dustbin-liner might make as he pushed something aside in there and reached in and removed what looked like latex gloves. Yes, latex gloves. 'Here,' the man said, to whoever it was, 'you can have these,' and he dropped them onto the seat beside him. Then there were a lot of smacking rubber noises as the man held his hands very close to his face and put on *his* latex gloves.

It was then that it struck her.

That the "*She*" of "She's mine", was most likely her.

That would explain the gloves. Everything the other one was being told to only watch. It was all to do with her. She felt like she had that time at the hospital when they'd put the intravenous drug into her. She felt as though she wasn't in the least bit in control of her body.

She couldn't see Fanshaw anymore.

He'd gone completely.

Gone.

She couldn't hear any noises from the bus. She could only hear her heart and her breathing. She thought that she was hidden behind her book, that seemed the only positive thing, as she gulped repeatedly and opened and shut her mouth. Out of nowhere there was this gacky stuff in the corners of her mouth and her body was emanating the strongest of smells. The kind of smells you'd call acrid. She was vaguely aware that she was saying a prayer in her head to Jesus. The only one she knew. The one she'd said with her mother at bedtime when she was a little girl.

He was surprised by the way she reacted when he touched her shoulder.

'Jesus fucking christ-almighty,' he said, and he tilted his cap and straightened his tie.

'Way-ahh-way-ahh-ehhh,' she started going.

'For fuck's-sake. God,' he said, and he recoiled from her, going off as she was like a car alarm.

'Way-ahh-way-ahh-ehhh,' she continued. And then, in a voice that trembled as if she were being shaken violently, 'Please, let your friend do it,' she said. 'First,' she said. 'He doesn't have to *only* watch. I don't mind. I really don't. I'd rather he fucked me first.' He couldn't believe what he was hearing. He'd noticed this woman on and off the bus for years. What was wrong with her? Such language. You just couldn't tell nowadays. The quiet ones could be as crazy as the fucking others.

'You're very attractive,' she said. She reminded the driver of how his son had behaved, when he was tiny, when he'd have a night terror and be *there* in front of you shouting out but at the same time be *light years* away. Somewhere fucking else entirely.

Looking at a place somewhere behind the driver she said, 'He's... *normal* looking, and... and... I'd like to save you to fuck later.'

He still hadn't calmed down by the time he got back to the garage.

He told two other drivers about the ins and outs of it but they couldn't have been less concerned. He wondered if it was because they were white and he was black that they showed not the least bit of interest in the story of him and this mad woman. One of the white drivers had eaten a piece of cake he couldn't finish. Didn't feel like eating with all that had happened. He fantasised about maybe asking them if they wanted something else.

Other than his cake.

He thought that when one of them said, 'Like what?' he'd punch him as hard as he could in the fucking face.

# RAPING NURSE CUNNINGHAM

Vernon kept witnessing strips of litmus paper from a science lab back amongst the mockery of his childhood.

The glasses weren't good.

Discovering Manny had caused an unwanted hiatus—*an opening or gap; a break in something that should be continuous*—in the ongoing ascendancy of Vernon and his battle against the dark forces of narcolepsy.

Vernon's wearing of his glasses now was just a litmus to that.

The witnessing of constant stress related images was another.

He pictured an ancient cream Bakelite circuit box under some musty stairs, and in it, a simple, degraded section of wire, burnt out.

Indicators falling in on him.

Out of nowhere.

He felt he mustn't view the wearing of his glasses as a retrograde step; they could so easily become a dreadful conduit to doubt and all manner of negativity.

He had to remain confident. Make strong affirmations. He

pictured the aspirational wall back at his flat, with its carefully framed photographs of every manner of human endeavour: The ascent of Everest. The Coronation. Superhuman athletes of every discipline; including his favourite particularly petite and elfin oriental diver with the magnificent slim hips and the slightly boss eye. He witnessed her standing with her hands ever so gently linked behind her back. Linked by means of one or two beautifully, delicately intertwined slim fingers.

Vernon safely ruminated on that.

He pictured *himself* as an Olympic hero, striding towards the biggest race of his life.

He altered the position of his glasses slightly.

He checked his doppelganger. It was difficult to pick him out in the gloom, but Vernon believed the pair of them to be in perfect synchronicity.

He'd gained access to the flats behind a woman in a fancy fur coat. That woman and the reception area had made Vernon wonder at Nurse Cunningham living in such a place. How she coped financially.

One anonymous threat had delivered a duplicate set of Nurse Cunningham's keys via a PO box to a small votive table he'd positioned for that purpose in front of his aspirational wall. All thanks to a tenuous item of hearsay about the big Security guard idiot below. The big idiot asleep with his big untidy cross-dressing feet on the furniture and an omen quietly on his TV: a recently re-released Heaven Bentley DVD. Vernon could tell that on the basis of a homeopathic tincture of information; the slightest sound; an almost inaudible ghost of her notorious laugh causing Vernon to blink repeatedly. Definitely Heaven Bentley.

Her laugh.

Vernon shut his eyes and tilted his head to let his refined palette commune: Heaven Bentley / mixed in amongst the bass-baritone of Lincoln Ductmeister. Lincoln Ductmeister of the ungodly silhouette and the bovine moans. He pictured Heaven Bentley screaming her pleasures at being incrementally penetrated by Lincoln Ductmeister's abominable member. That was the light before the dark. The pleasure before the pain as the recognition of Heaven Bentley being Manny's ex came in on him like the unwanted receipt of a live handgrenade. Bouncing about the small enclosed confines of his mind.

He felt the weight of his body shift slightly on his heels.

He wondered exactly what kind of omen this was.

Heaven Bentley on the big pervert's TV.

He held on to the degraded section of wire that was his paltry connection to the universe. He firmly pressed the tip of each index finger against either opposing thumb.

For some reason, making a closed circuit with his firmly joined fingers, just like that, it seemed relaxing.

Therapeutic, even.

/

The Mumbo Jumbo blaring out of Nurse Cunningham's bedroom was a surprise. The volume of the music together with its
type, it set an unusual emotional tone.

Slightly frantic.

Ensconced amongst the shadows of the surprisingly rancid
smelling room, the part of Vernon forever checking the pulse
of his screwed perception sensed a glitch. A tiny frightening
vacuum. Vernon witnessed the pilot of a big aircraft about his
pre-flight checks with his eyes looking up but with his eyebrows down. Furrowed.

Here he was.

Finally.

Moisture already around his lips from the mask.

He couldn't stop blinking.

'*Here*,' he affirmed.

But everything was not as it should be. The laws of physics
themselves seemed on the kilter. Vernon felt this mean little lag.
Something akin to the separation he'd sometimes experience

while in his masturbatory training; with the stimulation thick and fast but the synapses strangely vacant.

Everything was coming at him too fast. Too loud. Too frantically. And with this long distance phone-call-lag. What long-distance-phone-call-lag? It wasn't a mean little lag or a *long distance phone call lag*.

No.

It was a *Chasm*:

/kazam/ *noun* **1** a deep crack or opening in the ground or the floor of a cave. **2** a very wide difference in opinion, feeling, etc. 17c : from Greek *chasma*.

He held his gloved hands up before the itching eye holes of his balaclava as though the witnessing of them might pinpoint him in the universe.

He blinked.

He could feel the general downhill drag of a cold sweat moving beneath his black, nylon killing clothes. He couldn't summon any awareness of having a penis at all. There was absolutely no sensation at all from that part of his body.

None whatsoever.

Every time he breathed, his spectacles, his glasses, they clouded over. Again, now. Misted completely.

Lifting his spectacles, he looked down towards his penis, opening and shutting his mouth beneath his balaclava.

He replaced his spectacles and looked up, blinking, towards the illuminated vision that was the nearly naked Nurse Cunningham.

He blinked.

He stared.

He blinked some more.

He swallowed.

Everything hung in the balance.

An elaborate system of delicate weights began impinging on

Vernon. Little polished cylinders swinging in from everywhere.

He attempted to govern himself.

He boldly removed his spectacles and rose to approach the diffused pink and white he knew to be Nurse Cunningham.

/

Later, when *so* much needed mollifying by a retrospective logic, she put it all down to what she'd been smoking.

She could only put it down to that.

Why else would she have thought, initially, IT—this thing—had looked quite interesting? have laughed at its tight black top tucked into its tight black trousers? The way you could so clearly see its bits. It was *so* comical.

It was the stuff for sure.

Bending her perception.

It must have been.

It just must have been.

Until the big, opaque, oscillating eyes stared at her through the black balaclava, that is. Until they began to set her straight. Blinking and blinking and blinking away against this blank look, as though things weren't registering for it properly. One minute it was there, still and blinking, like every blink was an effort to swallow something visual that wouldn't be eaten, then it suddenly headed off to the side of her, shouting, 'I *will* culminate with Nurse Cunningham.' Veering off towards some clothes hanging from a hook on the back of her door.

All in a flash.

Out of nowhere.

Relating to nothing she'd ever witnessed before.

It put its hands amongst her clothes on the back of the door and pulled them to the floor as if it believed them to be human. The opaque, oscillating eyes seemed to be looking for something on the ceiling as the IT struggled with her clothes and pulled down its tight black trousers. She watched it as if it were some curiosity on the TV.

*Retrospectively.*

*Retrospectively*—there was something about it acting on her like a big poultice. *Retrospectively*—she could see all the bad things forming a queue.

All the bad things about being with the urologist, and then not being with the urologist; all the bad things about being with the other men from before and then not being with them; and all the bad things about her family from before all that adult sadness.

From before all the adult sadness all that childhood sadness.

All of that.

All those bad things.

All those bad things.

All the frustrations and betrayals from every failed human interaction she'd ever had. Backed up behind her. Out of nowhere. Like a big, angry army; this whole big oncoming coup bent on all kinds of foul expressions of disappointment and hatred. *Retrospectively*, she thought.

*Retrospectively.*

*Retrospectively.*

*Retrospectively.*

That must have been what gave her the ability to act like that. In the way she had.

In a way she never would have dreamt she could.

Not in a million years.

The stuff she'd been smoking.

She wasn't used to smoking anything.

Let alone that.

She believed it best to hit it really hard before she confronted it properly; as though for every time she'd helped and tended and served and saved she'd actually been fashioning an antithesis to all that, which was this…as she hit it across the back of the head with the first thing that came to hand.

That being the preheating iron she'd had out to iron her uniform.

Before she'd been side-tracked by her hair.

It went down amongst the clothes and uttered some muffled words and came back up onto its knees again. She watched all this happen in the same way she'd watched every jilted, deserted, cheated and abused woman strike out before her on TV.

From a distance.

Separated.

Comfortably interested but not really fully engaged.

There was a whole clump of slightly smouldering debris on the hot iron.

And this smell of cooking meat. Cooking meat and burning hair.

She gently pushed the iron, on a hot setting, she pushed it in amongst the complaining black wool of its face and nose. There was an angry hissing as she rolled the edge of the iron over its tongue, as it attempted to speak.

All this five minutes after casually looking at herself in her dressing table mirror.

All this out of absolutely nowhere.

And her always just the most normal girl with her whole life up to this moment playing quietly out in a dreadfully dull minor scale.

She stood in front of it. She released her gown and pushed her hips forward. To give it a good look at her naked torso. Like five minutes into being really weird, she could be as weird as that. She'd never felt so sensual. Her body was a mass of goose pimples. She felt as though a localised electrical storm was discharging a current across the entire surface of her skin.

She felt more significant than a planet.

The thing in the burnt black ball of wool and hair looked all askew and odd. Its big opaque eyes blinking. Its jaw going from side to side like a tiny goat eating grass.

Beneath the acrid hair smell and the meat smell was the clean smell of her body. She looked down, beyond her goose pimpled belly and hips. She looked at her dark, shining, pubic hair and knew, then, without a doubt, that she was beautiful.

She *knew* she was beautiful.

In all her life she'd never known that with clarity.

She pulled off its balaclava, which complained, as it would do, being a big black wooly scab to its face. Medical procedures she might be using were running beneath everything like subtitles in a foreign film. She dropped the balaclava-exoskeleton with its few clinging bits of it into the things lap, near the point at which its penis poked from the top of its tight, black trousers. She could feel its breath against her pubic hair. Without the mask, it looked like some bird; it had this expression, like it had lived its entire birdy life without proper nutrition and was gazing, for the first time, at a wonderful field of corn. Its little beak opening and shutting and its great big eyes blinking.

She was so sexually aroused.

*So* sexually aroused.

She poured boiling water onto the henna, stirred it, and

pushed it into its face, like all this was the normal thing to be doing on a Wednesday.

On an evening like this.

New Nurse Cunningham noticed its knuckles whiten and its penis back off into the tight, black trousers. Like a mollusc.

It didn't make any noise.

Apart from the bubbles it was completely silent.

She felt as though there were an alter-rail between her and it.

That she'd just delivered it a communion wafer.

It collapsed amongst her clothes on the floor.

It said, fat lipped and wettish yet quite distinctly: 'Narcolepsy: a condition marked by sudden episodes of irresistible sleepiness,' and then it was silent.

She sat back down at her dressing table.

She felt unbelievably calm.

She looked down at the V of her thighs.

She felt as though she'd been properly introduced to herself for the first time.

Like a big wave coming from a flat sea.


Out of the nothing—the blank; it could have been five minutes or two hours, it was the sight of the back of its head that dissipated the first wave and caused her to see another one coming. The back of its head looked bad.

She wondered how she'd failed to notice all that blood.

She imagined the immediate future. She imagined trying to explain all this. The little she could see of its face was purple, under the henna. She thought, 'What had it done?' It had appeared in her room, late at night. It hadn't even touched her. It had attacked a pile of clothes. And look at the state of it now.

The other wave hit her.

It picked her up and took her a long way from where she

334

wanted to be. She wasn't sure she liked the new, calm, self-assured Nurse Cunningham. Look what had happened already.

The new Nurse Cunningham could end up getting the old Nurse Cunningham in a lot of trouble, she thought, pushing firmly at the black limpness of her It with a painted toe. That being the first time she'd ever taken a pulse like that.

With a toe.

She had an idea that there'd be a big debate about whether or not she'd used "Reasonable force" against the thing in black with the purple face and the bloody gash that was more than a bloody gash and was even decorated with a small spattering of what she really didn't want to acknowledge hanging from the back of its head. The unmentionable she was looking at having been slightly sautéed by her iron.

She kept repeating: Reasonable force.

Reasonable force.

Reasonable force.

Her mind kept vomiting up big after-the-event-things. Like it was baulking out a horrible new clue with every mouthful.

Another one:

Who this *it* was.

The technician from the hospital.

The technician with the weird eyes. Vernon something. The "Vernon," of have you seen *Vernon* today? The "Ohhhh, Ahhh—*Vernon,*" Vernon. Everybody at the hospital pulled the same face when contemplating Vernon.

*Her* It.

She sat there thinking.

Then she found its bag and looked inside.

# VERNON PRENDERGAST'S LAST STAND

He catalogued all the signs. He was trying to let them on board slowly; like some horribly deformed, random crew. There were mixed messages coming from his face. His buttocks felt as though they were high in the air and naked. There was a definite and precise pain coming from his anus. His face felt excruciatingly tender and tight and wet to one side.

That side tasted of banana.

Banana.

Definitely.

And something else; something rancid.

He couldn't see anything.

He had no idea as to where he was.

He tried to move his head. That caused a big pain. The pain ran around the top of his head and down in-between his shoulder blades and culminated somewhere between his anus and the base of his penis. He reached behind himself and patted his hand gently across his left buttock.

He was surprised his buttocks were naked.

He was surprised to find that he was defecating what appeared to be a cylinder of steel.

He tentatively grasped this new aberration and ran his hand up and down it while beginning to contemplate the wisdom of pulling it gently out.

/

She'd been wandering the streets for five hours; hopelessly lost.

She'd completely lost her bearings by remaining on the bus way past her stop. Until its last stop.

Because of that man.

It was all too much. Too much to contend with—the maniac on the bus; being convinced the maniac was going to kill her and God alone knows what else besides and all the turmoil that sprung from that and in amongst that turmoil her losing her purse for the first time in her life, ever. And everything to keep you safe in it being now gone and her at the mercy of the city.

Her at the mercy of the city.

She thought she better stop for a moment and gather herself. Prepare herself for one last big push home. She chose a quiet corner that didn't seem too threatening. She took the trouble to breathe in a slow and concentrated fashion; as though she'd just discovered the miracle of breathing for the first time.

She thought about her purse. She tried picturing it somewhere. She thought she could picture it on the floor of the bus.

Maybe.

An odd noise caused her to look down a little alleyway. It was very dark. It took her a while to be able to focus. To be able to focus on anything. She heard the odd little noise again. It sounded like a small, helpless animal in pain; very much like the small, muffled noises Fanshaw made when it was wet out and she'd neglected to let him in.

She could pick out something amongst the garbage in the alleyway.

In the middle of it, this blurry something, something else glistened and trembled—a small glint of shiny steel, like the silver disk on a dog's collar.

She was desperate to be home, but she couldn't abide the suffering of animals. She could *not* abide the suffering of animals. If there was one thing she couldn't abide, it was that.

The little disk caught fragments of light. It was a bit like naval semaphore. She believed it a signal for help. She believed that a small dog was trapped and suffering a few feet away. 'Hello, dear,' she said. 'Hello–Hello?'

A yet more pathetic noise filtered towards her through the darkness. 'Oh, dear, dear,' she said. '*Dear, dear dear*. Ohh, *my*. Don't worry, darling. Mummy's coming.'

She felt she might really appreciate the company of a small dog.

If it were in too helpless a state, she thought it might give her an excuse to call the police. They might sort out things for the dog and take her home, she thought. Surely.

She probed further into the alley until she came to the source of the glint.

It was like a strange and very upsetting visual game.

She tried to deduce what on earth she was looking at.

It looked like an obscene face, smoking a large, metal cigar. She was so transfixed by it. It was as though the colossal fear building up in her was being held in check by her complete inability to piece together this jumble of information. The steel tube metal-cigar appeared to be pulsating. Ever-so slightly. She felt as though she needed one more clue to convince her to die of fright. That's when the hand appeared out of the black and started feeling around on what she realised, now, thanks to the hand, was a buttock.

A light came on in a window nearby; it released a whole stream of disgusting information from the thing on the ground:

Its trousers were pulled down to its thighs.

It was wearing a back-to-front black balaclava.

There was hair and blood and stuff poking out where there might have been a face.

There were thick, bottle-bottom spectacles over this hair and stuff where there might have been a face.

One of its ankles was caught up in an upturned wheelchair.

The spectacles were attached to a thick, familiar band.

'Oh, dear, dear,' she heard herself say. 'Oh, my goodness, goodness-me.'

The thing made a grunting noise and turned its head slowly around. Lots of black, knitted wool, covered in what appeared to be some kind of fruit and other debris. What must have been the real face, behind it. Behind all that somewhere.

A section of the fruit moved around what might have been a mouth.

The whole concoction crumpled back amongst the garbage. The back of the head opening in the wool offered her again the thick, bottle-bottom spectacles and the hair and the stuff.

It looked like a back-to-front monster with a metal penis.

The metal penis had words on it: Something-vescent Vitamin C.

She knew it was "Effervescent".

She watched the hand emerge from out of the blackness again.

She watched it gently engage the tube.

She witnessed the slow removal of the metal tube.

She'd never seen anything like that in the whole of her life.

The hand disappeared around the other side of the head with the metal tube-cigar. The black balaclava moved from side to side in a confused way. The metal tube-cigar flailing as both of its hands started to try to remove the balaclava. It appeared to be stuck fast, though. Every time the hands made an effort, the thing emitted a dreadful sound. The hands tearing a hole in the other side of the balaclava involved a lot of dreadful, unusual noises, then the hands brought the metal tube in close to the black wool and the fruit. They passed the metal tube along in front of the torn, black wool and the fruit; scanning it.

She thought the noise it made then was slightly derisive.

It unscrewed the end of the metal tube.

It brought the open end back up to the balaclava and held it there for a while; like a sailor, looking for land, she thought.

It put a finger into the tube and pulled out a piece of paper.

As it read, slowly, in the bad light, as it read whatever was written on that piece of paper, it had some kind of seizure and started frantically writhing and feeling around underneath itself.

It began howling and shaking the tube in a downwards fashion.

The tube slowly began to release something puckered and pink and vile. Even she could recognise one of those, with it being circumcised, completely out of context though it was.

That was when the mad young woman with the very large piece of timber leapt out of nowhere.

The older woman just stood and watched.

The cafe that they sat in was rather nice. It was odd to think that this place had been right there, all along. That in here they'd been serving tea and food while all that business had been happening in the alleyway.

Mr. and Mrs. Fish just working away as if it were any normal day.

It was surprisingly busy. For the hour.

The older woman felt as though she were in a completely pliable state. She thought that a lifetime of orderliness, conformity and formality hadn't prepared her for an evening such as this.

The younger woman looked much prettier without the strange plastic Macintosh she'd been wearing earlier. Although there was something inappropriate tangled in her hair. It was small, though. Too small to know what it was likely to be, exactly—without a context.

The older woman looked the younger woman in the eyes as she talked on and on. Occasionally she chanced a look at the thing in her hair.

'I wouldn't even have considered it, never, hadn't I found all this stuff in his bag,' the young woman was saying.

It was as if they'd been on some late night shopping expedition and were comparing purchases. The older woman really didn't want to look in that bag, but she didn't want to offend the young woman, either.

So she looked in the bag. At all the horrible things.

'Can I get you two anything else?'

It was the waitress/proprietor. She had on a big apron. Printed onto it was a scene of a South-sea island beach. With palm-trees. The waitress/proprietor had big forearms. She was a big girl generally. She looked very bored but kindly. She had a tattoo of a small fish on her left shoulder. With some small loopy writing under the fish:

*Mrs. Fish Loves Mr. Fish*

The young woman looked at the older woman and raised her eyebrows. The older woman shook her head. 'No, I don't think so,' said the older woman. 'Thank you very much.'

'I'm starving,' said the young woman. 'I'll have a full-English,' she said.

The older woman didn't really want the young woman to have a full-English. She wanted to call for a minicab. Like she should have done hours ago. From now on she vowed to spend whatever spare money she had on minicabs.

She felt relatively safe, sitting in the cafe, though. Drinking tea.

She had a place to put cafes and tea and civility in general. She didn't have a place to put the likes of what had happened earlier. She wondered if that was why it seemed so distant and unbelievable. For it did. She thought that if anybody ever had, or ever might, witness an alien space ship landing, this is how they'd be likely to feel afterwards.

Divorced and separate.

Maybe even calm.

The older woman kept looking at a ring of small brown spots on one of the younger woman's wrists. That part of her wrist must have been unprotected, between her surgical gloves and the sleeve of the plastic Macintosh from earlier. That's what she thought.

She thought she might have expected to have gone to pieces, earlier.

But she hadn't.

She was sitting here, drinking tea, watching the young woman who was laughing now and couldn't appear to stop.

The older woman was surprised to notice that she, herself, was also smiling.

## DYUGU THE TURKISH ANGEL

'It's like you've got this pilot light inside you. And it's just burning away and waiting for something big to ignite.

'Maybe even love.

'Can you imagine? at Vince's arch, with all those machines laying down MDF dust onto everything, the water running down the walls, and one minute you're just sitting in the tearoom talking the same-old/same-old and then Vince brings in this Turkish Angel. Who's hurt her head. And she slumps down in a chair opposite as though she's fallen through a portal from a Botticelli painting and you're looking at her long limbs and her flat belly and her long neck and her blond hair and thinking that she must be freezing cold and how you can't ever remember having been in the same room as somebody as beautiful as this. Not since Russia anyway. And Vince has assumed that she's one of the graduate students from the college who're working in his arch next door, and he tells her that she's safe with you because you're just as mad as she plainly must be and he makes her a cup of tea and goes back to work. And this Turkish Angel, who isn't one of the students from Vince's arch next door, *is* actually just a Turkish Angel who's tripping on acid and everything else besides and was in the petrol station by the roundabout until she was asked to leave and saw the beautiful black dog that belongs to one of the men who comes to Vince's arch and she just walked towards it down the cut to the arch to bang her head outside where the students are working and be brought in by Vince for a cup of tea.

'And you get up and ask her if she's OK and she's noticed Vince call you Manny and she just says your name, "Manny," like that, and she strokes the red velvet of the old cinema chair next to her and pushes it down and runs the palm of her hand across it slowly and then asks you to sit there with her and to run the palm of her hand across your leg the same way as she had the fucked up red velvet of Vince's chair. And *now, only,* you know that that red velvet chair's just heavenly tactile information crowding into her and that's where you're at cross-purposes because part of you's thinking that maybe Turkish Angels like this are walking the earth with unlikely soul-mates to find and some conceit in you's led you to think that her unlikely soul-mate... is,

'well,

'is, might be...

'*you* .

'You don't want to think that you're just another tactile revelation of wonder like the velvet chair as you stroke her hair because she's just picked up your hand and kissed it and is holding it to her head. A couple of minutes in to the strangest hello of your life. And her head goes back and she takes your thumb in her mouth and then you kiss and the comic book magic-boomerang flies into the air and everything in the real world's skidding along like a juggernaut with the brakes full on and you feel her right nipple through her top and put your hand between her legs and she's just bombarded with everything running right through the *sublime-channel* and you're like some sailor after this long fucked up voyage that's gone on for half a lifetime and you just want to secure all the lines and revel in this with an intensity of love comparable in proportion to the loneliness you've been feeling for years. Having taken these three massive jumps from one huge flat steppingstone of affection to the next in the two minutes in which you've known this Turkish Angel who's kissing you and smiling with her head thrown back and her eyes closed like she's finally, finally discovered the modern equivalent of the Technicolor Joseph she's been sent to get.

'And the pilot light that's burning inside you flickers, it flickers and catches the reservoir of love that the Turkish Angel's made manifest in that small tea-room

'and

'goes

'Fucking

'Boom.

'And finally, out of necessity, after things have calmed down—because, despite not wanting to, you gave her the option to realise that you're just a nobody covered in paint who's got the glimmer of something in his eyes that she wants a lot more of solely because she's wide open and vulnerable and way off the normal template of things and's capable of witnessing even an old chair as sublime—you're reeling her in as Vince comes back and together you try to piece together where Turkish Angels might actually live in the real world. And she says, "Buckingham Palace" first, and, after that "amongst the earth" seems like a good place to come from as a second choice for a beautiful, darling fucking gorgeous Angel like her. And she's unwrapping all these bullshit, calloused, supposedly unwrappable layers you've laid down round your heart since Svetlana because that's what Angels like her can plainly do for fucked up paint covered mortals like you, while, in the real world, she's twisting her long

347

fingers in front of her like she's playing an instrument you can't see and bringing up her knees under her on the faded red velvet chair and holding onto your hand and squeezing it so tight and bringing it to her mouth and blowing her warm breath over your hand that she can feel's cold in this cold room and you wanting everything to just stop like that in this cold room, wanting the big old skidding juggernaut with the locked on brakes to stop its sideways journey down this ice-road, to draw up in the silence so, in this new world that's hers, as this big old machine releases the last of its heat into the cold, cold air, you out of all this vapour might receive a wonderful, accurate, beautiful memory of your love for Svetlana. And you want the whole universe to pause because things as rare and beautiful as Turkish Angels don't just walk into your life and jump across big flat stepping stones of affection with you as if it were just a daily thing that happens whenever you choose to stop for tea. Which it isn't and never will be. No matter how much you want it or how better you think the world might be for a normality like that.

'And the rest of the day, after she's gone, what she's left behind's so palpable that the whole workshop's governing itself to get back on course and leaning like a big old groaning, masted, wooden boat to find the normal template of things; with Vince and Xav and Traffic's Appalling making mistakes with measurements and you fighting the petty, mundane nature of paint as you attempt to hold onto the Turkish Angel's version of things and remember her

'warm
'breath
'on
'your
'cold
'cold
'hand.'

# A DOG IN THE BUNKER

I'm holding onto the memory of Dyugu. There's me and her, then there's the situation here. We're at a place that does Indian food but nobody's eating. We're only drinking beer. Xav's talking. Sitting on a small sofa. A long thin man straight out of a Brueghel. Talking about death. 'He did it to his dog before he'd do it to himself,' he says. 'Just to *check* it worked. Just to make *sure*. The Russians were *well* pissed off. *Well* pissed off.'

Everybody else is looking confused.

This conversation, as most all others, a framework for humour to prompt a rhythm that keeps us all rowing in unison. That stops us being completely diminished by the size of the ocean and the breadth of the sky.

'You what?' asks Traffic's Appalling.

I can't believe what's happened to Traffic's Appalling.

He's enormous.

Maybe he's developed some kind of glandular problem. His thyroid maybe. His face is so huge even blinking looks to be a problem.

He's blinking like a burn's victim.

I try to summon up images of Vince's tea-room.

'Hey, Manny. You OK?'

Traffic's Appalling's blinking at me.

'I'm OK,' I tell him.

He stares back at me with hardly an expression; maybe all the muscles in his face are too taxed by the stretched-tight nature of it; maybe they can't have any impact on his face.

Xav holds a finger up to his head like a gun. '*Hitler*,' he says. 'It *well* pissed off the Russians because of it being a *soldier's* death. *Shooting your brains*.' he slides his finger off his head, making a silent bang with his mouth.

'So, what are you saying? Hitler shot his fucking dog?'

'What a cunt,' says this other guy. Another carpenter. I don't know who he is. I've only just met him today.

'No, he gave it *cyanide*.'

'Hitler gave his dog cyanide? Fuck. Why?'

'Because he wanted to see if it worked. *Then* he shot himself.'

'He gave his dog cyanide? Then he shot himself? I don't get it. What's with the cyanide?'

'Well he's pressed for time, isn't he? *Down* in the Bunker. Trying to weigh up his options. *Everything* against him. His options *limited*. He knows he's not going to escape through a *real door*.' Xav looks about him. '*Is he*? No he's not. So he's got to *build* one hasn't he?

'A door to the other side.

'A door to Death.'

Everybody's blinking and drinking beer and looking at Xav: doing personal puppet shows of Hitler, Eva and the dog behind their eyes.

'And he's not going to try out the cyanide on *Eva* is he? Not with there being a fucking dog in the bunker anyway.'

These are the images in my head.

Work related rowing images.

Everything normal. Comprehensible. Fine. The whole structure in place.

Not being able to breathe.

That's the first symptom.


Dyugu, the thoughts of her, the target I've made of her for love, the intimacy I'm feeling for that, for her and Heaven, maybe, them the poultice anyway, to somehow breach a meniscus in my subconscious and out slide Svetlana.

With complete clarity.

Her face close to mine.

Our breath together.

The feel of her beneath me.

The smell

and taste

of her.

Whatever I've been using to hold her down, to secure her fast, gone. This little broken sarcophagus. Svetlana in front of me now.

Not being able to breathe…

That's the first symptom…

I think to just hold onto the words being said. To keep making mundane observations. Like so quickly I have to lash myself to this room or I'll be lost.

Completely and utterly lost.

Vince sets down another round of drinks.

I'm watching like my life depends on it. I feel as though I've been thrown into very very cold water.

'What kind of dog was it?' asks Traffic's Appalling.

'Who's dog?' asks Vince.

'Hitler's. The one the cunt poisoned.'

'Isn't that irrelevant?' says the new carpenter. 'I'd like to know more about the poison,' he says. Why didn't the poison work? That seems more to the point. If it *had* worked, then surely Adolf Hitler, the infamous Nazi leader, would have taken it himself. Something must have gone horribly wrong with the poison. I expect the dog died in dreadful agony. That's in all probability why Adolf Hitler took the poison. I mean didn't take the poison. The cyanide. I mean that's why he shot himself.'

I'm thinking just observe.

Everybody's staring at the new carpenter.

Observe and listen, two words flashing in my head like the swinging illumination from a lighthouse.

The Cloud, even in my condition it's surprising. He joins the conversation: 'I think you'll find,' he says, 'that Hitler's alleged to have both taken cyanide and shot himself. The concensus being that he felt the cyanide pills, which had been supplied by the SS, Himmler's SS, were likely not to be cyanide at all. Himmler, as Hitler had recently heard, had been trying to negotiate a peace treaty independently. In any event Hitler didn't trust the potency of the pills. The validity of them. Hitler had a personal physician in the bunker with him. Werner Hasse. Werner Hasse had a dog. It was with him at the time. In the bunker. His dog's name was Blondi. Hitler insisted the supposed cyanide pills were tried out on Blondi. To test their efficacy.

'Blondi died.'

The Blondi Died.

The last two words.

The Cloud said them from behind his newspaper.

'I think it was maybe an Alsatian,' says Traffic's Appalling. 'The dog. You reckon?'

'What?'

'Hitler's dog?'

'Yeah.'

'I don't picture it as being an Alsatian.'

It's like when you're in a public place and you suddenly feel the need to vomit or defecate. That's what it's like.

'What then?'

I'm trying to deny my mind what it seems so keen on balking.

'I don't know. Something more like a Mexican hairless or a chihuahua?'

'Yeah, right. Hitler, in the bunker. Hitler and Eva and a Mexican fucking-hairless or a cunting chihuahua.'

'Fancy shooting a cunting chihuahua.'

'He didn't shoot a chihuahua. Nobody shot any chihuahua. Adolf Hitler, the infamous Nazi leader, didn't *have* a chihuahua,' says the new carpenter.

'He might have done. He could have. Maybe. Why not? What the fuck's wrong with chihuahuas?'

Traffic's Appalling's clothes are ridiculously tight on him. That's how it seems.

I think I've done this all before, holding onto Traffic's Appalling when everything else is pitched and on the slide.

'For fucks-sake.'

'Bastard. Probably burnt it as well.'

My phone's buzzing in my pocket. I take it out. look at it. It's a message from Heaven Bentley:

YOU'RE WELCOME TO HIM.

'Yeah, that's where that famous post-war German sport started.'

'What post-war German sport?'

'The one with a whole lot of chihuahuas and a catapult. You know, they poison one, wang it in the catapult, set it on fire... fly it up into the fucking air...'

'And shoot it with a fucking gun.'

'That's it. See. Knew you'd have heard of it before.'

353

'For fucks-sake.'

'I suppose he threw it off the roof as well?'

'He was in a fucking bunker.'

Every time I breathe in there's Russia and I'm inhaling the smell of Svetlana.

'I've always thought it's a bit like falling,' says Traffic's Appalling, one fat hand obscuring his face.

'What's a bit like falling?' asks Vince.

'Life,' says Traffic. 'Life. It's like when you're born you're pushed out of this plane... and life's the distance you've got to fall and figure it all out. Yeah,' he says. 'You're pushed, and out you go, and you're falling. Attempting to figure it all out.

'It's like that...

'And the cloud's middle-age...

'...One minute you're young and above it, you can't see the ground, and, consequently, you've no fear of fucking death. None at all. Then—whoosh. You're in it and wondering how much air there might be left the other side between this whatever and the whatever it is you've always had an inkling about beyond. So to speak. Yeah. Middle age is the cloud. You come through it... whooosh—you start seeing the ground.'

'Fuck.'

'The ground? The ground being death, right?'

'That's right,' says Traffic.

There's a pause. There's eyes looking out and falling puppets coming down.

'It's not cloud, actually, Traffic,' says Xav. '*Not at all.*'

'What is it then?'

'It's...fucking...mist,

clinging

to

the

fucking ground.'

I lose the conversation like a man a cliff by his fingernails.

There's a lot of noise that's not the conversation that's gone but me with each big effort I'm making to breathe in against the big shudders that are a running commentary to the long-awaited surge of grief and sadness and confusion coming out.

All of this, seemingly, completely outside of my control.

I picture a small man trying to get *in* an *out* turnstile to a huge sporting event just ended. I can see him perfectly.

It's that difficult

to breathe

for picturing the letter that arrived a month ago and is stifled in the box with the gun.

The letter I can feel has a photograph in it.

The one from Russia.

# THE DISGUSTING RUG AND THE BOWL FULL OF AMPULES

My breath, all the way back to the flat, each gasp, another bucket from the well full of everything forgotten about Svetlana.

I arrange all I have by way of distraction about the floor, around my bed—opiates to whiskey through everything in-be-tween—like a child the contents of its toy box. It's not clement, the weather, it's cold. I open the curtains and the windows. Turn on the laptop. News clips start flashing up. Short stories with images: a twelve year old girl, sucked into the drainage system of a swimming pool; the pumping system—drowned. Looking for her goggles at the bottom of the pool. That's what it says. Then cat stories. How two cats survived various misfortunes. Two cats, by way of apology. I open windows on the laptop. I get to a swingers' site. (I can feel the proximity of the gun / the box / the envelope to my right as sure as there's a monster waiting in the wardrobe there. All the right side of me cring-ing.) A whole listing of live member webcams and thumbnails from Asia, Africa, The States. Fifty or so global women mostly masturbating to their webcams. Live. I watch my cursor click a few thumbnails. I feel I could be out there about London with a shovel, digging up graves; nothing would make any difference to the way I'm feeling now. Blank. A forty-seven year old woman in London with a nice vagina, she's masturbating with a blue dildo and a silver vibrator. Every now and then she reorganises herself, rides only the blue dildo while typing messages and moaning. 80'sdoll69's dressed in an American football shirt. In Chicago. She's throwing herself about her room, playing air-guitar to some big track, lifting her shirt and stroking at her vagina. It's shaved. She's got a blonde-bubble-perm. She takes her shirt off. She keeps darting coquettish looks to the camera. She's got implants. Under my computer chair, the central bit of the base, where it nearly meets the floor, there's this big wadge of dust and hair. I just dropped my tobacco and saw it. I've never noticed it before today, it having obviously been there a long time unseen; just another indication of a slowly unravelling reality. benice'n cum, from New Jersey, is nineteen. Beautiful. Skinny. Naked apart from a g-string she's pulling up into the slit of her vagina and a couple of handfulls of oil. Three thousand eight hundred and twenty-three people are watching her. There's a still life thumbnail vignette from Baden-Wurttemberg—seven dildos; all different shapes, sizes, reflectivity and colours. I click on the thumbnail. All the video's showing is the dildos on a table. That's all. One dildo's made from clear plastic filled with what looks like glitter. Two hundred and eighty-four people are watching the dildos. The woman from London's got a big, veined, yellow/pink dildo now. The blue one's gone. She has nice hands. Jabba's on his Xbox in the background. I've got a glass of wine, a cigarette and I've taken some pills. I type a message to the woman from London: londoncuntforu—IT'S BEAUTIFUL. YOUR CUNT. IT REALLY IS. YOU HAVE NICE HANDS TOO. REALLY NICE HANDS. I send her the message.

The box with the gun, the monster in the wardrobe, it's to my right about a foot, two feet away from my right thigh. On a shelf in there. londoncuntforyou's the big veined dildo only now. She's on that. You can hear her typing. No message comes back. There's a picture of the twelve year old girl. Subsequently, there are pictures of the two cats. I take my trousers off. My pants. I stroke my cock and watch lodoncuntforu's pretty cunt and her nice hands. Listen to her moaning. There's the whack of Jabba in the front room hitting pixillated golfballs and the area on my thigh that's screaming the position of the box with the gun. There's another news heading: Soap star's murder trial to commence. I click on that. It's not Heaven. It's somebody else. londoncuntforu's stopped broadcasting. Her screen's just black. White writing on black saying londoncuntforu has stopped broadcasting. Black, like there's been a death in the family. 80'sdoll69, her room's empty. There's a drum kit in the background of her room. I stare at that for a while. A small black dog walks across 80'sdoll69's carpet and disappears.

It comes back into view.

Gazes up towards the camera.

Tilts its head slightly.

There's only me and this dog in the whole world.

I shut the londoncuntforu window and the 80'sdoll69 window.

There's the drowned twelve year old girl, the dead soap star and the cats.

I open the wardrobe.

I open the box.

I open the letter.

Everything else is a blank.

/

If I dredge back there's a door banging. It's cold. Really cold. I'm on the bed and there's the smell of shit. The cold and the door banging and the smell of shit. And somehow, the smell of shit, it's not unpleasant. It's comforting. The smell of shit, for a while it's like an anchor. And Jabba. There's warm water and a cloth and Jabba like something from the bible, Jabba, washing me and bundling my sheet and coming back and throwing the quilt over me and holding the box with the gun and the letter, all that cradled in his arm like a baby…and I think maybe reading the letter and stroking my head and saying something kind.

The quilt over me now. Over my head. Cocooned. A thought firmly imbedded in me like a parasite:

*The premise on which I've been living has been a false one.*

I don't really care much for what's going to happen next.

What I know now, it's killing me.

All I know is it can't be sustained. The bad bad feeling. It has to stop.

any
which
way.

Short of the gun, which I seemingly don't have the courage to use.


He's obviously looking at his phone now, seeing it's me calling; whatever noises I'm making by way of communication enough to tell him accurately the severity of the situation I believe myself to be in. A little dance on the phone with him, talking, mollifying me, without a reason forthcoming as to why I'm so de-railed. Svetlana and that business from him the only secret I've ever managed to keep. Me, finally saying that whatever happens, I've just got to lose it for a while. A few days. Have a big blank. While things settle. I ask him can he pick me up, can we go and get whatever it'll take together. Will he hang onto me for a bit.

He picks me up. We drive off. Saying nothing much. We get to this big block of flats in the East End, a lift, a hallway... beyond the hallway, a room with people in it neither of us has been to before waiting.

The Cloud's telling me that the block of flats, it was designed by Erno Goldfinger. Do I remember? He's saying it was a dry run for Trellick Tower. Balfron Tower, he's saying. This is. This is Balfron Tower. He's saying, did I remember? Didn't I remember? Do I remember? We did a job here last year, a location for a film. That's how the flat we're going to, we know about it. The locations guy had told us about it. It's notoriety. The Cloud says do I really want to be doing this. Am I sure? I tell him I'm sure. I'm positive. It's not his fault. If he didn't come, if he hadn't come, I'd be here on my own or finding someplace like it. Its alternative. And really fucking up.

The lift works.

I feel safe with The Cloud. As if somehow I might still just have a longterm.

There doesn't seem to be anybody much about. The whole place smells of Indian/Pakistani/Bangladeshi food. Curry. We keep ringing different bells. Looking into cameras. Being buzzed through different doors. The Cloud looks like I'd imagine he'd look if he had a child and was concerned about that child. Its welfare. Whatever we normally do by means of conversing, gesture, expression, whatever we're normally able to generate, I've let go my part of that bargain. Somehow, it seems like a big deal. Never having managed to have done that before. Not participate. The hallway we're walking along, it's giving off to front doors and kitchens, front doors and kitchens. All along the right hand side. The smell of cooking really intense. The hallway's enclosed. There's a wall with windows to the left. Where there could have been a balcony there's just this long wall with windows. The passage we're making, The Cloud and I, it seems incredibly insignificant. My heart beat feels really flat. If I drift, I can see an out of season seaside town. Pictures by Erwin Olaf or Aaron Corey. Under these circumstances I feel myself unrecognisable. There's some sort of comotion half way along the hall. A lot of noise from behind a section of window off to the left. It's flapping. The noise is. The commotion. There's a bird, a pigeon, trapped in-between the window on our side and what looks like an even dirtier section of glass beyond. We both watch the bird, look at one another.


There's no obvious way to help the bird short of breaking the glass. We walk on.

By the number on it, we're at the right door.

The Cloud rings the buzzer.

/

There's the reality of what you're free to be seen yearning for and searching for on the streets, and then there's the reality of this room, whatever they're searching for in here. This room with the disgusting rug and the bowl full of ampules. There's a coshed courtesy and formality, scratches something in me. The walls are painted over unprepared surface—conduits, degraded plaster, brick, tiles, all with bold linear black on white. The black looks to be sprayed. The floors are concrete. Blood red paint. There's a table covered with the makings of what they're all after, these people, besides that there's not much else—this old filthy rug, a couch and some kitchen chairs. There's an ipod on the floor wired to big speakers. Playing RL Burnside. There's about eight to ten people here. I don't know about the people. I figure on the basis of what I've been finding out it's not my position to pass any kind of judgement.

I think how maybe, a while ago, coming into a place like this would have made me feel nervous, a bit excited at least.

Now, way back in my head,

way in the distance,
there's a single bored figure sitting...
watching this bad bad movie unravel.

I sit down on the floor. The Cloud, he's saying yes, we'll stay
for a while. He haggles for a small percentage of what's on that
table.

He brings it over.

/

There's some small movement in the periphery of my vision.
My consciousness embedded.
Tiny.
Minute and shrinking yet.

/

Hitting it at 3am, wrapped in a stinking rug, abandoned in a wood and left for dead. Because that's what junkies feel obliged to do, somebody OD's and dies, apparently. In their front room. On their gear.

They take you out like the garbage.

Way out down some track in the middle of nowhere. Off that and into undergrowth.

Some bulshitter like you who lies about having taken ampules before and then goes blue on their floor.

Hits his personal rock-bottom.

You look around the studio from your vantage point by this bucket and the sink and try to read something significant in other people's faces. Like they'll be able to tell you what's expected from you, this bucket and the paint. You look at an open tin of burnt umber and an open tin of raw sienna that are by your right knee. There's ten litres of white to your left. Five litres of black. You look into the colour you're mixing in the bucket.

Some kind of taupe.

Nothing.

Traffic's Appalling's nearby, leaning up against the work-bench, reading his newspaper. You remember enough to know that Traffic's Appalling + Electricians + the camera = You're on standby. You look away from Traffic's Appalling. There's a whole bunch of electricians. Beyond them the camera. You try and remember who the art-director is on this job. You try and remember what this colour is that you should be mixing. You look around for a colour chart, in case you've been handed one as reference.

There's no colour chart.

Whatever you'd normally be doing now, you'd normally be telling Traffic's Appalling about last night. Any other foul night in the past, you've had no problem.

But you can't. You can't elucidate on that.

You, who can tell anybody most anything.

You can't tell him that.

You're only just being able to think it yourself, little at a time, peeking over the edge of your psyche to your personal rock-bottom.

You look around some more: there's a living room set, a hall set and a bedroom set. You think you must be working on a commercial but you can't be sure. There's a feeling of slippage in your head; as though a mechanism's come adrift and won't properly engage. It's not an unpleasant feeling. It just makes operating in the real world impossible. You shake your head a bit, in the same way you might kick a faulty machine.

It makes no difference.

The t-shirt's really tight on Traffic's Appalling's shoulders as he leans around and looks at you.

'You OK, Manny?'

You just look at him for a bit. 'What am I doing?' you ask.

'Hey?'

You remember your arms tight by your sides, the foul smell and the sound that rain makes on a sodden rug with a human being inside it and vegetation and suchlike all around.

'With this paint. What am I doing with this paint?'

You think it says a lot for Traffic's Appalling that he looks at you in a reasonable way, as though you've just asked a reasonable question.

You remember thinking, for a while, before the rain, thinking you'd been buried alive.

Your body shot through with an electric current.

When it all seemed helpless.

Before the rain.

Lying there remembering the letter.

The consequence of that being your predicament. You being buried. Justly so. The letter your ticket to this. *Fuck you, you cunt.* You can hear it now, a whisper, from outside the rug - you, inside, berating yourself. Her father dead. Having attempted to address certain things. Like what he'd done to you. Had had done to you. Rapewise. And everything. Everything, such-as images and videos of him amongst a look-alike prostitute.

That looked just like Svetlana.

Doubtless shot from ornate, gilded cornaces.

You in the stinking rug.

A big wet rancid cocoon.

Getting all reborn.

With information.

With the rain coming down. Knowing yourself not buried. Starting to wriggle about and be liberated amongst wet vegetation because junkies don't do knots.

To find a road because junkies don't carry anything farther than they have to in the middle of the night.

The only car that came stopped.

And the man in that car—*God only knows what gave him the courage to do that, to stop, you thought*—he didn't mention a single thing about you being in the state you were in: filthy, wet and smelling of shit for the second night running. He said he was a Christian. He said he had a Christian duty to help. That's what gave him the courage to ease on his break for a looming monster like you.

His Christianity.

'It's that wall colour. For the bathroom,' Traffic's saying. 'You know?'

You look around. 'What fucking bathroom?' you ask him.

He's not looking as though he's being judgemental in any way when he says: 'The one for tomorrow, Manny. The flattage we've got next-door.'

You keep stirring the paint as you picture standing outside your flat with the sun coming up. Your arms away from your body; everything about you trying to disown itself. Home, just in time to take a shower and swallow some pills and put on your work clothes and phone The Cloud and listen to his big silence as you relate your story. You, telling him that he drove you and him to the junkies' place last night, you remember that much, but then What? And it turning out he'd got a phone call. That was the what. Another junkie-suicidal. An ex-girlfriend. An old art college acquaintance who wanted to be ending everything right there-and-then plainly even more than you, calling, as she had, from Battersea Bridge. A parapet. She was the what. Him going to help her with your insistence that you'd be fine amongst all these strangers, their ampules and the rug.

You still saying nothing about Svetlana because it didn't seem the time for sudden ancient stories of male rape and loo-kalike Russian prostitutes, what with lunacy enough sprouted everywhere for the pair of you. And you only really being able to cope with ironing out the practicalities of where you stood with The Cloud. As to whether he'd actually abandoned you or not.

It must have been nervous energy that meant there was nothing left to do but laugh.

So you did that.

The pair of you.

Laughed.

And you listened to him ask if you were OK.

And you saying Fine.

And him saying what are you going to do.

And you saying go to work.

Because you figured it better, all things considered, to get to work, rather than stay in the flat with the letter and the gun, because, all things considered, reborn or not, death, as an entity, it still felt close at hand as an easy option.

'Manny,' says Traffic.

He's blinking down at you.

You look up at him.

'Take it easy… Fuck-sake,' he says.

## MONSTROUS DEBRIS

He's perched in his swivel chair. You've seen the look he's giving you before. It's the look a man who's got his life under control can easily give a man like you, who hasn't, while trying to look as though he feels empathy.

For you.

For your parlous state.

There are pictures of him and his family on his desk. In the pictures, and, sitting there in the real world, he looks clean and orderly. He looks like he has self-discipline. He looks as though his life's something he gets up and does every morning after a calm nourishing breakfast. With ease.

'What is?'

'Everything,' you tell him.

'How do you mean?'

'Everything's mashed up and degraded.'

He's turning his biro in his hand and giving you that look.

'You know those cartoons?'

'Which cartoons?' he asks, with a big grin.

'The ones where the character runs over a cliff—just shoots off and remains hanging in the air, for a moment, before it falls.'

'Yes…' he says, as though he's cautiously opening a door to the madness that's you.

'Like the coyote—Wile E. Coyote—in Roadrunner?'

'Yes.'

'That's where I am.'

You can see he's having trouble adjusting that look. He's right at the end of what that look's capable of. He's got nowhere else to go as far as that look's concerned.

'And you say your memory's a major issue in this?'

'Yes.'

'And how's that manifesting itself?'

'With the soap, for instance.'

'The soap?'

'Yes—that's where it started.'

You don't know whether he's looking bored or frightened now.

'I couldn't figure out whether I'd washed myself or not. I just kept staring at the soap as though it could tell me. But I was none the wiser. It didn't.'

'*Right.*'

You knew he was going to say "right" like that.

'You do realise, that drinking the amount you are, without any of the other considerations, drinking that amount alone can cause serious, permanent damage.'

'To what?'

'To a lot of things…to your *brain*, for one,' he says.

He's looking at you with another look. A look of disdain born out of being the kind of man who's never seen the point in risking any kind of damage to himself, whatsoever.

'I know,' you say, 'I've stopped.'

'You've stopped drinking?'

'I've stopped everything apart from the smoking—tobacco. Apart from smoking tobacco.'

He's writing this down.

'I gave it all up…eight weeks ago. Yes, eight. The drink, the drugs,' you take a look at him, 'and the prostitutes,' you say.

His expression betrays a little blip with your mention of prostitutes.

He's running a finger across his right temple. 'Eight weeks?' he says.

'Yes.'

You explain to him how you went completely blank on the way home. A while back. How only your trousers saved you. That you didn't know where you were going or where you'd been. That you hardly knew who you were but for the paint on your trousers whispering a prompt.

Whatever you say, you're not going to mention the wood, the rug and the ampules.

You know he doesn't need the *i*'s dotting in relation to the extreme nature of you.

He starts tapping at the keyboard of his computer. 'I'm going to ask you a series of questions,' he says. 'Just a formality.' He gets himself set. He looks at the screen of his computer. He looks at you.

'Who's the Queen of England?' he asks.

You're really surprised by that question. Shaken. You think how he's getting back at you. How he doesn't empathise with your self-destructive tendencies and your visiting prostitutes. You look at him. You haven't answered him yet. He's writing something down.

Your mind goes blank.

'OK,' he says, really slowly. 'We'll try another one…'

He's looking at his screen. You're looking at his family photograph. You're looking at his son, who looks happy and must be about five.

'What day of the week do you think it is?' he says.

You're blinking as you look at this man's son; at his little arms and his little pod of a body, all stripy in a t-shirt.

He's saying something about the tide going out. About how when you stop drinking, excessively, your brain is hit by a massive vitamin B deficiency. He says that that can create a condition that manifests itself in strange ways. He's piecing together the analogy. He says it's rather like the tide going out, leaving you standing amongst all this monstrous debris.

You must be looking completely blank because he says it again, 'Standing amongst all this monstrous debris,' he says.

He's smiling as he tells you this.

'Debris that's remained invisible,' he says.

You haven't a clue what day of the week it is when he asks you but you can see lots and lots of debris.

The last thing he does is to get up and stand in a corner and ask you to walk towards him. This is the last gauntlet he throws down to you. To your poor proprioception. He's smiling as you walk towards him like you're some kind of miracle big boy who might just make it.

/

That's why you're here, now—with them pushing in massive doses of vitamin B to fill the void in your head and save whatever's left of Manny.

You, with more than enough time to start taking stock of debris.

You can see yourself standing on this beach.

The tide's way out.

You—

surrounded by all this junk.

Looking back over things, it's like watching a horrible dance—now that all the filters are gone and it's just you and the vitamin B. You figure the real business of this horrible dance started with the letters from Beatrice and ended with letters from Svetlana; the ones that started coming nine weeks ago. Like Beatrice's letters were the "Excuse Me" at the beginning of this mashed-up dance and Svetlana's letters, they were the music stopping.

And the old dog-handler, right about your black prostitute

mother Gladys.

Your 100% mother.

And her beautiful beautiful black face.

And Vernon the V.

Vernon, your brother, the complete mess that was him and his face so similar to yours.

Vernon and Gladys both finally introduced to you by the TV and hanging about the rest of the substance of your misery now as decoration.

Them both badly dead without you ever having had the chance to say a proper hello.

To your family.

You think you saw him once and that'll have to do. Both of you stopped for a second to place one another in a hospital corridor but not managing to find the significance in the familiarity; not finding it in the real world for it being found by you both only in a mirror before then.

You lie there doing this big, retrospective jigsaw: your life up to vitamin B.

## THE FIRST REAL PIECE LAST

I'm holding Beatrice's letter between my thumb and forefinger.

I watch the bottoms of my curtains billow. The pattern of their cloth, it's letting in a pattern of sunlight that's speckling my room. I watch the curtains as though whatever they're telling me about the big respiration going on out there, it might be important. As if it could solve everything.

I can hear the river.

It's the end of a very hot day.

I can hear the noise of a plane as it fights the atmosphere to rise over London. I can hear people in the flats around me. All of this, part of some palette I've determined to turn my back on.

The curtains are carrying on regardless.

The pitch of another plane building.

I slowly picture my tunnels collapsing; I think how the only tunnel that ever got things done was the gun.

I'm holding that one in my other hand.

The patterned light's all over it. It's speckled with these gleaming freckles of light. They slide along it with the slightest movement of my hand.

Beneath Beatrice's letter, there's the last one from Svetlana.

I picture both these letters falling to the floor, imminently.

Both these letters and the one, small photograph:

The real thing.

The only real thing ever.

I've got my other tunnel up on the screen in front of me. The word count on that is up over eighty thousand.

I figure all I need do is drag it to the trash.

To empty the trash.

With only the vitamin B to lean on I think that whatever I felt I was doing with this tunnel, it doesn't need to be witnessed by anyone else. It would be too much of me hanging about to haunt people that didn't deserve it.

I can see two lines clearly: a rising one and a falling one—the rising one represents the questions being asked of me, the falling one my ability to answer those questions. I don't know how to address the obvious disparity between these two lines.

I don't have the first idea about that.

I take the small photograph from between the two letters and look at it.

I look at Svetlana.

She's smiling.

I stare at the little boy on her lap.

Him, the only real thing ever.

There's an address written across the back of the photograph.

A date only a few weeks back.

I watch the curtains billow.